DARK STRANGER

THE DREAM

THE CHILDREN OF THE GODS
BOOK ONE

I. T. LUCAS

The Story Behind The Children Of The Gods Series

Myths as persistent and as prevailing as those of the vampire, the shapeshifter, and other mythical creatures, as well as modern-day UFO and alien sightings, may not be purely the product of overactive imaginations. What if at the source of those myths were events and personalities that left an impact so profound that their echoes could be heard in the mythologies of civilizations continents and millennia apart?

Could they perhaps originate from realistic hallucinations induced by members of an advanced species who exhibit some of the characteristics of those mythical creatures?

More than seven thousand years ago, the first advanced human civilization appeared out of nowhere. Archeological records show that the Sumerians knew about the solar system and placed the sun at its center, had schools for children, girls and boys, established laws to protect personal property, and afforded women the kind of rights they hadn't enjoyed since Sumer's decline and up until modern times.

The Sumerians accredited their gods with providing the blueprints for their civilization and their advanced scientific knowledge, as well as the creation of humankind itself—a hybrid the gods engineered by combining the genetic material of a god with that of a lesser creature.

The abbreviated version of their creation myth isn't the only one to find its way into the Bible, albeit modified to fit its monotheistic agenda. Adam and Eve and the Garden of Eden are there as well. Though in the Sumerian version, the snake is a sympathetic god who decides to grant humans knowledge of a carnal nature—the way the term knowledge, or to know is used throughout the Bible—giving humans the ability to procreate, which as hybrids they previously lacked. Another god, the head of the Sumerian pantheon, considers humans' rapid procreation a threat to the gods (implying that the gods were not as fruitful) and throws them out of the gods' garden.

The Children Of The Gods series is best read in order.
Not intended for readers under the age of 18.

PRELUDE: SYSSI

Premonitions are tricky.

And although Syssi had been having them for as long as she could remember, she could never predict how they'd come to pass.

Yet in one way or another, they always did.

It was a curse.

Knowing something was coming, but not the when or the how, left her perpetually anxious.

Lately, she sensed a dark shadow descending over the world, a malevolence that had an oddly familiar flavor to it. An old and powerful force was on the rise, readying to plunge the world into darkness. Yet again.

It alarmed her.

So much so that she dreaded watching the news or reading a newspaper. To witness global events unfold according to her predictions only fueled their potency. And like one of those biblical prophets of doom, the foreknowledge she was burdened with was too vague to heed—even if anyone cared to listen.

And yet, although the portents were mounting, it seemed as if no one was concerned. Blinded by one trifling thing or another, most of her friends were convinced that their future was secure.

As if weapons of mass destruction were not threatening to annihilate the world, and the slaughter of thousands in Africa and in North Korea and in other godforsaken dictatorships wasn't happening. Not to mention that hunger was still a serious problem in parts of the globe, and basic human rights were rapidly eroding in those and other parts: specifically, those of women.

It weighed on her.

Being a powerless observer sucked.

There was nothing she could do.

Except, some small part of her was rebelling against this perceived helplessness, whispering in her mind that she was wrong. It was like an itch, a nagging suspicion that she was forgetting something important, and that just around the corner, a life-altering adventure awaited.

Perhaps it had something to do with the dream that had been tormenting her for months. Infrequent at first, lately it had been a nightly occurrence, and she would wake up gasping, sweaty, shaky, and with a mean headache.

The dream always began in the midst of a heart-pounding pursuit.

Out of breath and desperate, she was running for her life through a dark wood—a pack of vicious wolves on her heels. With the hellhounds' terrible red-glowing eyes and snarling muzzles never far behind, her panting breaths were the only other sounds to disturb the quiet of the night.

What am I doing here?

Why are they chasing me?

Dear God, I'm going to die—horrifically—they are going to tear me apart.

Her eyes darting frantically in search of help, Syssi could see nothing besides the elusive shadows the moon was casting on her path.

She was losing hope, her legs threatening to give out, when up ahead in the distance she discerned what looked like a silhouette of a man. She couldn't be sure, though. The tall shape was barely visible below the limbs of a large tree—it might've been just another shadow.

It remained a mystery. She'd never reached him, not even once, always waking up before getting close enough to find out if he'd been real.

Trouble was, Syssi didn't know what to make of the dream. Was the dark stranger friend or foe? Was she supposed to run to him? Or from him?

On that, her premonition remained undecided, churning up a strange mix of contradicting feelings: a sense of trepidation, but also excitement.

Yes, her premonitions were definitely tricky.

1

SYSSI

"Watch out!" Syssi threw a hand out, bracing against the Porsche's front panel.

Her new boss, the most talked about professor on campus, Dr. Amanda Dokani, was going to get them killed.

"Would you chill?" Amanda cast Syssi an annoyed glance before accelerating again to take advantage of an opening in the next lane over.

Syssi held her breath. The space didn't look big enough for a motorcycle. The Porsche was a small car, but not that small. When Amanda managed to slip it into the tiny space without causing an accident, Syssi sagged in relief.

Would telling her boss she was driving like a maniac get her fired?

Nah. Not after all the trouble Amanda had gone through convincing Syssi to come work for her. Besides, they were friends. Sort of. "You're dangerous. I'm never going to hitch a ride with you again."

Amanda snorted. "I don't know what your problem is. I'm an excellent driver."

If she wasn't holding on to the dashboard for dear life, Syssi would've crossed her arms over her chest and huffed. "Why can't you stay in one lane? Do you really think all that weaving between cars will get you there faster? And anyway, what's the rush? You have plenty of time until your first class starts."

Amanda let out a resigned sigh. "Fine, I'll slow down. But you need to tell me what's gotten into you. Yesterday, you had no problem with my driving."

True. But that had been before the disturbing foretelling that had forced itself into Syssi's mind this morning. Amanda was in danger, the premonition had been clear on that, but the details had been fuzzy.

"I had a premonition about you."

"Aha, I knew it. Let's hear it." Amanda looked excited as she peered at Syssi with a pair of big blue eyes that seemed to be glowing from the inside. It must've been a trick of the light—a reflection from contact lenses—because people's eyes didn't emit light. Though, it sure as hell looked like it.

Syssi shook her head. This wasn't the first oddity she'd noticed about her new boss. Not that any of it was a big deal, just small things. Was Syssi the only one who noticed that there was something peculiar about the professor?

Probably.

Amanda's students were too busy gaping and admiring to actually listen to her lectures, let alone notice that there was something off about her.

Tall and lean, with dark, glossy, short hair, deep blue eyes, and full, sensuous lips that were red without the benefit of a lipstick, Amanda's beauty bordered on the surreal. Distracted by her looks, most people could see nothing beyond it, and at first, Syssi had been no different. But with each passing day, since she had first walked into Amanda's lab a little over two months ago, it was getting easier to see the person inside and ignore the cover.

Upon discovering that Professor Dokani was conducting experiments on extrasensory perception, Syssi had volunteered to be a test subject. What better way to explore her ability to foresee glimpses of the future than having a neuroscientist examine it?

Her results had been so exceptional that even though neuroscience hadn't been her field of study, Amanda had pestered her to join the research team.

Syssi had politely declined.

She had an internship lined up with a wonderful architect. Tragically, though, the poor man had died of heart failure a few days before she'd been supposed to start. So here she was, working at the lab and getting valuable insight into an ability that had haunted her, her entire life.

At least until she could find another architect to intern with.

"It was vague, as they all are, so I didn't want to worry you for nothing, but I sensed that something major was going to happen to you—not life threatening, but life changing."

Amanda smirked. "Hey, maybe the groundbreaking paper we are working on will get published in *Nature*? That would be major and life changing."

Syssi shook her head. "The premonition wasn't bleak, but it wasn't sunny either. Besides, we are not ready. Even I know we have to do a lot more experiments before we can prove your hypothesis."

Tapping a long-nailed finger on the steering wheel, Amanda frowned. "I know. Tell me something, are you still getting those nightmares? The ones with the wolves?"

Syssi blushed. "Yeah, almost every night." She'd told Amanda about the dreams, but not about the recent changes in their nature. Last Saturday, she'd gotten a little closer to her would-be dream rescuer, and closer yet each night since. His facial features were still obscured by the shadows, but she could tell that he was tall, exceptionally so, and that his body was beautifully built—lean and strong like that of an athlete.

Even though it was only a dream, his proximity was doing all kinds of weird things to her, affecting her in a most disturbing way. The man was like the epicenter of a force field, emitting some kind of attractant she was powerless to resist.

The way he held himself, his entire body language exuding an aura of power and confidence, was calling to everything female in her. Syssi yearned for her dream guy like she'd never yearned for any real man.

To be with him would differ from any sexual experience that she'd ever had or even fantasized about. Before the dreams had taken on this new twist, her fantasies had been quite tame, as well as the men starring in them. Kind of like her ex-boyfriend, or perhaps just a little more exciting. Gregg had been as far removed from intense as it got.

Not this guy.

He would demand nothing less than her complete and utter submission.

The shocking part was that she found herself yearning for his dominance. The concept was so foreign to her that she should've found it abhorrent, and certainly not titillating. Still, it was hard to argue with the very physical evidence her dream arousal was leaving behind.

Wet panties weren't a big problem first thing in the morning, but the arousal carried over to her waking hours. Syssi could've banished it, forcing it off her mind, but the truth was that she didn't want to. It made her feel alive. There was something naughty and delicious about her constant state of arousal, her yearning for the forbidden sensation, and she refused to give it up.

Not yet, anyway.

She would cast these fantasies aside once she started dating again and had a real guy in her life. It didn't require a degree in psychology to figure out that there was a connection between the dreams and her extended dry spell.

Amanda cast her a sidelong glance, no doubt puzzled by Syssi's blush. "The dreams are affecting you, and this is why you see trouble lurking in every corner. I think you are mixing up real premonitions with a bad mood."

"Not likely. I know the difference. A premonition has a very distinct feel to it." Syssi sighed. "I'm just tired. All I need is one good night's sleep to regain my sunny disposition." One without disturbing dreams about a sexy dark stranger.

"What you need is to get laid. One good tumble and the nightmares will go *poof*. Isn't a handsome guy part of the dream? You need to catch up to him and turn that nightmare into something naughty instead of scary; something fun like several screaming orgasms." Amanda squirmed in her chair. "I could use some myself." She winked at Syssi, the seductive smile on her beautiful face so sinful it had Syssi squirm a little herself. Amanda was such a sexual creature that it was impossible to remain unaffected. Especially given Syssi's already elevated state of arousal.

If it were anyone else other than Amanda, Syssi would've been freaked out, thinking she was that transparent and that everyone could figure out what her dreams were about. But the woman had sex on her mind twenty-four seven. She would've turned a dream about a trip to the supermarket into something sexy.

But even though Amanda was very open about her sexuality, sometimes shockingly so, Syssi didn't want to share this with her boss. She hid her discomfort with a shrug. "I don't know if he is handsome or not because I never get close enough to see him. It's not that kind of a dream."

Liar, liar, panties on fire.

2

AMANDA

"Where the hell is he?" Amanda murmured and took another quick glance at the time before fixing her gaze back on the lecture hall's door.

From her elevated vantage point on the podium, there was little chance she could miss Kian. At six foot four and with two distinctive bodyguards at his side, he wasn't exactly inconspicuous, or easily overlooked.

She was just anxious for him to show up.

At last, after endless nagging and cajoling, her brother—the all-important Regent and head of her clan on the American continent—was making the time to come see her teach.

He should be here already. Kian was punctual to a fault. *Unless, he isn't coming after all.*

Snatching her phone out of her purse, Amanda turned her back to the class.

Where are you? I have to start in a few minutes, Amanda texted, then waited, tapping her heeled shoe on the podium's hardwood floor.

Don't get your knickers in a twist. Parking the car. Be there in two.

Letting out a relieved breath, she smiled and texted back. *Knickers? Really? What century are you stuck in? It's a thong now. Get with the times, old man. And unless you can fly, you won't make it in two.*

Old man walking as fast as he can while texting. Stop bugging me.

Amanda chuckled, but as she shifted her attention back to the rapidly filling classroom, her eyebrows dipped with worry. At this rate, Kian might not find an empty seat, let alone three, which might provide him with a perfect excuse to leave.

"Professor Dokani, I just wanted to tell you that I love your lectures," called out a brave soul sitting in the first row.

Gutsy boy.

She smiled and gave him the thumbs-up.

The room, already one of the largest in the department at one hundred and fifty seats, was nearing full capacity. Amanda's class, "Mind: The Final Frontier," was quickly becoming a favorite of the student body. Not that she had any illusions as to why her class was so popular.

It wasn't due to a sudden interest in the philosophy of neuroscience, or appreciation for the title's reference to *Star Trek*. And sadly, it wasn't due to her fascinating lectures or her amazing teaching skills either. No, the course's popularity had mainly to do with her looks.

Owing to her exceptional hearing, Amanda couldn't help but overhear her students' murmurs; most of which were flattering, though some were not just rude, but outright derogatory. She would've loved nothing more than to slap those boys around for talking like that about a woman, any woman. Unfortunately, she couldn't. Not only would it get her fired from the university, but it would expose her supernatural hearing and uncommon strength.

Amanda sighed. Beauty wasn't all that it was cracked up to be. What most people didn't realize was that it was both a gift and a curse. No one bothered to look past the cover to see what was on the inside.

Even Amanda herself hadn't been immune. For most of her life she'd let this exquisite exterior define her, but lately it just wasn't enough. She wished to be admired for her skill as a teacher, and not the looks her unique genetic heritage had bestowed upon her.

"Just look at her," she heard one of the boys whisper. "She looks like something straight out of an anime illustrator's fantasy."

Nice. But although what he'd said was flattering, and not vulgar like some of the other comments she'd heard, Amanda had to disagree. Unlike the nearly naked anime beauties, she was dressed, modestly and impeccably.

Still, at the back of her mind, shoved into a hidden corner she managed to ignore most of the time, Amanda often felt like an anime character: an exaggerated exterior masking a hollow interior. But then she covered it up well, projecting a confident attitude and dressing the part.

This morning she'd taken particular care, choosing an outfit to best fit the role she was playing—a distinguished and respected professor, yet a hot one. The slim-fitting black trousers and blue silk blouse revealed very little skin, leaving the job of accentuating her figure to the exquisite cut of the luxurious fabrics.

Amanda didn't own a single article of clothing that wasn't a top designer label or that didn't cost more than most folks' monthly mortgage payments. Not that she could afford that kind of stuff on a professor's pay; that wouldn't have covered her shoe budget alone. But her shares in the clan's extensive holdings ensured she could buy whatever struck her fancy without ever needing to work for it.

The research she was conducting had a higher purpose than earning her income or even prestige.

Still, she liked feeling important for a change. And besides delighting in her students' reactions—amusing and thrilling as they were—she had to admit that she truly enjoyed teaching and was surprisingly good at it.

With a thinly veiled smirk, Amanda watched the young men—some freezing in place, awestruck as they stared at her, others tripping over their own feet as they tried to find a seat without taking their eyes off her.

Some tall, some short, some pale, some dark. Most were average-looking. A few were worth a second glance.

Yummy, so many to choose from.

She loved their attention, their lust. Drinking it in, Amanda was in her element: the hunter in a field of ogling prey.

Mortals, with their weak, malleable minds, were easily snared, their memories of the hook-ups easily erased, and the men themselves just as easily forgotten.

Regrettably, it was a modus operandi for her kind.

Repeatedly thralling partners messed with their brains, while hiding her true nature for extended periods of time was tiresome and carried the risk of exposure.

Long-term relationships were simply impossible.

Those of her kin who'd tried had gotten burned, most figuratively, some literally.

Case in point—the witch hunts.

In days past, a woman like her might have been called a femme fatale, a succubus, or even a vamp. Nowadays, there was a new term, cougar, which she liked better. It didn't carry such negative connotation and was, in fact, closer to the truth.

Not that anyone would dare think of her as an older woman. Amanda shuddered at the thought.

She was a beautiful, young female.

Her fake birth certificate stated that she was born on the sixth of May, 1984. It got the sixth of May right, but the actual year of her birth was 1773.

Amanda was over two hundred years old.

The funny thing was, for a near-immortal she truly was young. Kian was four years shy of two thousand—the old goat. Compared to the life spans of mortals, though...

Well, what they didn't know didn't hurt them. She was what she was—what biology and her kin's traditions made her—a lustful, hedonistic, near-immortal.

Amanda liked who she was, and she loved her life. Most of it anyway.

At last, as the classroom began to settle down, she spotted Kian, flanked by his trusted sidekicks—number one and number two as she nicknamed Brundar and Anandur. The three headed for the back row, where seats immediately became available, vacated by their occupants who scurried to find a place elsewhere.

Good.

Amanda would never admit it, but Kian's approval meant a lot to her. Being that much older, he fulfilled both the roles of the father she'd never had and a big brother.

Lately, the clan's holdings were increasing at a staggering pace, and managing their family's extensive affairs was taking up most of Kian's waking time. It had taken relentless nagging to pry him away for a couple of hours to come see his baby sister teach.

3

KIAN

Kian was taken by surprise when the lecture reached its end with a lively discussion concerning free will. Enchanted by Amanda's rendition of the mysterious nature of consciousness and the brain's uncharted neural pathways, he had lost track of time just like the rest of her students. Even Brundar and Anandur, who'd expected to be bored out of their minds, had been listening—riveted throughout the entire class.

"It's time to go," Kian whispered, motioning for them to follow as he pushed to his feet. Leaving Amanda's mesmerized audience behind, they sneaked out of the lecture hall unnoticed, which in itself served as another testament to her skill. More often than not, the three of them attracted a lot of unwanted attention—be it admiration from females, or apprehension from males.

Then again, establishing their headquarters in a big city that was home to the film and music industry had its perks. On the streets of Los Angeles—with all of its actors, musicians, and wannabes of the same—a bunch of tall, good-looking men wasn't an unusual sight.

Once outside, Kian squinted at the glaring sun and pulled on his custom-made, heavy-duty sunglasses. Unlike his native Scotland, it rarely got cloudy enough here for him to forgo the shades.

And at this time of year in particular, the bright orb's glare was brutal on his over-sensitive eyes.

Not that it got significantly better during what passed for winter in Southern California.

Pulling up to the curb, his black SUV with its dark-tinted windows attracted the interest of the few people on the street. Thankfully, no one lingered to gawk.

"She's really good. Even I got it," Anandur remarked as he opened the passenger door for Kian.

With a slight nod, Brundar seconded his brother's opinion.

"I still hate the idea of her being so publicly exposed. It's risky. All it will take is for some nosy reporter to go digging into her fake dossier, and all hell will break loose." His temper on the rise, Kian slammed the SUV's door.

He had to admit, though, Amanda had had her students spellbound. Some of it was no doubt due to her beauty, and some due to her special ability to influence. But as he was immune to both and had still found the lecture fascinating, he had to give her the credit she was due.

"Where to, Master?" his driver asked, easing into traffic.

"We are having lunch at Gino's."

Mindful of the amount of work still waiting for him, Kian pulled out his phone and began scrolling through the avalanche of emails and texts that had managed to accumulate during the two-hour class. He'd barely gotten through a fraction of them when his driver parked the SUV in front of Amanda's favorite place for lunch.

Gino's was a short drive away from campus, close enough for her to grab a quick bite to eat during her lunch break, but too far for her students to get there on foot, which meant the risk of her bumping into one of them was low. She'd discovered it two years ago when she'd gotten her first job at the university.

A generous grant provided by one of the clan's subsidiary corporations ensured Amanda had free rein to test her ideas. But even though Kian was funding her research, he didn't put much stock in her achieving her main objective. His reasoning was that even if Amanda failed to find anything useful for the clan, her research could potentially benefit humanity, which, of course, was the ultimate goal and justified the substantial monetary investment.

"Is it we, as in you and Amanda, or are we invited as well?" Anandur asked as they stepped out of the vehicle.

"No. I will have you guys stand sentry, salivating while Amanda and I eat. This is not the Middle Ages, and I didn't do so even then. Really, Andu, sometimes I wonder if it's part of your act or are you really that thick."

Brundar chuckled, a jab directed at his obnoxious brother never failing to bring a rare smile to his austere face.

"What I mean, ladies... are we all sitting together as one big happy family, auntie and uncle with their beloved nephews? Or Amanda and you upstairs, while we guard from a safe distance—out of hearing range—downstairs?" Anandur arched both of his bushy red brows.

"I don't know. It's up to Amanda. I'm not sure what she has in mind." Kian frowned, remembering she'd mentioned that there was something she wanted to talk to him about.

"Aha, you don't know. So I'm not so thick, am I?" Anandur smirked.

Kian shook his head but smiled despite himself. Anandur liked to act the big brainless oaf. At almost six and a half feet tall and about two hundred and fifty pounds of muscle, he looked like a pro wrestler. Add to that a head full of crinkly red hair, a bushy red beard and mustache, and he could play an extra in a Viking movie.

In contrast, Brundar looked almost feminine. A little over six feet, he wasn't short, but his lean build, pretty angelic face, and his choice of hairstyle—keeping his pale blond stick-straight mane so long it reached the small of his back even when bound with twine—made him look delicate. Metrosexual.

Their appearances couldn't have been more misleading. Of the two, Brundar was the deadlier force—cold, calculated, and skilled. A true master.

Anandur's reliance on his brute strength, though, didn't mean that he could be easily fooled or manipulated. He was a keen observer, capable of quick and accurate assessments of sticky situations, never acting on impulse. The big oaf act fooled his opponents into underestimating him, which naturally was the whole point.

Together the brothers, who'd been serving as Kian's bodyguards for centuries, were deadly to anyone posing a threat to him or the clan.

As expected, Gino's was packed with customers waiting in line on the sidewalk to be seated. The few round bistro tables on its narrow veranda were all taken—some by young mothers with their strollers blocking whatever little space remained, and others by business types from the nearby offices.

Bypassing the crowd, Kian took the worn stairs leading directly from the back entrance up to what Gino called his VIP section. It was a small room on the second floor reserved for his special guests—those who for various reasons didn't want to mingle with the rest of the clientele, or members of his large, extended family.

The room looked like an old lady's parlor. Old-fashioned wallpaper in green and yellow hues covered walls which were decorated with the fading portraits of stern matriarchs and patriarchs posing in their Sunday best—their disapproving expressions staring from their frames. Six upholstered chairs surrounded a round dining table in the center, and the serve ware came from a peeling sideboard laboring under the weight of piles of china.

Looking at it, Kian imagined that one of these days the thing would collapse, and Gino's heirloom collection would be history. But each time he'd mentioned it, Gino had just smiled, saying not to worry; his grandmother's sideboard had held for the past fifty years and would keep on holding for at least that many more.

With another glance at the wood's widening cracks, Kian

shrugged and sat down. He would hate to tell the guy, *I told you so,* when it eventually fell apart.

As he peered at the street through the open French doors that led to the tiny balcony overlooking the front, the lacy curtains fluttered in the light, warm breeze.

Feeling his tension ease, Kian realized he liked it here. It was cozy and intimate, despite the tacky decor, or perhaps owing to it.

4

ANANDUR

"Hey, Gino!" Anandur waved the proprietor over. "How are you doing, buddy? Life treating you well?"

"Can't complain. Business is doing good, the family is good, so I'm good. Eh? What can I do for you, gentlemen?"

For some reason, Gino was always nervous around them, despite the fact that since Amanda had gotten the job at the university, they were eating here at least twice a month and leaving extravagant tips. Anandur had often wondered if it was the small guy's instinctive wariness of men their size, or Gino suspecting them of being Mafia goons.

Calling Kian boss certainly didn't help matters. But what the heck, Anandur liked messing with the old man.

"The boss is upstairs. Could you please set us a table down here next to the stairs?" Anandur leaned down to Gino's ear. "We need to watch both entrances. If you know what I mean," he whispered, pausing for effect. "Oh, and the lady is going to join him shortly, so it will be two upstairs and two downstairs for lunch today."

"The lovely Ms. Amanda?" the small man breathed, wiping his spotless hands on his pristine apron, his mostly bald head glistening with perspiration.

"The one and only." Anandur chuckled. "And speaking of the devil, here she is in person, the beautiful Dr. Amanda Dokani." He pointed at the front door.

"Hi, boys!" Amanda sauntered into the restaurant, causing a momentary halt in the chatter. She hugged Brundar, then stretching to reach, kissed Anandur's cheek. "Kian is upstairs?"

"Yep, he is waiting for you. But before you go, I just wanted to say, you totally rocked today!" Anandur high-fived her. "I didn't snooze even once." He pulled her into a hug.

"Congratulations on the promotion," Brundar added, for once not skimping on words.

Gino was still wiping his hands, waiting for her to acknowledge him.

Amanda turned, flashing him her megawatt smile. "Gino! Sweetheart!" She leaned to give him a hug.

"*Bellissima*!" He blushed the color of beets, returning the hug and planting a kiss on each of her cheeks. "So happy to see you again."

"You always brighten my day, Gino. The way you say bellissima… Makes a girl swoon. Be a darling and bring me my wine upstairs? I'm in the mood to celebrate. You still stock it, I hope?"

"I keep it just for you, bellissima!" He beamed.

Amanda's favorite wine, a 2005 Angelus, was too rich for Gino's regulars, but he always kept a bottle just for her. Excusing himself, Gino scurried to the kitchen to fish out the bottle he was hiding behind the onions in the pantry. The unmistakable scent always clung to the bottle, and Anandur wondered if Amanda could smell it as well. Female immortals' sense of smell wasn't as acute as that of the males, but still, this one was quite pungent.

Starting up, Amanda paused mid-stair. "Aren't you coming?" She arched her brows.

"Sorry, princess, we are on guard duty, keeping an eye out from down here. The two of you together in public always makes me twitchy." Anandur waved her off and dragged a chair to the small table the waiter had placed near the stairs.

"As you wish." Amanda shrugged and kept climbing.

5

AMANDA

Amanda wasn't about to argue. The conversation she was planning to have with her brother required privacy.

Argh, he is going to fume and rant, she cringed.

For a good guy, he sure had a very short fuse. But this needed to be done, and giving up was not an option.

The future of their clan depended on it.

"I'm so proud of you!" Kian got up and pulled her into a hug.

"It's about time someone was!" Lingering in the comfort of Kian's warm embrace, Amanda sniffled, blinking back the tears that were threatening to ruin her carefully applied makeup. "The naughty party girl is finally making a contribution." She chuckled.

Nine years ago, Amanda had decided to enroll in college, surprising everyone, most of all herself, with how brilliant she'd turned out to be. In just seven years, she'd earned a PhD in the Philosophy of Neuroscience, and was now hailed as a new and fresh thinker, a leader in her field. Her papers were published in the most respected scientific journals.

"Oh, sweetheart, when you look ahead to a lifespan of thousands of years, two centuries of partying seem like nothing at all. And after the sorrow you had endured, you deserved all the joy you could find."

Why the hell did Kian have to bring it up?

Her day had been going so well until he opened the trapdoor on the old pain she'd buried deep down behind thick walls and a moat. Surfacing, it dragged its serrated edge through her insides. "You know I don't talk about it!" She pushed away from him, wiping the few tears that found their way out despite her best efforts.

In the silence that followed, the sound of Gino's light footfalls echoing from the stairwell announced his arrival. A moment later, he rushed in with a loaded tray in one hand and a folded stand in the other. Setting it up by the table, he proceeded to pull out a chair for Amanda. "My lady?" He gestured for her to take a seat.

Donning her well-practiced cheerful mask, Amanda did what she'd always done when unpleasant thoughts intruded. She pushed them back into their little jail, redirecting her train of thought to a happier place; like whether Gino insisted on always serving them himself because he coveted their generous tips, or because he believed they were celebrities. "Thank you, Gino." She sat down, sneaking another discreet swipe at her eyes before offering him a bright smile.

Gino removed the red-checkered napkin from the basket of freshly baked rolls, letting the steam out, then fussed with the placement of the wine glasses. Once he was satisfied with how everything looked, he proceeded to make a big production out of opening the bottle and pouring Amanda's wine.

As he pulled out two menus from his apron pocket and was about to hand them out, Kian stopped him with a chuckle. "Please, we have no need for these. Unless new items have been added since our last time here, I can recite your menu verbatim. I'll have a Caesar salad and the vegetable lasagna, please."

"The garden delight fettuccine and your delicious house salad, *per favore*." Amanda smiled at Gino and reached for one of the fragrant rolls.

"Very well!" His face beaming with satisfaction, Gino puffed out his chest and stuffed the menus back in his apron pocket. "I'll be back with your salads momentarily."

Sipping her wine, Amanda stole a furtive glance at Kian to assess his mood as she thought of a way to broach the delicate subject she needed to discuss with him.

"You're plotting something." Kian narrowed his eyes. "I know that contemplating look, the one you have when you want to tell me something you know I'm not going to like. Let's hear it then and get it over with so I can bite your head off, and we can eat in peace."

Amanda pouted. "You could be nice and agreeable for a change."

"Spill!"

"I want you to meet Syssi," she blurted in a hurry, cringing in preparation for his retort.

"Syssi?" He arched a brow.

"Yes, Syssi, my research assistant, remember? I mentioned her before." Amanda looked hopefully at Kian. He didn't seem angry. Yet. Maybe this would go easier than she had expected.

"Last I heard you mention that girl, you were blabbering about an architecture graduate who excelled at predicting coin tosses."

"I hired her," Amanda said while trying to look remorseful.

"And what credentials did she bring to the job? Arranging the functional MRI machines in an aesthetically pleasing manner? Painting the lab in designer colors? I understand you wanted to test her, but why hire the girl?"

Kian's level of aggravation was rising with each sentence. He had this tendency to fuel his own temper over minor issues. And yet, when things hit critical mass he somehow managed to be as cool as a cucumber.

"Syssi is an amazing person, smart, dedicated, and hard working. The internship she had lined up bummed. The poor schmuck died of a heart attack on a fishing trip of all places. I needed a research assistant, and she was both available and the best test subject I had to date. She is off the charts, Kian. And it's not only the coin tosses, which in itself is beyond impressive; she guesses with eighty-seven percent accuracy. The random-computer-selected-images test? You know which one I'm talking about?"

When he nodded, she continued. "She was spot on, or close to the correct image in ninety-two out of a hundred pictures. She has the strongest precognition ability of any mortal I've ever tested. I'm telling you, Syssi is a Dormant, Kian. I just know it." Amanda could barely contain her excitement.

Kian ran both hands through his hair. "I can't do it, Amanda. It's just wrong. Pick another male. It doesn't have to be me."

"I don't know what your problem is, Kian. You bang random women you pick up at clubs and bars, and I know for a fact that you've even paid for it on occasion. So why not Syssi? Why not someone who has the potential to change your life and give hope to the rest of us? We know there must be Dormants out there; carriers of our unrealized genes who can be turned into near-immortals like us. Potential mates we could bond with for life. And I think I finally found a way to identify them. You know why I started this research in the first place, searching for anomalies, paranormal abilities. Once we realized DNA testing was useless, instead of giving up, I took a different approach. Don't you want children, Kian? Immortal children? Don't you want a life mate?" Amanda was exasperated. If it were up to her, she wouldn't even pause to think. But only males possessed the venom necessary to activate the dormant DNA.

It was a cruel twist of fate, or as Kian believed, the work of a crazy geneticist. Only the immortal females contributed the special genetic material to their offspring. And only males could activate it in a Dormant.

An immortal mother and a mortal father produced mortal offspring who possessed the dormant immortal genes and could be activated by venom. If not activated, the dormant genetic material would remain inert, but still pass from mother to daughter, and so on. It wouldn't pass to the sons, though.

The immortal heredity was matrilineal.

To facilitate the activation of a Dormant, an immortal male would have to inject the latent with his venom. When sexually aroused, the male's fangs elongated and venom was produced in specialized glands; the need to bite and release it into the female's system congruent with the need to ejaculate.

Aggression toward other males triggered a similar reaction. Though the venom produced for the purpose of immobilizing or even killing an opponent was obviously more potent and carried a different mix of chemicals. A large amount of it pumped into the victim's system paralyzed the body and stopped the heart. Even in immortals.

Kian just stared at her, looking stunned by her audacity. But she did not back down. Holding his stare, she challenged him to pick up the gauntlet.

"You really want to know what the big deal is? I'll tell you. I hate it! I hate what I have to do. I feel like a drug addict—needing, craving the release sex provides and despising the need. I wish I could abstain, or at least have the luxury human males have of taking matters into their own hands, so to speak. But I can't bite myself, can I? If I could put my hands on the sick fuck who designed us this way, I would kill the fucker... slowly." Kian took a fortifying breath in an obvious attempt to calm down, then continued in a quieter voice.

"I use these women. I don't remember their faces or their names. They are all interchangeable in my mind. Not to feel like a jerk, I try not to objectify them, giving them as much pleasure as I can, and when tampering with their brain, I leave the memory of pleasure intact, erasing only the biting part and replacing my features with those of another. That's all I can do to ease my conscience. But there is nothing I can do for myself, for the way I feel, as if I'm a goddamned animal with no control over my baser needs."

Reaching over and taking Kian's hand, Amanda purposely kept pity out of her expression. "I had no idea it got so bad for you."

She did not understand his misery. She loved sex. Loved the

variety of partners. Perhaps it was different for the females of the clan because supposedly, there was a purpose to their sexual appetite. Conception was extremely rare for her people, and pregnancy was hailed a miracle. With the females of the clan holding the key to its continuity, as only their progeny could turn immortal, they were encouraged to seek a variety of human partners in the hopes of conceiving.

Their plight was not as bad as that of the males. The possibility of having a child to share their long life with, to bear witness to their journey, made the lack of a life-mate tolerable. But for the males there was no such solace. If their dalliance with a human resulted in a child, that child was mortal, with a mortal's short lifespan and vulnerability. But wasn't that exactly what she was trying to rectify? Find Dormants that were descendent from other matrilineal lines?

As all members of her clan were the progeny of one immortal female, they were forbidden to one another.

A taboo.

Kian took her hand. "You're still young, Amanda, so it's still fun for you. But I bet it will get old by the time you reach my age."

Amanda looked into his eyes and spoke softly. "Forgive me for pushing. But I still don't get what all of that has to do with you attempting to activate Syssi. If she turns out to be a dud, all you did was have sex with another faceless, nameless female. But if she is the real deal, isn't it worth a try?"

As his handsome face hardened, Kian pulled his hand away, leaned back in his chair, and crossed his arms over his chest. "Here is the thing, sister of mine. She will not be another faceless, nameless girl. We don't know how long it takes to turn an adult woman. Don't pimp me out like I'm some man-whore." He uttered that last bit acidly, his expression turning menacing.

She had known her holier-than-thou brother would find her request objectionable, but she hadn't expected him to be that adamant about it. Nevertheless, she had to give it another go. Tempt him. Too much was at stake. Shaking off her despairing mood, Amanda straightened her back and leaned forward. "Syssi is beautiful, Kian, and smart. You're going to love her…" She paused, realizing that the word love did her a disservice in the context of this conversation. "I mean, it's not like you'll be suffering. She is exactly your type. She is blond, very pretty, with a deliciously curvy figure. I'm sure you'll find her attractive. And engaging. Did I mention already how smart she is? And nice?"

"I'll take your word for it, but I'll pass. Ask someone else. If she is so wonderful, I'm sure you'll have no shortage of volunteers." There was a finality to his tone that would have deterred a lesser opponent. But Amanda remained adamant.

"I'm not going to choose someone else," Amanda hissed, then hushed as she heard Gino climbing the stairs.

Sensing the heavy tension in the room, Gino's smile faded. "Here are your salads, and more rolls. Enjoy!" He turned and beat a hasty retreat.

Amanda waited till Gino was out of earshot before resuming her offense. "You are my only brother, and what's more, you're our mother's only living son. You're the closest to a pureblood male the clan has. Your venom's potency is Syssi's best chance of turning. And when she turns, she will have the potential to create a new matrilineal line. Don't you want to be the one who creates it with her? Who knows if I will ever find another one? Maybe she is the one lucky shot? Are you willing to bet on it? To forfeit your one chance because of pride and arrogance?" Amanda was practically huffing with righteous indignation.

Kian regarded her coolly, still leaning back in his chair with his arms crossed over his chest. "Nice speech, Amanda. One problem, though. The 'when' is an 'if'. If she turns, and if I were a betting man, I would not put my money on this one. And the answer is still no."

Amanda set her elbows onto the table, dropping her forehead on her hands. "You are such a stu… stubborn old goat. Just sleep on it. Don't decide anything yet. Maybe when you meet her, you'll change your mind."

"I don't think so, princess." Kian's tone got a shade warmer as he leaned in and patted her cheek as if she was a petulant child. "Look, you will have similar chances of success using another male. The only thing I'm spoiling for you is your romantic fantasy. It's not a big disaster. Put on your big-girl panties and deal!"

Amanda smiled at his feeble attempt at levity. Despite his stubbornness and gruffness and bad temper, she knew that he loved her. "If I were leaning that way, I would have snatched Syssi for myself in a heartbeat. I like her that much." She pouted.

Kian rolled his eyes and dug into his salad, letting her know that as far as he was concerned, this discussion was over.

6

SYSSI

"Why Amanda thought I could do this is beyond me," Syssi muttered as she stared at yet another print-out. The freaking computer had been spouting nonsensical results all morning, and she was no closer to finding the error than she had been five hours ago.

Taking a hammer to the thing was looking more and more enticing.

Heaving a sigh, she ran her fingers through her hair. Again. Sticking out in all directions, it was tangled and knotted from the number of times she'd pushed her fingers through it.

I probably look like Einstein, and not because of what's under my cranium.

It was time for a break, the hollow feeling in her belly reminding her she hadn't eaten yet.

The two espressos, one cappuccino, and eight cups of coffee she'd consumed before lunch—which was excessive even for a caffeine addict like her—didn't qualify as nutrition.

It crossed her mind that she reached for coffee the way other people reached for alcohol. When agitated or worried, or just in need of a break, the ritual of making it, pouring it, and stirring in the precise amount of sweetener relaxed her.

Drinking a truly good cup of coffee was her idea of bliss.

Pushing up from her chair, she stretched her back, listening for the familiar popping sound. A stretch wasn't as satisfying without it. When it came, she did a couple of side to side twists and then turned toward the two postdocs. "I'm going to grab a sandwich. You guys want anything?"

Hannah shook her head, pointing to the empty protein shake container on her desk. Her latest diet craze consisted of protein shakes, protein bars, and water. Nothing else.

David, the other postdoc, smiled his creepy smile and took a big bite of his salami sandwich.

Ugh, she must have been really engrossed in her work not to notice the nauseating stench.

"I can bring cookies."

Hannah made a sad face. "Rub it in, why don't you. Waving sweet, delicious carbs in front of the fat girl. Meanie!"

"Fine, so no cookies."

"Hey, what about me? I want something sweet..." David leered.

"In solidarity with Hannah, no dessert." Syssi pretended not to get it—her usual line of defense against unwanted advances.

David was a jerk. He didn't flirt or tell jokes, or any of the other things guys usually did to get Syssi's attention. He ogled, made inappropriate comments, and habitually invaded her personal space, believing for some inexplicable reason that he was God's gift to women everywhere. His delusional beliefs aside, his problem wasn't that his features were unappealing, David was an average-looking guy, but that he was schlumpy and unkempt. More than his personal hygiene or taste in clothes, it was his personality that needed a major makeover.

In the lab's kitchenette, Syssi slapped together her favorite sandwich of goat cheese, tomatoes, and basil on whole wheat, then ate it leaning against the counter.

She wasn't ready to go back yet.

Out there, she would have to deal with David. And unfortunately, as she'd learned from experience, he wasn't done. Once

David started with his idiotic comments, he'd be on a roll for the rest of the day.

Oh, the joy...

"Good afternoon, darlings!" Syssi heard Amanda make her grand entrance. "Missed me terribly, I hope? And where is my girl Syssi?"

"Over here!" Syssi called over a mouthful.

Amanda poked her head into the kitchenette, then stepped in and leaned against the counter next to Syssi. "What's up? You look troubled."

"I'm dying out there. I can't find what's wrong with my programming. The computer has been spouting nonsense all morning, and I'm ready to go at the thing with a sledgehammer."

"Why didn't you ask David for help?" Amanda crossed her legs at her ankles and her arms over her chest.

Syssi cast her boss a sidelong glance. "Are you serious? He will never let me live it down, probably demand a hookup as payment. The creep."

Amanda's expression turned serious. "I know you don't like David, heck, I don't like him either. But he is very good at what he does, and you need to use him. There will always be people like him trying to mess with you, but if you let them, you'll find it damn hard to accomplish anything. You need to be forceful and refuse to take shit from anyone. Sometimes a girl needs to be a bitch not to get pushed around. Be a bitch, Syssi! You might even enjoy it." Amanda winked, her gorgeous face returning to its usual brightness.

"Thank you for the advice, mommy."

Joking aside, Amanda was right. Syssi needed to deal with David, or working in the lab would become intolerable.

What puzzled her, however, was Amanda's admission that she didn't like David either. She was the boss and no one dictated to her who she should employ and who she should not. With a frown, Syssi asked, "What I don't understand, though, is why you hired him if you don't like him?"

"He was the best applicant for the job. And besides, I hired him *because* I don't like him."

"So am I to assume that you don't like me either? Since you hired me..." Syssi pretended offense.

"No, my dear, sweet Syssi, I adore you. You know that!" Amanda slapped her cheek playfully, then kissed it. "I hire females I like and males I don't."

Searching her face, Syssi realized Amanda wasn't joking. Her boss seemed sincere. "I don't understand."

"Better shun the bait, than struggle in the snare," Amanda quoted, looking down at her stiletto-clad feet.

"Oh, Amanda, you're not that bad. I don't buy the whole femme fatale act."

"Who said it's an act? I am bad. You have no idea how bad!" Amanda made a wicked face.

"You witch!" Syssi laughed, mock-punching Amanda's shoulder.

Amanda shrugged, pushed away from the counter, and headed for her desk with the sensual saunter of a practiced temptress.

Syssi didn't buy Amanda's sex-on-a-stick act. It was nothing more than the theatrics of a drama queen. Being so strikingly beautiful, her boss naturally expected to be the center of attention wherever she showed her face.

Except, was it possible that she really was as sexually active as she claimed to be? Maybe.

And why not? Amanda wasn't married—didn't even have a boyfriend—she could and did as she pleased.

Good for her!

Reflecting on her own nonexistent love life, Syssi cringed. She hadn't been on a single date since things had finally fallen apart with Gregg. For two lonely years, she'd mourned a relationship that had been dying a slow death long before it had ended. Though, in retrospect, she realized it was the sense of failure more than any lingering tender feelings that had her stuck on the sidelines while everyone around her was having the time of their lives, or at least pretending to.

Syssi had met Gregg her first week of college, and they'd stayed together until his graduation four years later. Being her first serious boyfriend, and her first and only lover, there had been this expectation that their relationship would lead to marriage. Except, when he had moved to Sacramento for a job, it had been a relief for both of them.

So why was she still alone? Syssi had no good answer for that. Men found her attractive, and she didn't lack propositions, but there was no one she found even remotely enticing. Except the guy from her dreams, that is, but he didn't count.

Her relationship with Gregg had left her wary of starting a new one. For some reason, being with him had dimmed her spirit, and two years later it hadn't bounced back yet.

Most of the time he probably hadn't been aware of acting like a jerk, never actually saying or doing anything that could have been perceived as outright offensive or belittling.

Instead, he'd just always managed to twist things around and blame her for everything that hadn't been working to his satisfaction. His grades falling short of spectacular had been her fault because she had taken too much of his time. They hadn't gone out enough because she hadn't scheduled and planned it. They hadn't had enough friends because she hadn't been outgoing enough... and so it went.

But the worst part had been the sex. There had been no intensity to it, no excitement, it had felt like a chore. Was it a wonder then, that she hadn't been looking forward to it? And of course, it had been all her fault. She hadn't initiated enough, she hadn't excited him enough. She hadn't been hot enough.

Blah, blah, blah...

Logically, she knew he had been full of shit. Where had been his contribution? Had he been just a bystander in their life together, waiting for her to do everything? But on the inside, in that irrational place where her fears and insecurities hid, she sometimes thought that maybe he had been right. Maybe she really wasn't assertive enough, outgoing enough, sexy enough...

Lacking... She felt lacking.

Syssi shook herself. *That's definitely enough self-pity for one day.*

And besides, not all of it had been bad. Gregg had stood by her side in her time of need. He had been loyal, and apart from the never-ending complaining, a pleasure to talk to.

But when the relationship had ended, she'd focused on the negatives; the bad parts had been vividly remembered and endlessly reexamined, while the good parts had been marginalized, forgotten.

It was time to move on, though. Maybe she should try some of the blind dates her friends were trying to set her up on. Or even look into those dating sites Hannah had suggested. But although Syssi had promised herself she would do it, she still hadn't taken a single step in this direction. Tomorrow, next week…

"Yo! Syssi! Your cell phone is ringing!" Hannah called from the other room.

"Coming!" Syssi hurried to retrieve her phone from her purse. But by the time she fished it out, her brother's call had already gone to voice mail. And if that wasn't frustrating enough, David's salami breath assaulted her as he bent over her shoulder to look at her screen, invading her personal space.

"Amanda said you needed my help," he breathed into her ear. "For a kiss, I'm willing to do you a favor," he added with a smirk, amused by his own wit.

"Cut it out, David, and please move your salami breath away from me. You know I can't stand the smell of meat," Syssi snapped. Pushing to her feet, she almost toppled her chair backward, forcing David to back up.

His eyes widened. "That was such a bitchy retort, so unlike our polite, proper Syssi. It was hot!" He leered before taking the seat she'd vacated.

"You want me. I know you do. That's why you're so flustered." He winked and started scrolling through the program. "Don't worry, sweetheart. I'll take good care of you." His hands flew over her keyboard, his concentration not at all affected by his sorry attempts at flirting.

She had to hand it to him. David had a way with computers that he definitely lacked with women.

With his face almost touching the screen, he kept going, "Nothing turns me on like a strong, assertive woman. I'll scrub my mouth with thorny roses for a kiss from you." Riding on a wave of his fetid breath, David's whispered poetic attempt did nothing but trigger Syssi's gag reflex.

She couldn't believe it. Instead of discouraged, he seemed even more determined.

"Look, David, I'm going to return this call, and you are going to find out what's wrong with my program. Not as a favor, but because it's your job. Amanda hired you for your programming skills. It sure as hell wasn't for your charming personality!"

"Oh, baby, you have no idea how hot you look when you're angry."

"Ugh! I'm going to strangle him!" Syssi kicked the leg of the chair he was sitting in.

Snorting, Hannah shook her head.

"It's not funny!" Syssi barked and walked out the door.

She hated confrontations. Especially futile ones like this. But at least David was going to fix her programming. Except, what would it take to fix him? For some reason, a vet with a scalpel came to mind.

Leaning against the wall, she banged her head. Today was such a shitty day, with her shortcomings and insecurities popping up like teenage zits. Just when she thought she was rid of them for good, they returned sprouting white heads. More than the confrontations themselves, she hated how ill-equipped she was to deal with them. Why the hell was it so hard for her to assert herself or show her temper?

Even now, her hands were still shaking, and she had to take a long calming breath before returning her brother's call. If Andrew detected her agitation, he would start a full-blown interrogation. And she was so not in the mood for that.

He answered on the first ring. "Hi, Syssi, how's the new job?"

"It's okay. Though I really suck at programming. Other than that, Amanda is a great boss and the work is interesting." Syssi paused before plunging. "You really should come visit. The woman is a stunner, and I would pay good money to see your jaw drop when you see her. The great Andrew Spivak will be speechless!"

Syssi was joking. Nothing ever fazed Andrew. But he was single and so was Amanda. Who knew what might happen if the two got together...

"You have piqued my curiosity. Though I doubt she's all that. Anyway, I spoke with Dad today."

"Yeah? How are they? What are they up to?"

Their parents were volunteering in Africa. Her mother, Dr. Anita Spivak, a retired sixty-six-year-old pediatrician, was working twelve-hour shifts in the harsh conditions of the ravaged region, providing much needed medical care to its children. Syssi's father, who had spent his professional career as a pharmaceutical sales rep and later as an executive, was enjoying his retirement; photographing nature and wildlife while helping his wife.

They rarely called.

Syssi wished she could blame Africa for that, but it was nothing new. Her parents had always been too busy with their careers, their social life... each other.

Andrew had been the responsible adult in their household, practically raising Syssi and their younger brother, Jacob.

Their mother had had Andrew at twenty-eight, and had given up on conceiving again when long years had gone by and nothing had happened. It hadn't been a big heartbreak. With her workload, raising even one child had been difficult. Lucky for Andrew, their grandparents had stepped in, providing the care he had needed. Syssi's arrival had been a miracle, the pregnancy taking Anita by surprise at the age of forty-two. A year later, she had been blessed again with another miracle. Jacob.

The two babies had been welcomed and loved but left mostly to the care of nannies. By the time they had arrived, their parents had been too established in their routines to make any changes for their sake.

"Dad sends their love. He says he has enough material to publish his first book, and he promises to send us the files to look through and choose the pictures we like most."

"I wonder when that will happen. You know him; lots of promises and little delivery." Syssi could not help sounding bitter. Their dad had been promising to drag their mother away from her work for a few days back home. Syssi was still waiting... two years later. She had hoped they would at least show up for her graduation, wishing they'd surprise her at the last minute. How naive of her. They never had.

"How are you doing, Andrew? Still bored at your desk job?"

It had been a while since he'd been sent away on one of his assignments abroad, and being stuck in the office usually made him restless.

Syssi had often wondered about Andrew's frequent trips. After retiring from a hush-hush Special Ops unit, he had joined the Internal Antiterrorism Department—supposedly as an analyst. Why then, had he been spending months at a time abroad? Doing what? Research?

"Actually, I'm swamped with work here, and truth be told, I'm tired of living out of a suitcase. I think you'll have to tolerate my annoying presence in your life for a little longer this time."

Andrew sounded happy to stay home... Intriguing... Was it possible he'd finally met someone?

"There must be a woman involved. I can think of no other reason for you to sound so cheerful about staying put. So tell me, who is she? Did you find someone special?" Syssi asked hopefully.

Andrew chuckled. "No, there is no one special. Who's crazy enough to stick around me?"

"You're a great guy, Andrew. Someday, you'll make some lucky girl very happy."

"I doubt it."

"You'll see. I have a feeling... Soon."

When Syssi had a feeling, those who knew her listened. Her premonitions had a freakish tendency to come to pass.

"I hope you're kidding because if you're not, you are scaring the shit out of me. You know I'm not built for anything serious!"

It was funny how scared he sounded. The brave warrior afraid of being snared by some mystery woman. "Nah, just messing with you," she lied.

"Wow! You had me there for a moment." Andrew took a deep breath and exhaled it forcefully, exaggerating his relief... Or maybe not.

"I have to let you go. I have to get back to work and deal with a pesky problem." Syssi sighed.

"Need me to come beat that problem up? I will, you know..."

"I just might take you up on that offer," Syssi answered, not sure she meant it as a joke. "Bye, Andrew."

Andrew leaned back in the swivel chair and laced his fingers behind his head. He wondered what Syssi wasn't telling him. The pesky problem was probably a guy, he smiled knowingly.

Nothing new there.

Syssi was so lovely, there would always be some poor schmuck making a pest of himself over her.

Maybe he should visit that lab after all, and not just to admire the infamous Dr. Amanda Dokani.

7

AMANDA

"Promise me that you are not going to drive like a lunatic." Syssi put her hands on her hips and glared at Amanda.

Folding her tall frame into the driver seat of her Porsche, Amanda buckled up and lowered the passenger side window. "Would you get in already? You're jumpy because of the nightmares, not my driving."

With a frown, Syssi opened the door and leaned against the frame. "If you don't promise, I'm not getting in. I'd rather walk."

"I'll be good. But only until I drop you off. After that I'm going to drive this baby like it should be driven."

Syssi got in and turned to look at her, worry lines furrowing her forehead. "You should be careful. Remember my premonition?"

Amanda shrugged. "You don't know what or when or how. I'd rather live dangerously than not at all."

With a wince, Syssi looked away.

Oh, shit, she shouldn't have said it. Hurting the girl's feelings hadn't been her intention. "I'm sorry. I didn't mean it like that. Please don't take it personally."

"No, you're right. I'm too cautious. I don't go on dates because

I'm afraid the guys will end up being jerks, or boring. Worse, I'm anxious about having to tell a guy that I don't want another date even before I have gone on the first one. Pathetic. My money is in a savings account, earning zero interest, because I don't want to chance losing any of it in the stock market. I could've doubled what I have if I had trusted my gut and bought Apple stock even though it was already high." She let out a sigh and slumped in her seat.

"What you need is a pattern interrupt. Something to zap you out of your comfort zone and force you into action." Amanda knew exactly what that something was, or rather who, but he'd refused to cooperate.

She needed to come up with a plan of how to get these two together in the same room. Kian was basically in the same situation as Syssi.

His days consisted of work and his nights of meaningless hookups. Day in and day out. He'd never taken a vacation, had never gone to see a concert or a play, and he'd been to the movie theaters exactly once. Kian wasn't living, he was functioning. He just wasn't aware of it.

Amanda was betting that once Kian and Syssi laid eyes on each other, the encounter would shock both of them out of their stagnation. It was only a gut feeling, but it was a strong one. She just knew that they would make each other happy.

But she was getting ahead of herself. One thing at a time.

First she needed to get them together, then let nature take its course on the express lane to the nearest bedroom. After that was accomplished it was a matter of waiting to see if Syssi transitioned.

Amanda believed she would.

Leaving the university grounds, she accelerated, and the Porsche glided along at what she considered an excruciatingly slow pace. It was late, and most of the rush-hour traffic was over. There was no reason to go so slow. With a quick glance at Syssi, Amanda let her foot press down on the gas pedal a little. The girl didn't notice a thing. She was busy looking out the window and moping.

Amanda kept accelerating until she was cruising at a more reasonable speed.

Turning her head toward her forlorn passenger, she was about to tease Syssi about her bad mood, when suddenly a stupid suicidal squirrel decided that it was a good day to die.

The furry thing jumped from a low hanging tree branch, right in front of her car. Amanda slammed on the brakes and the car swerved, skidding out of control. She managed to right the Porsche a split second too late, hitting a water hydrant head on.

Metal groaned, Syssi cried out, and Amanda held her breath, waiting for the airbags to deploy and the hydrant to erupt in a geyser. But the impact hadn't been powerful enough to cause either. Evidently, she'd managed to slow down sufficiently to avoid more serious damage.

Throwing the door open, Amanda unbuckled and got out, rushing around to open Syssi's door. "Are you hurt?" The impact had been mild, but humans were so damn fragile.

Syssi tried to shake her head, then winced, rubbing the spot where the seatbelt had cut into the skin of her neck.

"Hold on, darling. I got you." Amanda leaned inside and unbuckled her.

"What happened?" Syssi asked.

"A good for nothing stupid squirrel. I should've just run him over."

"Don't say that!"

"Just kidding. But I'm mad as hell. I have plans for tonight." Amanda went over to the front and examined the damage. "Not as bad as I thought. It's just cosmetic." She got inside and turned on the ignition. "It's good that the Porsche's engine is in the back. Get inside, Syssi."

"What about the hydrant?"

"It's fine. Let's go."

Amanda waited for Syssi to buckle up before backing away from the hydrant and easing into traffic.

She'd better call Onidu and tell him to get her a loaner. Pressing a button on the steering wheel, she called home.

"Onidu, darling. I had an unfortunate fender bender with a hydrant. I need you to get me a rental."

"Of course, Mistress. Are you well? Do you require medical attention?"

"I'm perfectly fine. But my beautiful car isn't. Would you take care of it for me?"

"Naturally, Mistress."

"Thank you." Amanda ended the call.

"Who was it?" Syssi asked.

"Onidu? He is my butler."

"Figures," Syssi murmured under her breath, thinking Amanda couldn't hear her.

When they reached Syssi's place, Amanda parked next to the curb and turned to her personal seer. "So that was it, I guess," she said.

"That was what?"

"The bad thing you were predicting was going to happen. I was in danger and it wasn't life-threatening. To either of us." She winked. "Case closed."

Syssi shook her head and winced, rubbing her neck again. "I don't think so. Not unless parting with your Porsche for a couple of days is a monumental, life-changing event for you."

"So what is your advice, my sage oracle?" Amanda asked as Syssi stepped out onto the sidewalk.

"Just be careful and watchful. There isn't much else you can do."

8

MARK

"To us!" Mark saluted.

Mark's team from SDPD was celebrating their latest breakthrough at Rouges.

The local bar catered to a mixed crowd: students from nearby Stanford, young professionals from Palo Alto, and the occasional riffraff. Most days of the week a live band provided entertainment. Except tonight.

Tuesdays, the band was off, so the place was not as packed and not as loud. Which was why they had chosen tonight for their celebration.

"Peace, love, and rock 'n' roll!" Logan downed a shot.

To outsiders, SDPD stood for Software Development Programming Department. Only those on the inside were privy to the special programming that the firm masquerading as a gaming developer was really working on.

In fact, the Strategic Defense Programming Division was a civilian outlet serving the federal government, its substantial pool of genius tasked with the development of viruses that could disable enemy weapon systems, specifically, WMDs—weapons of mass destruction.

Top programmers, gifted hackers, and brilliant mathematicians were secretively lured into its fold. Some were seduced by promises of big money, others by a chance of changing the world, and a few were simply blackmailed.

Once in, they were never let out.

Not that anyone really wanted out.

Realizing the significance of what they were working on, they knew there couldn't be a higher calling or a greater purpose for their skills.

They were literally saving the world. Regrettably, as anonymous heroes.

"To Mark!" Armando raised his sixth shot of tequila. "Our boy genius. The one and only. The king of hacking. May he keep producing more fine lines of code!" He downed the shot, his cheering friends banging the table as they tossed back their drinks.

Mark felt a ripple of apprehension course through him. The salute was generic enough not to divulge anything specific and yet, potentially, it could have clued someone in.

SDPD, and Mark in particular, had provided the basis for the most famous computer virus in history. The virus that had infiltrated and damaged a dangerous rogue regime's nuclear facilities.

It was just the beginning.

They were well on their way to developing something even better. Soon, there would be no advanced weaponry that they couldn't disable, providing a safety net for the US and its trusted allies.

Naturally, some governments and terrorist organizations didn't appreciate their work, therefore Mark's life and the lives of his coworkers depended on their anonymity.

They were supposed to be invisible.

Heck, they were not supposed to even exist.

They were all drunk.

Well, everyone except for Svetlana, who was a bottomless pit. The tiny Russian mathematician had an off-the-charts IQ and a not-so-secret crush on Mark.

Holding her shot glass, she stood up to her full height of five feet nothing and saluted.

"To Mark!"

Then downing the straight shot of Absolut vodka she favored, Svetlana proceeded to drop herself onto his lap, wiggling her tiny butt to get more comfortable or perhaps stir something up.

Mark tensed. Wrapping his arm around her waist to steady her, he held her in place, preventing her from burrowing further.

The girl took it as a sign of encouragement. Turning to face him, she planted a wet kiss on his lips.

The guys went wild, whooping and whistling. "Svetlana! Svetlana! Svetlana!" They cheered her on.

Getting bold, she straddled him, took his cheeks in both hands, and licked his bottom lip with her small pink tongue, urging him to let her in.

Gently, not wishing to offend her, he pushed her away and rearranged her position so she remained seated only on one of his thighs. Holding on to her waist, he reached for his drink and saluted. "To the team!"

"To the team!" the guys shouted.

Dejected, Svetlana pushed up from his thigh, and the sad look she pinned on him made him wince.

It was a shame that she chose him as her object of desire. Any of the other guys would've loved for her to get frisky with them. Svetlana was a pretty little thing, with skin so white it seemed translucent, huge, pale blue eyes, and long, wavy, white-blond hair. She was just a kid, really, barely over the minimum drinking age.

Mark liked the girl, just not in the way she liked him.

Winking at her, he playfully smacked her butt. As he had intended, Svetlana perceived the gesture as him flirting back. Smiling, the hurt look gone from her big blue eyes, she turned and went back to her seat.

Mark exhaled quietly. Being gay wasn't a big deal to anyone anymore, but he was a product of a different era and preferred to keep it private.

No one needed to know.

He didn't flirt with other gays or go to gay bars. Instead, he'd found a lucrative escort service that provided partners to affluent men like himself. As these establishments went, it was discreet, costly, and offered a good selection of prime healthy studs.

For Mark, it was the perfect solution. He made shitloads of money he didn't need; his shares in the family business were more than enough to keep him in style. So why not spend it on his insatiable appetite? Safely and prudently.

He even had a tryst scheduled for later tonight and needed to leave soon to get ready.

Mark was excited.

Jason's web profile had been promising. The guy was young, handsome, and a student at Stanford, which promised he wouldn't be a complete dolt. Mark had no patience with stupidity. To him, it was as big a turn-off as an offensive body odor or a potbelly.

At nine o'clock, Mark excused himself, claiming a headache. He left after a round of cheerful, drunk hugs from his friends and a lingering one from Svetlana.

As he waited outside the club for the cab that would take him home, he sought to sober up in the night's cool air. Except, his buzz was more about the thrill of anticipation than any lingering intoxication.

He got home with twenty minutes to spare—just enough time to grab a quick shower, decide on a flattering pair of slacks and a button-down shirt, and set his living room to the right atmosphere. His guest being a paid escort, the effort wasn't necessary. Nevertheless, as this was the extent of his love life, Mark was determined to get the most out of it.

Thinking about the wicked seduction he had planned for tonight, Mark paced around his living room impatiently.

At the sound of a knock, he took a deep breath, and with a last quick glance at the mirror by the front door, hurried to open it for his guest.

The young man standing on his front porch looked nothing like the guy in the picture on the escort service's website.

Mark's neck tingled. Something was wrong.

"You're not Jason," he said, debating if he should slam the door in the guy's face.

"Sorry, Jason could not make it tonight. I'm Gideon, his replacement." The man forced a fake smile that did not reach his eyes.

Something was definitely off.

The guy was handsome enough; tall, with broad shoulders and muscular arms, but he wasn't gay. Mark had centuries of experience and an innate sense about these things. He could sniff out a gay man from a mile away.

Gideon, if this was his real name, definitely wasn't one.

There was something oddly familiar about the guy's aggressive vibe, though, and Mark's sensation of dread grew worse. A moment later, an adrenaline surge tightened his gut as he finally recognized it for what it was. His body's natural alarm system had been triggered by the presence of another immortal male.

Except, this one wasn't a member of his clan. And as the only other immortals Mark knew of were his clan's mortal enemies—the Doomers—this man meant him harm.

Terrified, he tried to slam the door closed, but the guy blocked it with his shoulder and with a brutal punch to the face sent Mark staggering backward. Following with his own body weight, the assassin brought Mark down.

When they hit the floor, Mark struggled to get free. But he was no match for the strength and skill of his assailant. In mere seconds, he found himself pinned face down to the floor with the immortal's fangs sinking deep into his neck.

All struggle ceased the moment the assassin's venom hit his system—the euphoria blooming in his mind and the languid feeling spreading through his body effectively paralyzing him.

He felt the venom being pumped into his bloodstream, pulsing in sync with his heartbeat. Although still aware enough to understand that he was about to die, in his drugged state he couldn't bring himself to care.

Eventually, the assassin withdrew his fangs and licked the puncture wounds closed. Mark knew that his near-immortal body would heal the bruising in a matter of minutes, and shortly thereafter, the venom paralyzing him would stop his heart, then disintegrate.

There would be no trace left of any wrongdoing, and heart failure would be determined as the most probable cause of death.

The family would obviously know. Besides blowing it to pieces, the only way to stop a near-immortal's heart was to inject the body with loads of venom.

His Advanced Decision Card listed Arwel's phone number as his next of kin.

The paramedics would call him.

Arwel would know what happened.

"This is for giving your corrupt western pets your stolen technology, you queer scum! This is for the computer virus!" the murderer hurled, then spat at Mark's face. "You brought the war to your own doorstep. Fighting by proxy is over!" he hissed through clenched teeth.

Mark was only dimly aware of what the Doomer was saying, hearing the words but not truly comprehending them. Through the drugged haze of his mind, he heard two more sets of footsteps entering his home. Conversing in short, clipped sentences, the men were speaking in some foreign language he didn't recognize.

It didn't matter. Nothing mattered anymore.

As he drifted away, he wondered if there was anything beyond this reality. Would his soul go on to some kind of heaven? Was there anything besides dark oblivion waiting for him?

If there was, he wished other souls would be there, so he wouldn't be alone. The thought of spending an eternity of incorporeal existence aware, and yet with no one to communicate with and nothing to do, terrified him more than fading into nothingness.

9

KIAN

Kian woke up with a start, his sweat-saturated hair sticking to the back of his neck and his heart still pounding from the nightmare. Filled with an intense sense of dread, all he could remember was the endless running and getting lost in a maze of strange staircases that had led nowhere, and being turned around in corridors that had twisted on themselves in impossible ways.

What had he been running from? Who had been chasing him? Why had they been chasing him?

It was just a dream. Kian tried to shake off the uneasy feeling. Nothing more than his mind rearranging bits and pieces of thoughts and memories to create an action horror flick with him in the starring role.

Yeah, that's all it was.

Unlike his mother and sisters, he didn't place much stock in dreams or premonitions. Ordinary, everyday reality was strange enough without throwing that into the mix.

Kian flung the damp duvet and tangled sheets off and dropped his feet to the floor. Sitting on the bed with his elbows on his thighs, he let his head drop as he waited for his heartbeat to slow down.

After a moment, the smell of freshly brewed coffee wafting from the kitchen was just the incentive he needed to shrug it off and jump into the shower. At first, he'd planned to be quick about it, but with the hot water jets pounding his skin from all six showerheads, it just felt so good that he allowed himself to linger.

It was absurd that a man surrounded by so much luxury got so little use out of it. There was always too much to do and not enough time to do it. He was rushing everything; his showers, his meals, his interactions with others. And yet, there were always some tasks left undone and issues unattended.

Most of the time Kian didn't mind the intense pace and the heavy mantle of responsibility. It kept him far too busy to dwell on the fact that he was lonely, although rarely alone. Or that his very long and productive life felt futile, despite all of his accomplishments.

Just once in a while he would have liked to slow down. Savor life. Smell the coffee.

Coffee, he could really use some right now, followed by Okidu's decadent waffles, topped with fresh fruit and smothered in coconut whipped cream. It wasn't the healthiest of breakfasts, but what the heck. It was good!

He was fortunate to have Okidu as his cook, his butler, his cleaner, his chauffeur, and his companion. Lots of hats for one person to wear, but then again, Okidu wasn't really a person. Quite often, Kian had trouble remembering that his butler wasn't a living breathing man.

Okidu was a marvel of ingenuity; a biomechanical masterpiece posing as a person. He didn't require sleep, didn't require maintenance, was self-repairing, and could survive on garbage. He could even morph his form from male to female and vice versa by adjusting his facial features and body shape; sometimes alternating between the two just for the sake of entertainment, and sometimes because circumstances favored a particular gender. Inherently, Okidu had none. No reproductive system or sex organs to define him one way or the other.

No one knew who'd created Okidu, or how, or when. There were only seven of his kind known to exist. A priceless masterpiece that could not be replicated or replaced. Over five thousand years ago, the seven had been a wedding gift to Kian's mother, a token of love from her groom. They had been believed to be an ancient relic even then.

Kian couldn't remember a time without Okidu being around. Since he was a little boy, Okidu had been there to ensure his safety, to feed him, to dress him, and to keep him company.

Though uncomfortable thinking of Okidu as a possession, as such, he was Kian's most valued one. Regrettably, Okidu couldn't be a friend or a confidant, he just didn't function that way. With his decision-making ability limited to a preprogrammed set of instructions within which he could learn and adapt, he was incapable of feeling true emotions. Nevertheless, he easily fooled the casual observer by approximating the appropriate tone and facial expressions.

"Good morning, Master!" Okidu exclaimed with a happy face and a perfect British accent as Kian entered the kitchen. Lately, he had taken to acting out his favorite mini-series on BBC, featuring an aristocratic British family and their household staff. Okidu had been alternating between mimicking the snobby butler, the hurried maid, and the cockney driver. Lacking a personality of his own, he must've calculated that mimicking cliché characters would make his passing for a human likelier.

It had been amusing at first. The exaggerated gestures, the different costumes, the accents. It was like having a private comedy show—every day, all day long, for weeks on end. It became annoying, and this morning it really grated on Kian's nerves.

Furthermore, there were only two waffles left, with Anandur and Brundar ogling them like a couple of hungry wolves.

"I saved the last two for you, Master!" Okidu chimed.

Kian felt like punching something, or someone, or rather two someones. Pinning the two with a hard stare, he barked, "Do I have to see your sorry faces every morning before I've even had my coffee? And then you wolf down my waffles? Don't you have food in your place?"

The brothers had an apartment two stories down from Kian's penthouse, and though every Guardian had one in the family's secure high rise, they preferred to stay together and share one.

Smack in the middle of downtown Los Angeles, the building he had built for the clan's American arm was a luxurious dig. To preserve appearances, some of the lower floor apartments were time-shared by international corporations in need of lodging for their visiting executives. The upper floors and an extensive underground facility served the clan. A private parking level, with elevators that required a thumbprint to open their doors, ensured his family could come and go safely and discreetly.

It took hiding in plain sight to a whole new level.

"Sorry, boss, but our kitchen doesn't come equipped with Okidu. And to be honest, between Brundar and me, we can't even fry an egg." Anandur was still eyeing the surviving waffles.

Kian sighed. "Resistance is futile," he murmured and poured himself a cup of coffee. Leaning his butt against the counter, he took a satisfying first sip of the hot brew.

"Please make some more waffles for the kids, Okidu. You have underestimated their appetite."

"Coming right up, sire!"

"It smells heavenly in here." Kri, their only female Guardian, poked her head into the kitchen.

Tall and athletic, his young niece was a kick-ass kind of girl, which got her the approval of the male Guardians. And although muscular and wide shouldered, she still managed to look feminine.

As always, her long tawny hair was pulled away from her pretty face and woven into a tight braid. Today, the heavy rope was draped over the front of a red workout shirt.

"Okidu made waffles, and no one called me? I'm deeply wounded." She walked in and planted her rear on a stool.

"Come in. Why the hell not? It's a goddamn party!" Kian dropped a plate in front of Kri and poured her a cup of coffee.

He couldn't tell her to go away now, could he? She had as much right, or lack thereof, to invade his kitchen as the other two.

"Thank you, Kian. As always, you're so kind." Kri accepted the mug. Holding it in both hands, she took a sip. "Ugh, bitter, I need sugar." As his stern look made it perfectly clear that he was done serving her, Kri got up to get it herself. "I know. I've already used up my quota of hospitality."

"What are you doing here, Kri?"

"I thought I'd stop by on my way to the gym and see if you wanted to join me for a workout." Avoiding his eyes, Kri looked down at her cup.

The girl had a silly crush on him and was using every excuse as an opportunity to spend more time with him.

Kian ignored it.

Descending from the same matrilineal line, they were considered closely related despite the many generations separating them.

A serious taboo.

Not that he would have ever considered anything even if that wasn't the case. In his mind, Kri would always be his little niece.

He figured she'd get over it.

Being only forty-one years old, Kri was barely a teenager in near-immortal terms, and like a mortal teenager, he assumed she suffered from a case of transitory, immature infatuation.

One she would laugh off later in life.

Kian glared at her, then turned to glare at the guys. "From now on, no one comes up here before nine in the morning, *capisce*?" He regarded their despondent faces. "And I want you to knock and wait to be allowed in. No more waltzing in whenever you feel like it. This is not the goddamn subway station!"

They had the same exchange every couple of weeks. Like spoiled kids, they'd behave for a while, then go back to pissing him off.

That was the trouble with employing family. What could he do?

Couldn't fire them, couldn't smother them either. It would upset their mothers.

Kian sighed.

"But the waffles, Kian! The waffles!" Kri lamented in mock despair.

"Get the fucking recipe!"

A loud knock announced another member of the team. Okidu rushed over to open it for Onegus, the head of the Guardians.

Taking one sniff of the tantalizing aroma, Onegus smiled his Hollywood smile, and, what a surprise, immediately beelined for the kitchen.

At least the SOB was actually supposed to show up for his morning meeting with Kian.

"Oh no you don't! Everybody out! Let's move the party to the other room!" Kian passed through the butler's pantry into the dining room, which was never used for its primary function. Kian ate at the kitchen counter and never had the kind of guests he wanted to invite to a sit-down dinner.

He liked to work from home, though, so when needed, he used the room for informal meetings. Not that this was a meeting.

More like a home invasion...

His home office was his quiet place to work, and he didn't want the gang invading it and messing with his neatly arranged stuff.

On some level, the fact that the whole force could fit easily inside his dining room was depressing. The number of Guardians had shrunk in recent years, and with only seven of them remaining, their duties were limited to providing security detail, mainly to him as Regent, and internal policing—enforcing the clan's laws.

Back in the old country, when the force had still been the size of a small battalion, Kian had led it into more battles than he cared to remember. In the days of hand to hand combat, when the Guardians had been tasked with protecting and guarding the clan's turf, the force had numbered between sixty and eighty warriors. But as times had changed—the USA becoming a relatively safe place for them to live and hide in—it had dwindled down, its defense services no longer needed.

Kian, as the clan's American Regent, was in charge of the Guardians as well as heading the local clan-council. And that was in addition to managing the clan's huge business empire.

He snorted as he remembered thinking that acting as Regent, over what were now two hundred eighty-three people, would be an easy job. It wasn't.

With their business empire growing and branching into various industries, Kian was working harder and longer than ever. There simply weren't enough goddamned hours in the day. Was it a wonder then that he was short-tempered and irritable?

He couldn't remember the last time he had some time off.

Just as his uninvited guests, and Onegus, were preparing to plant their butts on the chairs surrounding his long dining table, Kian's cell phone vibrated.

He pulled it out and glanced at the caller's name before answering. "Arwel. What's up in the Bay Area?"

There was a moment of silence, then a sigh.

Kian felt a ripple of anxiety rush down his spine. "Talk to me!"

"Mark was found dead in his home this morning." Arwel paused.

Kian remained silent, stunned by the impossible news.

"His cleaning lady found him on the floor of his living room and called 911. He had my number on his Advanced Decision Card, listing me as next of kin."

Arwel's speech faltered. It had been a while since a member of their family had been killed. The security and anonymity the clan enjoyed in their adopted home made them complacent. The pain of loss had faded into distant memory. Facing it once again was hard, more so for Arwel.

The poor guy had enough trouble coping with life as it was, with his over-receptive mind bombarded relentlessly by the emotions of others. To protect himself, he often drank excessively. Though he sounded sober now.

"His body was intact. The paramedics declared heart failure as the probable cause of death. Obviously, we know what that means —fangs and venom. We checked his house for clues." There was another pause. "Doomers got him, Kian. They are here and have somehow found Mark."

As Kian's mind processed the implications, the chill that had started in his heart upon first hearing the disturbing news spread out to encompass his entire body.

DOOM—the Devout Order Of Mortdh Brotherhood—was his clan's ancient enemy. Sworn to annihilate every last member of his family and destroy any and all progress Annani was helping humanity achieve, they sought to plunge the world back into ignorance and darkness.

Theirs wasn't an idle threat.

Time and again, the order had manipulated mortal affairs by planting seeds of hatred, triggering wars, and dragging humanity down—successfully halting and reversing social and scientific advancement all too often.

The DOOM Brotherhood was a relentless scourge.

It was Kian's worst nightmare made manifest. He had believed that hiding in plain sight among the multitudes of mortals would keep his family safe from this powerful enemy. And yet, the Doomers had somehow gotten to Mark.

"Are you sure he was murdered by Doomers?"

"They left a message taped to his computer screen."

"What did it say?"

"Nothing and everything. It's a drawing. Two sickle swords crossed at the handle, flanking a disk. Their fucking emblem. I took a photo of it."

"Send me the picture."

"Hold on."

Kian switched screens. The image of the crude drawing was blurry, but there was no mistaking the DOOM's emblem.

As grief and impotent rage warred for dominance over his emotions, he pushed up from his chair and began pacing.

As a man of solution-driven action, Kian felt an irrational, overbearing need to do something, anything, that would make this all go away. Except, there was no action that would bring Mark back. No going back in time and changing the decisions that had led to this.

The only thing left for him to do was to mourn the dead and safeguard the living.

"Bring our boy home... Take the jet and bring him here," he told Arwel, then paused to realign his mental gears and get them in motion.

"Check his body and make sure they didn't plant any tracking devices on him. The bastards know we'd bring Mark home for a proper service. Can't risk them following you here. Go through his place again, see if anything is missing. Check for any clues that can point to us; letters, photos, personal mementos, and the sort. If you find anything like that, bring it here. I'm sure his mother will want to have it. Pay attention to details. I need to know if they found anything."

"I'm on it!" Arwel was about to hang up.

"Arwel! I'm not done. I want all clan members from your area evacuated. Have Bhathian contact them and explain the gravity of the situation. Provide each one with a different route and mode of transportation. I don't want a mad rush to the airport. They are to take nothing and tell no one. Just get up and go. We'll take care of the details once everyone is safe."

"They are not gonna like it, boss."

"I know, but until we figure out what went down, they'll be chilling their butts over here. I'd rather have them pissed than dead."

Kian ended the call and turned to the Guardians. By the look of their somber faces, they were ready to hear the bad news, waiting for the boulder to start rolling and come crashing down on them.

It was one of those moments everyone dreads; the unexpected disaster striking out of nowhere, destroying the illusion that you're in control, and shoving the cruel reality in your face.

Shit happens! Deal with it!

Squaring his shoulders, Kian delivered the grim update. "As you've probably figured out, we have a situation. Mark, son of Micah, was murdered in his home last night." Kian lifted his phone to show them the DOOM emblem. "This was left behind, taped to his computer screen."

"Fuck!" was the only response from Anandur. Brundar and Onegus looked ready to kill, and Kri sniffled, trying to hold back her tears.

None of them knew Mark very well, but they knew of him; the clan's genius programmer. His loss was devastating not only on a personal level but also as an asset that would be difficult to replace.

Kian sat down and dropped his elbows on the table, then hung his head on his fisted hands. "It's all my fault. I take full responsibility," he admitted, the guilt eating at his gut.

With a curse, Onegus brought his fist down on the table. "How could it be your fault, Kian? Beyond your usual spiel of being Regent and responsible for everyone and everything. Yadda, yadda, yadda."

"It is my fault. I might as well have placed a neon sign, pointing to his head and blinking: *Here I am. Come get me!* Anyone with half a brain could've figured out that a code this sophisticated couldn't have been developed with current knowhow."

Kian had known he was taking a big risk by allowing Mark to leak too much info too soon. But he had felt he had no choice. The risk of WMDs in the hands of power-hungry despots outweighed the risk of exposure. And besides, he had never imagined that the Doomers would come after Mark. He'd assumed that if they'd retaliate, they'd do it the same way they had always done, using the mortals under their influence against those the clan was helping.

Kian continued, "After so many years with no casualties, we've become complacent. And even before, the few of us the Doomers managed to snare were random cases of a male being in the wrong place at the wrong time. They've never been able to hunt us down successfully; there are just too few of us, and we hide too well.

Except now, I feel like I've drawn the fuckers a goddamned yellow brick road!"

"Maybe they just got lucky with Mark?" Kri suggested. Which earned her the condescending you-don't-know-what-you're-talking-about look from the others.

"No, guys, just hear me out. Think of how the Doomers always retaliated before. They went after our humans or helped theirs against ours. Suppose the Doomers were seeking revenge on the team that worked on that code. They somehow find them, identify Mark as the top programmer, and decide to take him out; send us a message. I bet they didn't even know he was one of us."

Kri got more animated. "We never used to work so close with mortals. We'd supply a bit of information and back off, let them work on it, figure it on their own. Then we'd supply some more, so it would look legit—home grown. No way the Doomers were expecting to find an immortal working on the same team with mortals. No freaking way!" Kri stared them down, daring them to try and refute her logic.

"She might have a point," Onegus admitted.

"Even if Kri is right, that doesn't change the outcome. Doomers still found and murdered Mark. And now that they have a clue as to what to look for and where, they might find more of us." Kian pushed to his feet and walked over to Kri. "Good thinking, though. You're a smart girl." He squeezed her shoulder.

At any other time, under different circumstances, Kri would've been ecstatic to receive this kind of praise from Kian. Now, she just nodded and reached for his hand on her shoulder, squeezing it back.

"Sire, the waffles are ready!" Okidu chose that moment to bring in a loaded platter. He placed it carefully on the sideboard, then scurried away, expecting a stampede. But the food was ignored.

"Thank you, Okidu," Kian dismissed him. "Actually, I need you to do one more thing. Make sure we have four clean, vacant apartments ready, and if you could, please air Amanda's penthouse. We are about to have overnight guests."

"Certainly, sire!" Okidu bowed.

"Thank you." Kian nodded to Okidu and faced the Guardians.

"Onegus, I want you to call an emergency council meeting for nine in the evening today. Don't tell them what it's about. I don't want anyone calling Micah to offer condolences before I see her. No one should get news like that over the phone. We'll meet in the big council room. Instruct everyone to wear their ceremonial robes. I'm going to demand sequestering for all council members, which they will surely bitch and moan about. But we don't have enough manpower to provide security detail for each of them separately. I need them here, protected. Hopefully, the formalities will impress upon them how serious I am about this. That will be all."

Kian's eyes followed his people as they pushed away from the table and silently trudged toward the living room. Onegus pulled open the front door, and with a slight nod, left followed by the somber brothers. Kri remained behind, looking lost.

Walking up to her, Kian took her in his arms and let her burrow her nose into his neck, hugging her for a long moment. Being so young, she had never faced the loss of a friend, and unlike the men's emotions which had been deadened by centuries of countless battles, hers were still raw with pain and grief. When she sighed and let go of him, he looked into her eyes, making sure she was okay.

But there was a reason he'd taken Kri on as a guardian. Squaring her shoulders, she pushed her chin up, and the determination he saw in her eyes proved to him that she really was the hard-ass he'd hired.

"Go, I need time to plan." He dismissed her with a pat to her back.

Alone, Kian allowed himself to drift on the waves of guilt and dread for a few moments, letting his mind go in different directions, envisioning every foreseeable danger and coming up with creative if not feasible solutions. It was an old and tried technique of his. Like purging out the pus from a malignant wound; eventually the blood would run clean, and healing would start.

Regrettably, other than the steps he'd already taken, he came up with nothing.

First thing on his agenda was persuading his sister to move into the keep. Out of all the council members, he expected her to give him the most trouble. He'd better talk to her before the meeting and prepare her. It would save him the public drama. Besides, getting Amanda to safety was a priority.

Good luck with that.

Preparing for battle, he pulled out his phone and called her.

After the initial shock over the news had worn off and her sniffles had subsided, she protested, "I can't just abandon my lab or not show up for classes.

Kian cut her short. "So come to the meeting and vote against!"

"You know how the vote will go!" she hissed.

"Yes I do. And if you had an ounce of wisdom in that brain of yours, you wouldn't be fighting me over this. More than your life is in danger. If they find you, they wouldn't kill you, you'd just wish they had."

Amanda huffed. "You're overestimating the risk. They are not going to find me. And if you're that concerned about my safety, assign a couple of Guardians to watch over me."

"You know we are short on Guardians. That's why I'm calling for the sequestering of all council members. I just can't keep everyone safe unless they are all in one location."

"Find a solution. I'm not leaving my work." She ended the call.

Kian sighed and ran the fingers of both hands through his hair, smoothing back the flyaway strands. He'd have to go over to her place himself and convince her it was the smart thing to do.

Or, what was more likely, drag her out kicking and screaming.

10

KIAN

It was oppressively quiet in the SUV on the way to Amanda's lab. The Lexus's almost soundproof interior filtered the outside traffic noise, leaving Brundar and Anandur's tight-lipped silence undisturbed.

Kian craved a cigarette, desperately, and a shot of whiskey or two.

He'd quit smoking years ago, but here and there the craving returned with gusto. Like it did now. It wasn't concern for his health that had prompted him to get rid of the habit, after all, his kind didn't get cancer or heart disease. He just hated smelling like an ashtray. The way the stench had used to cling to his hair and clothing had disgusted him.

Though he would kill for one now.

Comforting the devastated Micah had been excruciating. It had left him empty and deflated. There was no good way to deliver this kind of news to a mother. You offered your sympathy, said how sorry you were, offered your help in anything and everything.

Blah, blah, blah... The words hadn't even registered. In the end, he'd just held her while she'd cried.

And in the aftermath, he'd been left with no energy to deal with Amanda.

Heaving a sigh, Kian gazed out the window and watched the cars passing them by. He wondered what kind of sorrows their mortal occupants were hiding behind their impassive expressions.

There was so much anguish in their short, miserable lives, and family dying on them was such an integral part of their experience that it defined the whole of their existence. He suspected humans coped with the depressing certainty of their own mortality by keeping it out of their thoughts in any way they could. It sucked.

To lose a loved one was the worst experience ever. He wouldn't allow that to happen to him.

Not again.

There was nothing he could've done to prevent Lilen's death all those centuries ago, but he'd be damned if he'd let anything happen to his obstinate sister.

Not on his watch.

Fisting his hands, he felt his lips curl in a snarl as his resolve hardened. He would march into that lab, throw Amanda over his shoulder, and carry her to the SUV. And he didn't give a damn if he had to do it while she was kicking and screaming the whole way. To keep her safe, he'd even lock her in one of the underground cells.

Yeah, that sounds good. Easiest way to deal with the brat.

Kian took a deep breath. Okay... *like that will fly.*

He needed to chill.

Patience is a virtue, he repeated. *Patience is a virtue.*

Yeah, it just wasn't one of his.

Let someone else get that merit badge. Kian didn't plan on applying for sainthood anytime soon.

Taking the elevator down to Amanda's lab, he wondered if it just happened to be in the basement of the research facility or had Amanda chosen it because she preferred working underground.

It seemed to be a natural default, an unconscious preference for his kind. The older ones, like him, still suffered from some sensitivity to harsh light, but it was nothing a pair of quality sunglasses couldn't handle, and certainly nothing that bothered the younger immortals.

Still, the original race of gods had truly shunned the sunlight. Their sensitive eyes had to be covered in protective goggles to filter even the little light that could infiltrate through the sides of a more ordinary protective eyewear.

There had been no windows in their dwellings. Instead, shafts positioned diagonally through the thick walls had provided airflow while minimizing sunlight.

The flip side of this handicap had been an excellent night vision, which near-immortals shared to some degree with their ancestors. The gods had been nocturnal creatures, more comfortable in the relative darkness of the night when the soft glow of the moon and stars replaced the harsh sunlight. So much gentler on their sensitive eyes and skin.

Not for the first time, it crossed his mind that his ancestors must've been at the source of the outrageous vampire myths.

Creatures with fangs that sucked blood and burned in sunlight...

Right.

Mortals and their wild imaginations running amok with exaggerations and embellishments.

They got the fangs and sunlight part right, even the mind control was spot on, but where had the blood-sucking part come from? Or the red eyes for that matter? An immortal's eyes tearing up from too much exposure to the sun's harsh light? A careless one forgetting to lick the puncture wounds closed?

Who knew?

The truth was that the gods of old were at the source of many intriguing stories, with the vampire lore being one of the most imaginative. In his opinion, however, the legends of the snake people were more fitting. What was it about bats that so fascinated mortals that they preferred them to snakes? Not that he was all that fond of reptiles himself. Besides, the things couldn't fly, and as this particular ability was part of what made the vampire stories work, the bats kind of made sense.

His bodyguards were still uncharacteristically quiet as they made their way down the corridor, the rhythmic beat of their boots on the concrete floor the only indication that they were still with him.

He wasn't expecting Brundar to be chattering away, but Anandur's silence bothered him. Kian turned to look back at the brothers. Though grimly focused, their eyes were following their feet instead of scoping the place.

Not good.

"Snap out of it, guys! And stay alert! You think it's safe down here just because there are people all around us?"

"What jumped and bit you on the ass, Kian! You think I don't pay attention? I have been doing the same shit for how long now? A millennium? I can do it sleepwalking." Anandur sounded more pissed than offended.

"Yeah, yeah. You may kiss my ass to make it all better, lick it clean too!" Kian jumped sideways to avoid the punch Anandur aimed at his shoulder.

At least the guy was smiling now.

Brundar shook his head and kept going, leaving them behind.

Stopping at the junction of corridors that terminated at the one leading to Amanda's lab, Kian called him back. "Stay here. This is a good spot. You can see everyone coming this way from either direction." He pointed to where he wanted them to stand guard.

"I'm going in by myself. The hellion is not going to like an audience."

Not exactly. Amanda loved drama. It was Kian who could live without it. "Try not to attract any attention to yourselves, and stay alert!"

11

ANANDUR

Leaning against the wall next to his brother, Anandur smirked as he watched Kian duck into Amanda's lab. The guy was in for one hell of a fight, and if Kian thought it would go down easier without an audience, he was deluding himself.

"Man, I would've loved to see that," he told Brundar.

His brother ignored him, as usual not interested in talking.

Anandur shook his head and turned his attention to the sparse foot traffic. A trio of giggling girls was heading his way, and he had to admit that staying out in the corridor was proving to be quite entertaining.

The girls were eyeing him and his brother with unabashed interest, smiling and sauntering as they got closer.

Gutsy, forward minxes.

Evidently, it was easier said than done for him and Brundar to avoid attracting attention.

Not that he had a problem with that.

With what the girls were wearing, or rather not wearing, he got himself a healthy eyeful of young female flesh. In addition to the painted-on, torn jeans all three were wearing, the tall brunette's T-shirt was open at the sides with her purple lace bra showing, while her friend's sported so many slashes that there was hardly any of it left to cover anything. And the one with the spiky pink hair wore a tiny thing with a Mickey Mouse picture on it that looked like something she'd swiped off her kid brother.

Got to love this generation, Anandur thought as he flashed them his best seductive smile and winked.

Their response to his blatantly masculine charm was as immediate as it was predictable, and his nostrils flared as the unmistakable, sweet smell of female arousal reached him, triggering his predatory instincts.

Brundar wasn't doing much better. Growling quietly beside him, his brother's body tensed as he got ready to pounce.

Adjusting himself, Anandur wrapped a restraining arm around Brundar's shoulders, holding on tight and squeezing hard while smiling at the girls.

"Damn, why are the good-looking guys always gay? It's so unfair!" the tall one whispered to her friends.

Anandur chuckled, his hearing more acute than the girls could ever suspect. Squeezing Brundar even harder, he kissed the top of his brother's head.

"I'm going to break your fucking arm if you don't let go," Brundar hissed.

Frowning, Anandur released his brother with a pitying sidelong glance. The poor guy suffered from a crippling lack of a sense of humor.

When the disappointed trio disappeared behind a corner, turning into another corridor, Brundar hastily cast a shrouding illusion around Anandur and himself. Obscuring their presence from any mortal passerby, his illusion made them appear part of the wall—undetectable unless someone bumped straight into them.

12

SYSSI

Syssi focused on the images flashing at evenly spaced time intervals on the screen: square, circle, star, triangle, star, circle, triangle, square...

The shapes were popping randomly in a never-ending sequence, and her task was to guess which one would flash next and hit the appropriate key—before the image appeared.

It was mind-numbingly boring, mainly since she'd been at it for the past couple of hours.

Any other day, she would've just quit. After straining her mind for so long, the test results were iffy anyway, but not today.

Syssi had never seen Amanda in such a bitchy mood before. The woman was scary. Something or someone must have pissed her off big time during her lunch break because she'd come back sullen and practically snarling at everyone.

Hannah and David had done the smart thing and had left an hour ago... Ran for their lives was more like it.

But not Syssi, no, Amanda's precognition experiments favorite test bunny had to stay behind.

Soon, she'd have to stop. Her eyes were tearing and her headache was blooming into a full-blown migraine. In a few minutes, she'd have to tell Amanda she couldn't take it anymore.

Sighing, she rubbed her blurry eyes as the lab's door opened with a creak.

Curious to see who it was, Syssi peeked between one flashing symbol and the next...

And lost her concentration.

Or rather had it blown to pieces.

The man closing the door was breathtakingly handsome; tall, broad-shouldered, and perfectly proportioned under the conservative charcoal suit he was wearing. The suit looked expensive, and it had been probably custom made for him, but she was sure it wasn't hiding any flab. The guy looked like he was all muscle.

Holding himself regally as he scanned the lab, his posture was somewhat stiff, until he found Amanda and loosened marginally.

As he glared at her, his deep blue eyes were hard and sad, making him appear angry, or frustrated.

He smoothed back his chin-length tawny hair in what seemed like a nervous habit, brushing the curling ends with his fingers and forcing them away from his angular, beautiful face.

Holding her breath, Syssi felt faint, her heart racing wildly and her legs turning to rubber. With an effort, she pulled air into her oxygen starved lungs and rubbed her tingling arms.

"You can save your breath, Kian. I'm not going to let you drag me away to your lair. There is nothing you can say that will persuade me to abandon my work. It's too important, so turn around and go home." Amanda circled her finger and pointed it at the door.

When he didn't budge, she crossed her arms over her chest and narrowed her eyes, staring him down while tapping her high-heeled shoe on the concrete floor.

So, this is Kian, Amanda's brother. Wow.

He looked nothing like Syssi had imagined he would. On the few occasions Amanda had mentioned her brother, she'd referred to him as the old goat, or the stupid old goat, painting in Syssi's mind an image of an older guy sporting a goatee and thinning, wispy hair.

In her wildest dreams, Syssi couldn't have imagined him as the magnificent Greek-god-facsimile standing before her. Although, with Amanda as his sister, she should have known better. A stunning woman like her boss just couldn't have an unattractive man for a brother.

Syssi felt like an ugly duckling next to these beautiful swans. Who wouldn't? No mere mortal could achieve this level of perfection.

Forcing her eyes away, she tried to do a disappearing act by sliding down in her chair and hiding behind her computer screen. Too shook up to continue the experiment, she went through the motions and pretended to be working, using it as an excuse to stay out of sight.

There was no way she was attracting attention to herself. If she were lucky, Kian would leave without ever noticing her.

Syssi didn't think she could survive an introduction.

Her reaction to him was so immediate and so overpowering that she had no idea what to do with it. She'd never responded like this to a man.

Syssi had never been one of those girls who idolized movie stars or rockers, and their big muscles and gorgeous faces had left her indifferent. Looks just hadn't been all that important to her. All she'd ever wanted was a nice, intelligent guy who was decent looking.

And yet, here she was, yearning with terrifying intensity for a man that could never be hers. Men like him didn't exist in her world.

He was beautiful, yet all male, there was nothing feminine about his perfect features. And his sophisticated business suit didn't fool her. Kian exuded a kind of primitive power and dominance that terrified her.

Because instinctively she felt compelled to submit to it.

Where the hell were these thoughts coming from? Even the terminology was foreign to her. What was happening to her?

Oh, God, just make him leave already.

She was going to take these embarrassing thoughts with her to the grave. No one, and she meant absolutely no one, would ever find out that such absurdities had ever flitted through her mind. She might not be a bra-burning feminist, but she would never let anyone dominate her either.

"Why are you being so stubborn? Did I really need to drop everything and come over here because you wouldn't listen to reason? There is real danger out there, and I can't let you—" Kian stopped mid-sentence as Amanda held a finger to her lips, shushing him, and pointed toward the back of the room.

"Syssi, stop hiding and come meet my brother Kian." Amanda was getting closer, waving her hand in invitation.

Syssi remained glued to her chair, hoping the floor would split open and swallow her up.

"Come out, girl. He doesn't bite... much." Amanda's snort sounded like a cackle.

Syssi shrunk away from her. The woman's sarcastic tone sounded positively evil, evoking in her imagination an image of the beautiful swans morphing into ugly vultures.

"Stop it, Amanda! You're scaring the girl with your idiotic comments!" Kian snapped.

Syssi felt like laughing—a crazy, cackling laugh. She wasn't scared of them. Why would he think that? What really scared her was her own reaction to Kian. She was intimidated out of her freaking mind, and now Amanda was forcing her to show herself.

No guy had ever terrified her like that. On occasion, she'd felt awkward, a little uncomfortable, and her accursed uncontrolled blushing had always been an impediment to her romantic life. But this was so out of her realm of experience that it was panic attack inducing.

As Kian's footsteps got closer, sweat broke out over her face and her stomach roiled. And then he was standing right beside her, extending his hand to help her up.

No-no-no-no!

Except, what choice did she have?

Lifting her head, Syssi thanked providence, her cursed foresight, and whatever else had prompted her to take a little extra care with her looks this morning. She had blow-dried her hair, put on a little makeup, and worn a nice pair of pumps that added three inches to her height.

At least she wouldn't look like a complete midget troll standing next to all that perfection.

But then, as her eyes made it all the way up to his face, her heart skipped a beat. This spectacular man was looking down at her with uncensored male appreciation.

Enthralled by the hunger in his eyes, she took his offered hand, the jolt of energy passing through her body bringing on such a strong blast of desire that it stunned and shamed her at the same time.

If her legs felt like rubber before, now her knees dissolved completely. She was holding onto his hand for dear life, her whole weight leaning on it. "Sorry, my legs must've gone numb from sitting too long," she managed in a hoarse whisper.

In the silence that followed, the hunger she saw in Kian's expression burned like an inferno before abruptly turning into scalding ice.

The change was startling.

As he straightened, his posture stiffened, his eyes hardened in disapproval, and his mouth narrowed.

He looked angry again. Forget angry, he looked savage, cruel. But this time his displeasure was directed at her, and not at Amanda.

Syssi felt her face heat up. She must've misinterpreted his expression, and her response had been totally inappropriate. Worse, her attraction to Kian must have been blatantly obvious for him to notice it, and he decided he wanted nothing to do with her.

Oh, God.

A guy like that probably had women throwing themselves at

him constantly; prettier women, elegant, sophisticated, assertive. He was so far out of her league, he might as well have been from a different planet.

Mortified, she lowered her eyes.

13

KIAN

Kian had been ready to chew Amanda's head off for shushing him, but then she'd pointed her finger at the girl hiding behind a large computer screen.

Curious, he'd dipped his head.

All he had seen under the desk were jean-clad, long legs and a pair of slender, heeled feet, but his enhanced senses had registered the girl's rapid heartbeat and the acrid aroma of her fear.

The two of them snarling at each other's throats like a couple of feral beasts, they must've scared the girl. And then Amanda had made it even worse with her sarcasm, sounding like a wicked witch and fueling the girl's fear instead of trying to ease it.

Intending to rectify the situation, he'd crossed the short distance to the girl, when it had suddenly dawned on him that Amanda had called her Syssi.

The same girl she wanted him to seduce.

Amanda's schemes aside, though, he needed to do something before the poor thing fainted. And at any rate, he was intrigued.

Extending his arm to help her up, he was curious to see her face, but it was hidden behind a curtain of wavy blond hair. It wasn't exactly blond, though. Several shades of light browns, blonds, and gold intertwined to create a spectacular whole. Taking a sniff, he knew it wasn't the kind that came out of a box. There was no residual smell of chemicals—just the light flowery scent of her shampoo. Not that he would've minded one way or another. Amanda colored her hair from time to time to change her looks, and it wasn't only about keeping her identity secret. She simply enjoyed it.

With a little sigh, the girl seemed to gather enough courage to look up at him.

Kian was dumbstruck.

Syssi was beautiful.

Staring at her lovely, blushing face, he was entrapped by her guileless gaze. The man who'd bedded thousands of women was rendered speechless by one blushing girl.

Kian couldn't explain it if he tried.

Yes, she was lovely, beautiful, with pale, flawless skin, and a small straight nose, and those perfectly shaped, plump, pink lips that were utterly kissable.

But what had delivered that gut-crunching punch was her big, bright, blue-green eyes.

In that brief moment, when their eyes had first met, he'd gotten a glimpse of her soul.

Startled, he kept staring, captivated, feeling as if he knew her—was coming home to her after being lost for a long time. It was all out there in her sincere, open face—the intelligence, the kindness, the shadow of sadness that shouldn't have been there.

And a hesitant, hopeful expression.

So sweet.

The girl was attracted to him, and she wanted him to like her.

Her lashes dropped over her expressive eyes, and she bit down on her lower lip before taking his offered hand.

Incredibly, that one small innocent touch stunned him, igniting an incinerating erotic current that burned a path straight from her fingers down to his groin.

What the hell?

Cursing the traitor in his pants, Kian was grateful for his suit jacket covering the evidence of his response. The girl looked flustered enough without getting a gander of that, and besides, he hated giving Amanda the satisfaction of being right.

Syssi was all that Amanda had claimed her to be and more.

Now that he had gotten her standing, Kian could also appreciate her deliciously curved body as Amanda had so aptly put it. Skintight jeans hugged long slim legs, the gentle curve of her hips narrowing into a small waist. Perfectly shaped breasts, substantial but not too big, strained her T-shirt, stretching it across her chest. And through the split neckline, he got a delightful glimpse of the rounded tops.

Damn! Amanda had been right. Syssi was exactly his type.

And she was blushing!

What girl blushed these days? None that he'd encountered lately, and for sure none so gorgeously delicious.

That demure demeanor just floored him.

Combined with the slight whiff of her arousal intermingled with that of her anxiety, the potent elixir cranked the dial of his lust all the way up, turning it into a burning need. His venom-glands began pulsating, swelling and dripping venom droplets down his elongated fangs into his mouth. The damned razor-sharp things were threatening to punch out over his bottom lip.

Kian pressed his lips tight. He could just imagine the sight of him flashing these beauties, a monster straight out of a horror flick. He'd bet Syssi's arousal would be gone in a flash. She would run screaming, and that hopeful infatuated look would be gone for good.

But oh, man, how he wanted her.

His imagination ran amok with the things he wanted to do to her, the erotic scenes flashing rapidly through his mind.

First, he'd tighten his grip on her hand and yank her to him, holding her sweet curves flush against his front, then grab her nape to tilt her head up and catch her lips, kissing the living daylights out of her. When he'd gotten her all breathless and panting, he would lower her to the desk and peel those tight jeans off her...

Yeah.

Kian shook himself. He had to stop that train wreck before it crashed and burned. Reining in his runaway libido, he shackled it with the steel cables of his tight self-control.

Bloody immortal hormones.

This whole thing was absurd. If that little chit had anything special about her, it was her ability to turn both his sister and him into blabbering, romantic dolts. He was too old and too experienced for these kinds of teenage fantasies.

Recognizing her...

Feeling like coming home to her...

He couldn't believe this kind of nonsense even crossed his mind.

It must've been just plain old lust.

For the past couple of nights, he had not gone prowling, and his sex-starved body was kicking his hormones into overdrive and making him stupid.

Sensing the change in him, Syssi pulled her hand out of his grasp and lowered her eyes, blushing again.

Oh, fuck, her timid response just threw more gasoline on the fire of his arousal, spurring on the predator in him.

Taking a deep breath, Kian hissed as he pulled it through his clenched teeth.

Oh, great, now he was hissing... charming.

He had to get out of there.

As he turned away from her to face his smirking sister, he felt the girl's hurt gaze burning holes in his back.

"Now, who has his knickers in a twist? Dear brother of mine." Amanda mocked his agitation. "Don't pay any attention to his foul mood, Syssi. It has nothing to do with you. It's just the way he is. An. Old. Grouchy. Goat." Amanda walked over to Syssi and wrapped a supportive arm around the girl's shoulders.

It was a ridiculous standoff, with Kian brooding on one side, and the two women forming a united front against him on the other.

When had he become the villain here?

He just wanted to get it over with, haul Amanda home and get that smoke and drink he was so desperately craving.

14

BRUNDAR

Out in the hallway, Brundar leaned his shoulder against the wall, twisting his dagger between his fingers as he observed the sparse foot traffic of mortals passing him by.

There was a common pattern to the way they talked, walked, the stuff they wore and the things they carried.

They fit a certain profile.

Some were leaving, walking in chatty groups of twos and threes, heading to the cafeteria or some other joint for their evening meal and making plans for later on. Others, holding on to their coffee mugs and their laptop cases, were coming in to do some late work at the labs.

Behind him, Anandur chuckled.

His brother was passing the time by entertaining himself with stupid YouTube clips on his phone, oblivious to the fact that he was on guard duty and was supposed to be invisible.

Idiot.

Brundar rolled his eyes as he imagined the ghost stories Anandur's disembodied chuckles might start. Glancing both ways, he checked to see if any of the students walking by them had overheard his idiot of a brother.

A girl clutching her laptop hurried by him without a glance, and another walked away, too busy talking on her phone to notice anything. But something about the three guys coming his way made the hair on the back of his neck tingle in alarm.

Snapping to attention, Brundar palmed the hilt of his dagger.

The men didn't fit the mold he'd discerned.

With no coffee or laptops, the young men were built like linebackers and marched purposefully with the gait of trained warriors.

They were heading straight for Anandur and him, staring right at them as if the fuckers weren't at all affected by his concealing illusion.

They shouldn't have been able to penetrate his shroud... unless...

Unsheathing his second dagger, Brundar assumed a fighting stance. Next to him Anandur did the same while speed-dialing Kian, proving he hadn't been as distracted as he'd appeared to be.

"Doomers in the hall. About to engage," he said when the shit hit the fan.

15

SYSSI

As Kian ended the call and returned the phone to his pocket, his face turned from brooding to grim to determined, and his body seemed to swell with aggression.

Something was up.

"Is there another way out of here?" he barked, confirming Syssi's suspicion.

"We can pass through the kitchenette to the adjoining lab; its front exit door faces a parallel corridor." Amanda hurried to grab her purse and laptop. "Syssi, take your stuff, we are leaving!" She was already in the kitchen.

Kian urged Syssi to follow.

"What's going on?" she asked while trying to walk as fast as Kian's hand on the small of her back was propelling her to. His stride was so long that she was forced to jog to keep up.

"Some unwanted company I'd rather avoid is coming this way," was his cryptic reply.

Syssi was afraid to ask any more questions.

Kian looked like he was ready to commit murder, and what's worse, she sensed that with him it wasn't just an expression. Which didn't really make sense considering the guy was supposedly the CEO of an international conglomerate. But her gut had an opinion of its own, and it didn't match the one her mind was comfortable with.

Come to think of it, he reminded her of Andrew. When her brother got like that, she knew to stay clear of him and keep quiet. In his line of work shit happened, a lot, and it didn't matter if he was on leave. Dealing with it, the last thing he needed was to be distracted by his little sister's curiosity.

Trotting behind Amanda, she wondered what she had gotten herself into. Who were these people? Was she in real danger? Or was it her imagination?

Except Amanda looked scared, she wasn't imagining that. And in addition to deducing it from her companions' urgency, Syssi felt it in her gut, which in this case was in agreement with her brain, confirming that something dangerous was coming their way.

Rushing through the adjoining lab, they exited into a corridor on the other side of the basement. But instead of heading for the elevators farther down the hallway, Amanda opted for the nearby emergency stairs. She threw open the door, and they ran up. While Amanda and Syssi's heels played a staccato beat on the metal stairs, Kian was somehow managing the climb soundlessly—his considerable weight not hindering his silent treads.

Interesting, what the mind focused on in an emergency.

Once outside, they hurried toward an SUV that had been conveniently waiting for them in front of the building, and the three of them crammed themselves into its back seat.

Had Kian summoned the car? When? She hadn't noticed him calling anyone. Had she been too preoccupied?

Duh, running scared from some unspecified danger would do that to a person.

The driver turned his head to face them, smiling a weird, fake-looking smile; the kind usually molded on the faces of store mannequins.

"Where to, Master?"

Master?

The situation was becoming creepier by the minute, and Syssi was going into a full fight-or-flight mode, or rather a fright and flight.

What did she really know about Amanda and her brother? Nothing. They might be the dangerous ones, and not whoever they were running from. Or perhaps she should be scared of both.

There were just too many things that didn't add up about Amanda and Kian. Though if asked, Syssi would not have been able to point to a single thing that would look suspicious to someone else.

They were just too good-looking, unnaturally so. Amanda had a butler who called her mistress, and Kian had a driver who called him master. Kian, who must've weighed well over two hundred pounds, could climb stairs soundlessly, and sometimes Amanda's eyes shone as if they were illuminated from the inside. Separately, each item on her list could be explained away, but taken together they painted a picture that was slightly off.

Or a lot.

"Drive for a few blocks, then park. I need to check on the guys."

Sitting squeezed between Kian and Amanda, Syssi clutched her purse with trembling hands, trying to hide how shaken she was—feeling like Alice in Wonderland right after she had fallen down the rabbit hole.

"Don't worry, sweetie, we're going to Kian's place and we will have a good laugh about this whole silly episode over drinks." Amanda hugged her stiff shoulders and patted her cheek.

Why the hell was Amanda treating her like a child?

But instead of feeling offended or at least peeved, for some inexplicable reason Amanda's words had a calming effect. Syssi's tension eased, and she felt herself relax, becoming comfortable, even languid.

How is it possible?

Her rational mind refused to accept the unexplained change.

Except, Amanda's hand kept stroking her hair and it felt so wonderful that Syssi's eyelids began drooping.

She was so tired...

How come? Syssi wondered again and tried to resist, but she couldn't fight the sudden compulsion to sleep.

16

KIAN

Amanda kept her mouth shut until Syssi's eyes closed and she slumped into the back seat, leaning against Kian's arm.

"She's out. So what's going on? And if this was all a trick to get me to come with you..."

Not deigning to respond, Kian only cast her an incredulous glare, then dipped his head to look at Syssi.

She was leaning against his bicep, her wild mane of hair covering half of her face and most of her upper body. Gently, he brushed it away from her cheek and tucked it behind her ear. Holding her carefully, he shifted so her cheek came to rest on his pectoral and wrapped his arm around her.

Syssi sighed contentedly but didn't wake. Tucked under his arm, her soft, small body felt as if it belonged there.

But Kian craved more.

In her sleep, she'd relaxed the death-hold she had on her purse, and her delicate hands were resting gracefully in her lap. Taking one small palm, he placed it on his thigh, savoring the added sensation. For now it would have to do.

Like hell...

Closing his eyes, he dipped his head to her hair and inhaled her fresh, sweet scent, then inched down to sniff at the soft skin in the hollow between her neck and shoulder.

Divine... So inviting...

Not surprisingly, his fangs distended and began throbbing with venom. Struggling against an overwhelming urge to sink them into the smooth, creamy column of her neck, he forcefully leashed the monster inside and pulled back.

With a wicked smirk, Amanda was eyeing him from Syssi's other side, no doubt debating between taking advantage of the opportunity to needle him some more and letting him enjoy the moment.

For now she kept quiet, but knowing his sister, she was patting herself on the shoulder. Observing his reaction to Syssi being exactly what she had predicted, she was basking in the success of her brilliant matchmaking.

Still, patience not being one of Amanda's virtues any more than it was his, a few moments later she asked again, "Seriously now, what's going on?"

"Anandur called from where I left Brundar and him to guard the hallway leading to your lab. Doomers showed up, and they were about to fight them off, giving us time to get away. That's all I know for now. It was right outside your door, Miss 'I'm in no danger,'" Kian bit out, glaring at her, his fury rising as the implications of what had just happened, or rather had almost happened, began sinking in.

"Because of your obstinacy, Anandur and Brundar are fighting for their lives." Throwing the accusation at her was unfair, but Kian was livid. If he had arrived just a few moments later, she would have been taken.

Imagining what horrific things those monsters would have done to her, he felt as if acid was slowly sliding down his throat and into his gut.

Amanda crossed her arms over her chest and shrugged, pretending she wasn't shaken. But she wasn't fooling him, not for a moment. Kian knew her too well. Amanda was just too proud to admit it, but the truth was written all over her face—she was distraught.

Taking a deep breath, he calmed his tone to something a little more human-sounding than a growl. "Was there anything important left in the lab? Something that might be useful to the Doomers?"

She shrugged again. "All the data from my paranormal research is on my laptop, and the lab's computers have only the standard university stuff. So no, I don't think they will find anything useful there. What I wonder, though, is how did they know where to find me?" She was trying to sound unaffected and matter-of-fact, but the slight tremble in her voice betrayed how rattled she was.

"It must have been something they found at Mark's place. Them showing up at your doorstep a day after his murder can't be a coincidence. Probably something about your work. Unless they hit your home as well." Kian glanced down at his phone again, anxious for news from his men.

"Onidu would've called if they did." Amanda had no reason to worry for her Odu; he was practically indestructible. But she pulled out her phone and called anyway.

"Onidu, darling, did we have uninvited guests today?"

"No, Mistress. Should I be expecting anyone?"

"Our enemy showed up in the lab and I wanted to check on you and give you a heads-up."

"You wish to give me heads, Mistress? What should I do with them?"

Kian chuckled. The Odus were very literal.

"Never mind. Just be watchful."

"Of course, Mistress."

17

BRUNDAR

The fight in the hallway would've been epic—if anyone had been able to see it.

Brundar was keeping the area shrouded in such a thick illusion of dread that anyone passing by hurried away, avoiding the turn into the short side corridor as if it were the anteroom to the fiery pits of hell.

The Doomers attacked with surprising skill, and the fuckers were strong and determined. But then, Brundar and Anandur had spent centuries honing their fighting techniques, and the younger immortals were no match for them.

The skirmish was over almost before it began. Daggers stabbed and slashed, most of them parried, some penetrating tissue, some only tearing at clothes. Punches and kicks found their targets with meaty thuds, eliciting strained grunts.

In the end, Anandur was choking the air out of one assailant, while Brundar had his dagger buried in another's chest.

The third managed to escape.

Brundar dropped his gasping opponent, the guy's body hitting the concrete floor and jerking up from the force of it. The impact put an end to the gurgling sounds of his desperate struggles for air.

For a split second Brundar contemplated giving chase, but

instead he sent his other dagger flying after the running man, nailing him between the shoulder blades.

The guy slowed only to yank the thing out and kept running.

Brundar had to let him go.

He couldn't maintain the shroud over the fight scene and at the same time cast another around the pursuit.

Unfortunately, Anandur's pitiful illusionist ability was limited to shrouding himself only, and even that was not done particularly well.

Brundar checked himself for injuries, satisfied that his many cuts and bruises were already healing. In a few moments, the bloodstains drying on his shredded clothes would be the only evidence left of the pounding he'd taken.

A glance at Anandur reassured him that his brother was just as banged up but no worse. The concrete floor where their downed opponents lay crumpled like ugly rag dolls was splattered with blood, and though some of it must've been his or Anandur's, most of it came from the Doomers.

Looking down at the incapacitated immortals, Brundar figured it wouldn't be much longer before their bodies repaired the damage.

It presented him with a dilemma.

Clan law prohibited injecting a fallen enemy with a deadly dose of venom. It was akin to execution, which neither he nor Anandur were authorized to carry out. Of course, the rules were different if it happened in the heat of battle; all was fair when fighting for your life. But in this situation, the boss had to give them the green light.

Anandur pulled out his phone. "Kian, we have two down and one escaped. What do you want us to do with the two we got? We don't have much time before they resurrect."

"Bring them to the brink, but leave them in stasis. How are you guys doing? Everything okay?"

"Nice of you to ask, but truly, it offends me that you do, boss."

Anandur was right. He and Brundar were invincible; the Doomers hadn't stood a chance.

"My offer from before stands. You can kiss my ass. Stay where you are. I'm sending a cleanup crew." Kian hung up.

Anandur pocketed his phone and grimaced as he turned to Brundar. "You heard the boss, we inject to the brink. Though I'll be damned if I know why he wants the scum alive. Maybe he plans to make hood ornaments out of their ugly carcasses." He chuckled. "I wonder who he's going to send to do the cleanup. Can you imagine Okidu in his suit with a white apron over it, on his knees, scrubbing blood from the concrete?" Anandur chuckled again.

He lost his smile as he glanced at the purple-faced, nearly dead male lying crumpled at his feet. "I don't believe I have to put my mouth on this filth." Anandur's face twisted with utter disgust.

He cast a quick glance at the other Doomer whose bleeding heart was already on the mend, slowly pushing out the knife embedded in it. "You'd better hurry." He crouched down and immediately turned his head sideways. "Whoa! Mine stinks."

Brundar was ready, his fangs were already fully extended from the heat of the fight, dripping venom and primed to go. Grabbing the male by the hair and twisting the guy's head, he exposed the neck and hoisted it up to his mouth. With a loud hiss, he sank his needle-sharp fangs into the Doomer's flesh, keeping them embedded as the venom pulsated, invading the man's bloodstream.

Injecting to the brink was a precise art. Too little did diddly-squat, and too much meant a permanent address in a hole in the ground. Listening carefully to the immortal's heartbeat, Brundar waited until it slowed down to almost nothing, then pulled his fangs out and sealed the puncture wounds.

The man could still die, but if he did, it was no sweat off Brundar's brow. He'd done what he'd been ordered to do. If he'd miscalculated, then oh, well; he'd done his best.

Anandur was still at his prey's throat, the man's undamaged heart taking longer to slow down. When he was done, he licked the wound closed and spat out.

"I need to rinse out my mouth after this shit!"

Anandur kept spitting out and wiping his mouth on his sleeve in between fits of spitting.

Eventually, Brundar took pity on him and handed him the flask of whiskey he had hidden in his jacket's inner pocket.

"Thanks, bro, you're a lifesaver."

Anandur took a big swig of the Chivas, gargled it in his mouth a few times and then spat it out. After the second and third swig had gone down his throat, he handed the flask back.

Brundar cranked his neck back and emptied what remained of the whiskey down his own throat. As his adrenaline level began dropping, Brundar's aches and pains made themselves known, and the beating his body had taken became hard to ignore. Slumping down to the floor, he propped his back against the cold concrete wall and let his head drop back.

Now, with their gruesome task done, all that was left was to wait for the cleanup crew. Until then, they had to maintain the shrouding and guard their prey.

Brundar felt tired, yet energized.

It was good to be fighting again, to feel the adrenaline rush, to use the skills he had practiced and perfected over the centuries.

Lately, he'd been feeling almost useless. What was the point of being a perfect killing machine if you never got to kill anymore?

As he reveled in the sense of power and utility, there was a small tinge of guilt in all that satisfaction. The enemy was attacking his family, but instead of the dread he should've been feeling, Brundar felt invigorated from the rush he'd gotten from the fight.

It was good to be needed; to carry out tasks only he and his Guardian brethren could.

Perhaps now, with this new danger looming over the clan, they could call in some of the others, those who had left the Guardian force for lack of purpose.

With a rare, fond glance at Anandur, he reminisced about their stormy past in the force. The battles, the brotherly revelry when they had come back home victorious, the pride of accomplishment, the gratitude of the clan.

Closing his eyes, Brundar welcomed the visions of his glorious past and smiled wistfully.

He missed those halcyon days.

18

SYSSI

Syssi's cheek was resting on something hard and smooth that smelled amazing.

Strong fingers caressed her cheek. "Wake up, sleepyhead. We're here." The deep, masculine voice reverberated through her rib cage.

Who? Where?

Suddenly, it all came rushing back.

Kian.

He was holding her tucked against him, caressing her and talking to her as if he gave a damn.

She stiffened, attempting to sit up and shake his arm off, but the sudden movement made her head spin, and she had to lean back against the seat... and his arm.

"Take it easy, beautiful, give yourself a minute; there's no rush." He kept stroking her cheek with his thumb.

They were in what seemed to be an underground parking structure, still sitting in the same car, supposedly still in the same universe.

Who are you, and what did you do with Kian the grouch?

The man sitting next to her had more mood swings than a hormonal teenager. She needed to tell him to cut it out, but it felt so good to be held like that. Syssi kept still, allowing herself a few moments of bliss to enjoy this surreal break in reality. Maybe she was still dreaming? And in her dream this gorgeous man was caring, kind, and warm, and called her beautiful.

She didn't want to wake up.

Just a few moments longer.

Then Amanda had to ruin it by sounding the wake-up call. "Syssi, if you're still sleepy, you can lie down on Kian's couch. I'm done sitting in the car. Let's go!" She opened the door and got out.

Nope, no dream.

Kian extracted his arm from around her shoulders and opened the other door. Unfolding his tall body, he stepped out of the SUV.

As soon as he left her side she missed him, his warmth, his closeness, his scent. Standing by the door, he offered her his hand —being gentlemanly, or perhaps thinking she needed help getting out.

As a matter of fact, she did.

Still woozy, she felt weak as if she'd been awakened too early from a very deep sleep, or perhaps had too much to drink. But neither of those applied.

What was happening to her?

She wasn't sick, wasn't hungry...

So why was she feeling like this?

Trying to make sense of why she felt so off-kilter, Syssi concluded it must've been the aftermath of all that adrenaline leaving her system.

Taking Kian's offered palm, she stepped out of the car and let him walk her to the elevator.

Once they reached the penthouse level, the three of them and Kian's driver stepped out into a beautiful vestibule. A round granite table stood in the center of a mosaic-inlaid marble floor, holding a huge vase of fresh flowers. Across from each other, two sets of double doors led to what she assumed were two separate penthouse apartments.

Kian's driver opened the one to their left, ushering them inside with the flair of a seasoned butler.

The place was beautiful.

If Syssi were to design her own dream home, she would make it look just like that.

The first thing that caught her attention was the wall of glass opposite the entry door, overlooking the magnificent, unobstructed cityscape. To its right, another glass wall opened to an expansive rooftop terrace, complete with a lush garden, a long narrow lap pool, and an elegant assortment of lounge furniture.

The living room decor was magazine-perfect.

Over the dark hardwood floor, a bright area rug delineated the sitting area. Three espresso-colored leather sofas surrounded a stone coffee table that must've been at least eight feet wide on each side. Vibrant, large-scale art covered three of the cream-colored walls, while a big screen topping a contemporary-style fireplace occupied the fourth.

To complete the perfectly put together room, vases filled with fresh flowers were strategically scattered throughout.

Syssi could think of nothing she would've changed. She loved the way Kian had managed to make the space warm and inviting despite its size and opulence.

Come to think of it, it made more sense that someone else had done the decorating...

A woman...

Of course Kian would have someone in his life, maybe even living with him, she had no reason to assume he was single.

Syssi rubbed a hand over her sternum, calling herself all kinds of stupid as she tried to soothe the sudden ache in the center of her chest.

Walking toward the glass wall overlooking the city, she decided to discreetly fish for information. "Wow, this is beautiful. You have amazing taste, Kian," she complimented.

Kian took the bait. "Can't take credit for it. This is all the work of our interior decorator, Ingrid. My only input was no clutter and no museum pieces, just a comfortable, livable space. Ingrid came up with all the rest on her own, and I basically approved most of her suggestions." He shrugged and walked over to the bar. Pouring himself a Scotch, he asked, "What can I offer you, ladies?"

"I'll have gin and tonic," Syssi called from her spot next to the glass wall, where she was pretending to look out at the view.

The relief she'd felt upon hearing his answer was just plain stupid. Even if there was no woman sharing his home, it didn't mean he didn't have one. And besides, he wasn't hers, and never would be. She had no business feeling jealous or possessive over him.

But oh, God, how she wished she did.

Kian unsettled her on so many levels, Syssi doubted she could have an intelligent conversation with the guy. Hiding her powerful attraction to him was taxing. Her acting skills weren't that good. The sooner she said goodbye the better, before she slipped and made a fool of herself by letting her insane desire for him show.

"Same for me." Amanda joined her at the view wall, slanting her a knowing glance.

"House! Open terrace doors," Kian commanded the smart-home system, sending the mechanized glass-panels sliding almost soundlessly into the wall.

Outside, Syssi chose one of the loungers next to the pool and sat down. This high up, the sound of the bustling city was nothing more than a distant hum, the drone disturbed only by the occasional car horn.

Tilting her head back, she gazed at the darkening sky, its wispy clouds illuminated by the orange and red hues of the setting sun.

"Beautiful, isn't it?" Amanda plopped next to her. Lying back with her palms tucked under her head, she joined Syssi in gazing at the color display in the sky.

"Yes, it is," Syssi agreed.

A glass in each hand, Kian stepped out and sat sideways on the lounger facing Amanda and her.

Even seated, he looked so big and so damn beautiful that he

took her breath away. And what's more, with his jacket off and his white dress shirt's top buttons open, she glimpsed the outline of all those hard muscles she'd felt when he'd held her close in the car.

Syssi stared, not quite gaping, but still her lips were slightly parted, and she felt her face reddening. With an effort, she shifted her eyes away from him and glanced up at the sky, discreetly observing Kian from the corner of her eye.

After handing Amanda and her the chilled beverages, Kian pulled a gold lighter and a pack of Davidoffs from his trouser pocket. Taking a cigarette out, he held it between his thumb and forefinger, lit it, and inhaled deeply.

His lids dropped over his eyes as he took several long drags, and the tension that was etched on his handsome face seemed to ease. With his craving assuaged, he lifted his eyelids a little, peering at Syssi from behind a column of smoke.

"Pew! Kian, you said you'd quit!" Amanda crinkled her nose in distaste, waving a hand in front of her nose.

Ignoring Amanda, Kian's eyes stayed trained on Syssi. "It doesn't seem to bother you, Syssi, does it?" he asked on a stream of smoke.

"No, I like the smell of cigarettes, even cigars. I find it relaxing." Taking little sips from her drink, Syssi inhaled, enjoying the smell of tobacco mixed with Kian's cologne.

It reminded her of her grandpa. When she was little, she used to sit cuddled on his lap while he'd read to her. His clothes had always smelled of cigars and cologne. No wonder she associated the mix of these scents with safety and love.

After a long moment of staring into her glass and swishing the ice cubes around, she squared her shoulders and turned to Amanda. "Would anyone care to explain what's going on?"

Amanda pushed up from the lounger and walked a few steps away, distancing herself from the offending smell. "There are those who believe that what we do in the lab is evil or unnatural, the work of the devil or some other nonsense like that. A certain religious sect declared war on our work, sending us nasty messages and threats. Luckily, Kian took it seriously and decided to post guards around the lab, believing the nuts may become violently incensed and actually carry out what they've been promising to do. As much as it pains me to say, it seems Kian was proven right. The guards called him to let him know they spotted suspicious characters in the hallway, and Kian decided not to take any chances with an unnecessary confrontation. The guards called again to say they were able to scare the thugs off, so hopefully this is the end of it."

Turning to Kian, Amanda smirked. "Anyhow, I'm going to leave you two lovebirds alone and head across the hallway to my place. I need to call Onidu and have him bring over my stuff. I have nothing here." Blowing a kiss at Kian, she winked at Syssi and walked away.

Syssi blushed down to the roots of her hair.

Did she really say it? Lovebirds?

She swore she was never going to forgive Amanda for embarrassing her so.

"I probably should be going too; it's getting late. I should call a taxi. I usually walk home from the lab, it's only about twenty minutes away on foot, so I leave my car at home to save on the parking fees. Sometimes Amanda insists on picking me up in the morning and then driving me home after work." Syssi was blabbering but couldn't stop herself.

So embarrassing. Now he'd think she was an idiot.

Not to mention that he might get the impression that she was stingy, or poor. She was neither. Syssi was frugal, preferring a hefty bank account to frivolous spending. Her girlfriends from the lucrative private high school she'd attended used to roll their eyes at what she considered fiscal responsibility, and some even had gone as far as calling her a tightwad. While they had been flaunting their parents' money, competing for who had the latest and most expensive things, she'd never developed a taste for it.

Syssi had no idea where this propensity had sprouted from. Growing up as she had in an affluent home, she knew her parents could afford all those things that had been so important to her friends, and they had never refused any of her requests. Syssi had never lacked for anything. But even as a kid she'd preferred getting money rather than toys or other trinkets as birthday presents, and had been thrilled to watch her bank account grow with every new deposit. Maybe it had been her mother's dislike for shopping that had influenced her. Anita simply hadn't had the time or the inclination for it. She'd ordered what she needed from catalogs. After all, her mother had spent most of her days wearing a lab coat and had deemed what was under it inconsequential.

That being said, Syssi didn't think it had been intellectual snobbism that had her sneer at unnecessary spending. Syssi valued independence almost above all else, and a big part of being independent was having her own money—and plenty of it—with the caveat that it had to be earned.

Her parents had covered tuition as well as room and board throughout undergrad and architecture school. But she'd refused to accept anything else. Syssi worked for her spending money as an SAT tutor. She was quite proud of the fact that her services had been in such high demand, she'd even managed to put away a good chunk of what she'd been making into her savings account.

Listening to her make a fool of herself, Kian smiled, but it wasn't the comforting kind, more the amused expression of a predator ready to pounce on his cornered prey.

And what do you know... that blast of desire hit her again even harder than before.

Come kiss me, she beckoned him mentally. *Touch me. Do something. Can't you see I'm burning?* Quickly averting her eyes, Syssi prayed Kian couldn't read her expression.

She wished she was the type who could actually voice these thoughts, or even act upon them. But she never would. Even intoxicated, she could never be that brazen.

Sighing, Syssi cursed her romantically debilitating shyness. She could lust after Kian on the inside, but she'd never make the first move.

Braving a glance, she expected Kian's expression to be smug.

Men like him were used to women fawning over them. They were empowered by it, expected it. Instead, he surprised her.

His beautiful eyes were full of regret.

With a resigned sigh, he pushed up from where he sat and offered her his hand. "Come on, beautiful, let me take you home," he said quietly.

Ignoring his hand, Syssi kept looking at him with wide questioning eyes, perplexed by the mixed signals he was sending her. "Why do you keep calling me that?" she blurted.

Usually, she was good at reading people, but Kian's mercurial behavior was impossible to figure out. One moment he looked like he wanted to do all kinds of naughty and exciting things to her, the next he regarded her as if she was a nuisance that he wanted nothing to do with. Then calling her beautiful again.

Make up your mind! Syssi wanted to scream at him.

"That's because you are beautiful." Kian's face softened, but his smile remained tight-lipped. Pulling her up to her feet, he held on to her hand as he led her out. At the front door, he paused to call to his butler, "Okidu, I'm taking Syssi home. I'll be back shortly."

The squat man rushed out of the kitchen. "Let me drive the young lady, Master. You do not have to burden yourself thus." Okidu was already putting his driver hat on.

"It's okay, Okidu. It would please me to take Syssi home myself." Kian held the door open for her.

"But, Master—" The guy seemed distraught.

Kian pinned him with a hard stare. "That's enough."

She wanted to tell Kian that she'd rather have the butler drive her, but after a quick look at his face she reconsidered. That hard, determined expression of his reminded her of Andrew, and she knew Kian wouldn't budge. She had enough experience arguing with her brother to know it would be futile to try.

It's gonna be torturous. Syssi grimaced, imagining the awkward silence that would most likely stretch between them on the drive to her home. Kian didn't seem like the kind of guy who did small talk, and neither was she. Hopefully, traffic would be merciful and the drive short.

She'd been right.

Starting with the elevator, through the car ride, it was just as awkward as she had imagined it would be. Kian drove stone-faced and quiet. She was stiff and nervous, anxious for it to be over.

It felt like a first date gone all wrong. Except, it wasn't even a date! Just two people who rubbed each other the wrong way, or perhaps the right way, which was even scarier.

As they got closer to her place, she began to worry. There was no doubt in her mind that Kian would insist on walking her to her door and not leave till she was safely inside. And after seeing the grandeur of his place, she hoped he wouldn't think that her tiny guesthouse-apartment was a dump.

Right behind her landlady's home, the converted garage was cozy and safe. And the rent was no more than what she would've paid at the dorms, while offering her more privacy and quiet. But compared to his penthouse it looked like a hovel.

Damn, sometimes being frugal and independent backfired. If she'd accepted her parents' offer to pay for a decent apartment, she wouldn't be fretting now about Kian getting the wrong impression about her.

He insisted not only on walking her to the door but on checking the interior for any possible threats as well. Thankfully, though, he didn't seem to mind or even notice the old secondhand furniture, or the mess. Syssi, on the other hand, added it to her long list of Kian-related embarrassments.

Standing like a doofus by the door, she waited for him to be done.

It took Kian all of thirty seconds, and even that took as long only because he decided to include the bathroom in his sweep.

Her neighbor's cat decided to take advantage of the open door and perform an inspection of his own. Walking around the small space, his tail held high in the air, he gave Kian serious competition for the whole aloof, regal, everyone-is-beneath-me look.

Crossing paths, the two males stopped to face and size each other up, and granting each other their royal approval, continued on their way.

Syssi cracked up.

Add snorting laugh to the list, she admonished herself, but it was just too funny. It was a shame she hadn't recorded the exchange, it would've gone viral on YouTube.

"What's so funny?" Kian regarded her like she was short of a screw.

Covering her mouth with her hand to try and suppress the giggles, Syssi just pointed at him and then at the cat—who, sitting on his hind paws, waggled his tail in agitation, apparently disapproving of the giggling as well.

"Whatever it was, I'm glad my feline friend and I were able to make you laugh. It was our distinct pleasure to amuse you." Kian bowed theatrically, his hand almost touching the floor.

Some of Amanda's flair for the dramatic must've rubbed off on her brother.

Suspecting he didn't get to be this way often, she found his unexpected playfulness endearing. It made him seem more approachable, easing some of the discomforting effect he had on her.

Syssi realized she liked him, and not just for his amazing body and his beautiful face.

Blushing, she lowered her eyes. But then his silence compelled her to lift them back up, and her breath caught.

Kian was looking at her as if he was dying to kiss her. Except, it wasn't the predatory look from before. His eyes were soft and full of longing—a deep wanting that for some reason was shadowed by dark clouds of sorrow and regret.

Gazing into those sad blue eyes, she knew he wasn't going to do it, and she would forever wonder what kissing him would've felt like.

It's better to live dangerously than not live at all. Amanda's words echoed in her head.

On impulse, Syssi brought her palms up to his cheeks, touching them lightly with her fingertips. Kian closed his eyes and leaned into her caress. Bending his considerable frame to just the right height, he all but invited her to stretch up on her toes and kiss him.

Her kiss started soft, gentle, with their bodies barely touching. Kian held her almost reverently; one hand cradling the back of her head, the other around her waist.

It was a nice, sweet kiss, but it wasn't what she wanted. What she needed. Underneath his reserve and his tenderness, Syssi sensed the wild beast he was holding back.

She wanted it unleashed.

Pressing herself closer to him and feeling the hard ridges and planes of his powerful body, she wanted more of him. With her hands streaking into his soft hair, she grasped fistfuls of it and pulled him closer, a soft moan escaping her throat.

It was all the encouragement he needed.

In a split second, Syssi found herself pressed against the wall, the hand at the back of her head fisting her hair, the other cupping her butt and lifting her up. Kian positioned her so their bodies aligned, grinding his hard length against her pelvis.

Hot, demanding, powerful.

As his tongue pushed past her lips—exploring and dueling with hers, retracting and invading in a blatant imitation of the act of sex—she felt her core bloom for him, flooding with wetness.

Now, that was a kiss! Syssi acknowledged with the few brain cells still functioning. Raw and intense, it ignited a burn that was about to burst into an all-out fire.

Touch me, she implored Kian silently, her breasts tight and heavy, craving his touch.

With her silent plea ignored, she resorted to rubbing herself against his chest, hoping the friction would provide some sort of relief. But all too soon he retracted, leaving her bereft.

Both palms cradling her cheeks, he touched his forehead to hers and closed his eyes. For a moment, they both panted breathlessly, waiting for their racing hearts to slow down.

As Kian lifted his head and looked into her eyes with that sad and resigned expression from before, her heart sank. The odd roll of her stomach portended that Kian was leaving and wasn't planning on ever coming back.

The one time she was actually considering taking a guy she'd just met to her bed, he didn't want her.

Syssi shut her eyes against the pain, concentrating on memorizing the feel of Kian's thumb caressing her cheek. He waited until she reluctantly opened her eyes to look at him.

An odd light shone in his dark blue eyes as he kept her mesmerized with that intense gaze. "Good night, sweet Syssi, you had a long day, and you're very tired, you need to get some sleep."

She was... so very tired... so confused...

Shuffling her feet, Syssi barely made it to her bed before collapsing on it—fully clothed with her shoes still on.

19

KIAN

Syssi was out for the night.

Standing next to the bed and watching her, Kian sighed and raked both hands through his hair.

The girl was proving difficult to resist.

She'd wanted him from the start, and even if he hadn't been able to scent her desire, it had been all over her expressive face—sweet and innocent in her shyness, still young and hopeful, so different from him.

He'd been tempted, breaking protocol and not taking his bodyguards with him so he could be alone with her. For a few moments, he'd even managed to convince himself that he was doing it for the clan.

Their future dependent on finding Dormants.

Except, he would've never forgiven himself if he'd taken her. It would've been deceitful, dishonorable. Kian had sacrificed enough of himself for the clan, for his family; the one thing he refused to give up was his self-respect, his honor.

As much as he craved her, he couldn't take what she so freely offered. The decent thing to do was to stay away.

Except, how could he?

When she had smiled at him, after his ridiculous bow, that

radiant smile had transformed her from sweet and beautiful to spectacular, and he'd wanted to vow that he'd always make her smile like that. Even if it meant making a fool of himself, it would be well worth it just to hear her laugh and giggle, carefree and unreserved.

Gazing at her beautiful face, he wanted to stay. Not for sex, although he wanted that too, but to embrace her and hold her tightly, caress her hair and whisper sweet nothings in her ear. To amuse her, to make her happy.

Just one kiss, he'd thought a moment before she'd kissed him—she wouldn't remember it anyway.

He couldn't allow it.

Knowing he would be leaving soon and erasing himself from Syssi's memories—most likely never to see her again—had twisted a knot inside him, bringing on a sense of loss and resigned sadness.

But it was the right thing to do.

For Syssi's sake.

His thrall had buried and muddled her memory of the day's events, starting from the moment he'd entered the lab. All she'd remember tomorrow would be going home with a headache and collapsing on her bed. If at all, the memory of him might surface in her dreams, nothing more.

With a sigh, he removed her shoes and tucked the blanket around her, making sure her feet were covered.

And still, he couldn't make himself leave.

Looking down at her lovely face, he brushed a strand of hair away from her damp forehead.

What an inferno blazed beneath that shy, reserved exterior of hers. So much so that Kian could almost believe Syssi harbored some sweetly dark desires—the kind he would've been more than happy to fulfill.

He'd never find out, though, would he?

Was he foolishly stubborn, just as Amanda had accused?

Why was he fighting this so hard?

Was he truly doing the decent thing and being chivalrous?

Kian wished he had someone he could talk to. Someone to help him clear his head and sort through all these conflicting and confusing emotions. Except, there was no one he was comfortable enough with, or close enough to.

With one last brush of his fingertips against her smooth cheek, he headed for the door. And as he closed it quietly behind him, Tim Curry's "Sloe Gin" lyrics echoed in his head. *I'm so fucking lonely.*

Kian shook his head as he walked down the long driveway back to his car, the cool air helping clear his head. He didn't have the luxury of allowing himself to wallow in self-pity. Even if a relationship with Syssi were possible, though he had no idea how such a thing could've worked with a human, there was no place for it in his life. Running the clan's international business conglomerate and keeping his family safe from the Doomers required his full and undivided attention.

Unbidden, his thoughts drifted back to how this never-ending war had begun.

20

KIAN

The story was one Kian had heard his mother tell many times. With each retelling, the details would change a little; some new tidbits added, others omitted. As a child, Kian had thought her forgetful, or fanciful. Only later, he'd realized that she'd been tailoring her story to her audience.

Besides, it wasn't as if anyone would've dared to accuse a goddess of forgetting, or making things up.

By now he had it memorized.

The tale would've sounded familiar to most mortals, as its distorted echoes had been recorded in the traditions of several of their cultures. Written in various languages, the names of the players had been changed and the story adapted to fit different agendas, different moralities, different sets of beliefs.

It had become a myth.

But as all timeless myths go, it had at its core a true story.

There had been a time when the gods lived among the mortals —bestowing their benevolence, providing knowledge and culture and helping humanity establish an advanced, moral and just society.

In gratitude, the people had worshiped the gods, expressing

their adoration with offerings of their best goods and their freely donated labor.

Obviously, these gods hadn't been actual deities. Still, whether they had been the survivors of an earlier, superior civilization or refugees from somewhere else, his mother wouldn't say. She either didn't know or was keeping the knowledge to herself. Annani took her godly status very seriously and made sure everyone else did as well.

Perhaps she sought to elevate her grandness, as if it was needed or even possible, by shrouding her origins in mystery.

The gods had unimaginable powers. They could cast illusions so powerful that they fooled the minds of thousands. Their power over the human mind was so strong that their illusions not only looked and smelled real but even felt real to the touch. They could project thoughts and images into the unsuspecting, inferior minds of mortals, influencing everything from moods, to moral conduct, to a call to battle, all the way to divine revelation and inspiration.

Physically, they were perfect. Stunningly beautiful. Their bodies never aged or contracted diseases, and healed injuries in mere moments.

But they could still die.

Even the gods couldn't survive decapitation or withstand a nuclear blast. For which, unfortunately, they had the means.

They were few.

The limited gene pool combined with an extremely low conception rate prompted the gods to seek compatible mates among the mortals. Those unions proved to be more fruitful, and many near-immortal children were born. But when those children took human mates, their progeny turned out to be mortal.

Upon closer examination, their scientists found a way to activate the dormant, godly genes, but only for the children of the female immortals. The children of the males were sadly doomed to mortality.

Annani, one of the few pureblood children born to the gods, and the daughter of the leading couple, became the most coveted young goddess.

The one fortunate enough to mate her would become their next ruler.

The chain of events following her coming-of-age wasn't surprising. A fierce competition ensued between two suitors. Mortdh, the son of her father's brother and, therefore, the first in line for her hand, was her intended. And Khiann, the son of a less prominent, though wealthy family, who on the face of things didn't stand a chance.

But Annani was very young and impetuous, and she chose the one she loved and who loved her back. Not the one she was promised to, who never really cared for her and had already numerous concubines and children of his own.

Mortdh was infuriated and demanded she mate him, as was his right. But his right was superseded by her choice. The gods' code of conduct clearly stated that any mating, even one with a lowly mortal, had to be consensual.

Madly in love, Khiann and Annani were joined in a grand ceremony.

Both gods and mortals were so infatuated with the great love story that they wrote hymns and created myths to commemorate it.

Khiann and Annani's love was the story everyone loved to tell.

The tale of love's triumph.

It drove Mortdh insane. In his mind, he lost not only his one chance for sovereignty, but the respect of all.

And it was: All. Her. Fault.

His hatred of Annani, and by extension of all women, burned with rabid intensity. He detested the females' right to choose a mate, he abhorred the matrilineal tradition of the gods. He vowed to seize power and change all of that. Under his rule, women would have no rights. They would become property, to be purchased and sold like cattle. Heredity would cease to be matrilineal, the chains of power would become patriarchal.

In his hatred and madness, Mortdh did the unthinkable; an atrocity so great that it shook the ancient world.

He murdered Khiann.

He murdered a god.

Savagely, he took the life of Annani's one great love.

The laments sung to mourn Khiann's passing and to grieve for the great love so tragically lost would become a ritual to be performed every year on the anniversary of his death.

Annani's father called for the big assembly to decide Mortdh's fate. His crime was the gravest of all. To kill a god was so unthinkable, their law did not even contain a punishment severe enough for what he had done. As executing a god was not allowed, the most terrible sentencing in their code was entombment. And the full assembly of all gods was needed to sentence one of their own to that horrific fate.

A god would not perish in the tomb; slowly his body would cease to function, going into a kind of suspended state. But it took a long time, a very long time, until consciousness faded.

A decision of that severity required a unanimous vote.

Mortdh fled to his stronghold in the north. Together with his near-immortal son Navuh, he assembled an army of mortal soldiers and his other near-immortal progeny. In his deranged mind, he concluded that if he could not rule the gods, he would eliminate them.

Lording supreme over mortals and near-immortals would suffice.

The assembly of gods listened to all the undisputed evidence and voted unanimously to pass the sentence of entombment. Mortdh's parents planned to plead for their son. However, upon hearing the damning testimony, the cold cruelty of the premeditated murder, they realized they had no choice but to vote with the rest. Their son had become insanely dangerous and had to be stopped.

Annani sat in on the council's deliberations, frozen in her grief. The only thing keeping her from collapsing into a despondent stupor was her need for vengeance. She had to hold on until the voting was done. She listened to the proceedings with her tears flowing down her cheeks and onto her lap. But when at last the voting was done and the sentence was passed, she felt no satisfaction.

She felt nothing but pain.

Annani wished she could die. Without her love, she had no reason to go on. There was nothing that could have filled the horrific void in her heart, and the agony of grief was more than she could endure.

Death would have been a mercy.

But as snippets of the debate pierced through the haze of her desperation, she forced herself to focus on what was being discussed, and was alarmed by what she heard. Apparently, the council had no clue how to detain Mortdh in order to execute the verdict.

Rumors of forces gathering under his banner suggested a war was brewing, and there was talk of assembling a force of their own. They were deliberating whether to go on the offensive and try to capture Mortdh, or remain in their stronghold and defend it against his attack.

From experience, Annani knew that the talk would go on endlessly, producing no definite action. What was the point of the sentencing if it could not be executed? How would her justice be served? Who would capture Mortdh? What if he attacked first and won?

If he ever captured her, her fate would be worse than death. Of that she had no doubt.

True to her nature, Annani did not hesitate long before deciding on a course of action.

She was going to run away.

She would take her flying machine and her love's precious gift of seven biomechanical servants and fly to a distant land the gods had never graced.

Mortdh would never find her.

Untouched by the gods, it would most likely be a primitive place, one without culture or an established society.

She would have to start a new civilization.

To accomplish that, she would need a set of instructions and a trove of knowledge. But then again, Annani knew exactly where to get it. She would steal her uncle's library, which contained much of her people's science and culture and was stored on a tablet she had seen him read often. He had even let her borrow it on occasion.

That decision and its prompt execution saved her life and the future fate of humanity.

That same night, while the gods still deliberated, Mortdh flew his aircraft over the council's fortress and dropped a nuclear bomb.

The only weapon guaranteed to kill the gods.

The devastation was so widespread that over half of the region's population died along with their gods. The nuclear wind carried the fingers of death far and wide, decimating everything alive on its way.

Including Mortdh.

Out of the ashes and ruins, humans and near-immortals rose and tried to survive on what was left. Nothing grew, and those the nuclear wind spared, hunger took.

The human population kept dying.

The near-immortals, as children of the gods, had bodies that could survive longer and heal faster and should have fared better. Some of them must have made it to distant lands and built new lives.

Annani sincerely hoped that was the case. Though over the next five millennia she encountered none.

The only part of the region unaffected by the nuclear devastation was its northern tip. Mortdh's stronghold. With Mortdh's death, his eldest son Navuh took over leadership of his people; several hundred mortal and near-immortal warriors along with their female broodmares.

Most of the unfortunate women had been mortal, but a few must have been Dormant or near-immortal because Navuh's immortal army had kept growing through the millennia, and with it, his power and his sphere of influence.

Navuh had sworn to uphold his father's vision of the new world order. And with his tight grip on the region's leaders, he had succeeded in plunging that part of the world into darkness and oppression the likes of which had never been known before.

It had been worse for the women.

They had become cattle: to be owned and sold by their fathers or brothers, to be bought by their husbands and discarded at their whim. They had been stripped of all personal rights. For all intents and purposes, women had ceased to be considered people. They had become things. Patriarchy had been born and was there to stay.

Annani fled to the far, desolate and frozen north. She never stayed in one place long, always fearing she would be found. Slowly, though, rumors of the disaster that befell Mesopotamia found their way up to her icy hideout, and she learned she was the last of her kind.

The only remaining goddess alive.

By now, all traces of the carefree young woman she used to be were gone. With her heart frozen just like her new home, she was numb and emotionless and lacked the motivation to do aught but get by.

And yet, she had to survive, for she was the custodian of a treasure: the knowledge, culture, and ideology of her kin.

The future of humanity was in her hands.

Without her, Navuh's darkness would spread until it consumed everything decent in the world.

She could not, would not, allow that to happen.

For five years, Annani ran and hid and survived with the help of her servants who made sure she at least had food and shelter.

Eventually, her grief and pain subsided sufficiently to allow her to move on. Not to forget, and not to stop hurting—that was never going to happen—but to start on her monumental task.

During her self-imposed stasis, she spent a lot of time thinking and realized she couldn't do it alone. She needed to create more of herself.

Annani knew of only one way to achieve that.

She had to procreate.

Except, she vowed never to love again. Her heart would forever belong to her one true love. Her soul would remain faithful to Khiann's memory.

To produce offspring, she would share her body with her mortal lovers, but nothing more.

She took many, using them and discarding them in short order. After the deed, she would fuddle her partner's mind, leaving behind a dreamlike memory of a heavenly encounter.

For the males it was no hardship to be used like that; after all, she was the most beautiful woman in the world. And to her surprise, Annani discovered it was not a great hardship for her either.

Her heart might have been frozen, but her body roared to life with insatiable heat.

Over the next five millennia, Annani was blessed with five children. Her first child was born after three thousand years, during which she almost despaired of ever conceiving.

Alena, her eldest, proved to be a blessing beyond measure. For an immortal, she was a miracle of fertility, delivering thirteen wonderful children in the span of five hundred years.

Kian was next, born only a few decades after Alena. Annani named her firstborn son in memory of her lost love. Except, she changed it a little so as to not bait the Fates. Kian would become the most instrumental in her quest to enlighten humanity.

A millennium later, sweet Lilen arrived. He grew to become a kind and brave man, well-liked by everyone. His tragic loss in battle plunged his mother back into the depths of despair, where she lingered till the birth of her daughter Sari pulled her out of that dark vortex.

Last but not least of the children was Amanda. The very young, and until recently, wild party-girl. The princess, as everyone called her.

Annani had never revealed the identity of the fathers, but she'd described them in detail, alleviating her children's natural curiosity.

They had been the most magnificent men. She had chosen the strongest, the smartest and most handsome males. They had been the fiercest warriors and natural leaders among their kind.

Kian wondered if the image she had painted for her children hadn't been exaggerated. Mere mortals were not that great. Had she done it for her children's sake? Her own? Had she even known whose seed had taken root? Or perhaps, she had just believed them to be so sublime because she had never stayed long enough to get to know them all that well.

With the human population growing and spreading to new and distant lands, Annani's clan needed two geographically strategic centers of operation. Kian had moved with some of the clan from Scotland to America, and Sari had taken over the European center, becoming his counterpart in the old country.

Annani's influence in the Western Hemisphere had grown. The gods' knowledge and wisdom had been slowly trickled to the mortals, helping them to evolve into the advanced society they would one day become. But the progress had been slow, thwarted time and again by Navuh's destructive power.

The Devout Order of Mortdh, as Navuh called his army of ruthless killers, was a formidable foe.

Lacking the intellectual resources Annani had stolen must have chafed terribly, as the Doomers had made a religion out of destroying and halting any progress she had helped mortal society achieve, whether scientific or social. Their dark sphere of influence had encompassed at times the majority of the civilized world. And each time, it had taken Annani and her clan centuries to recoup and push back the evils of ignorance and hate.

Annani's clan was small, numbering in the low hundreds, its slow growth limited by its single matrilineal line.

The Doomers, on the other hand, were legion.

As far as Kian could ascertain, they had an advantage from the start, with Navuh inheriting a few near-immortal or Dormant females from his father.

They must've guarded these females fiercely, as none had ever made it out of the Doomers' clutches.

Heavens knew, Kian and his nephews had searched near and far for centuries. They had followed rumors and fantastic tales of witches, nymphs, succubi, and other mythical creatures, in the hopes of finding an immortal female at the source of the stories. But as time and again the clues had led to nothing, they had eventually stopped looking; reluctantly accepting their fate.

Outnumbered and outmuscled, the clan's best strategy had always been to hide.

They had lived quietly and unassumingly, avoiding any undue attention. Of course, the ability to create illusions and erase memories had been instrumental in that effect.

Taking advantage of their sophisticated knowledge base, slowly but surely, they had developed a shrouded economic empire.

Owned and operated under myriad identities and entities, the clan's holdings included land, coal and ore mines, banks, manufacturing facilities, hotels and other real estate all over the world, adding in modern times a trove of patents and technology-based enterprises.

Occasionally, the Doomers had managed to snare a clan member, and several males had been lost that way. Kian shuddered at the prospect of the Doomers ever catching a clan female.

In their hands, she would long for an end that would never come.

Now, as the rules of the game had been irrevocably changed, Kian would have to reevaluate the clan's time-trusted strategy.

Annani was safe in her Alaskan shrouded fortress. The place was extremely well hidden under a manufactured dome of ice; undetectable even with the help of satellites. The only way in and out was on a specially designed aircraft, piloted by one of her trusted Odu servants. Even Kian couldn't find the place on his own.

Sari and the European clan should be fine as well. They all lived in their Scottish stronghold, which was defended with the help of the best surveillance equipment there was and clouded by its occupants in a perpetually maintained illusion.

That left his people.

They were scattered all over California and trusted their safety to living unseen among millions of mortals.

This would have to change.

Kian grimaced, imagining the hell they'd give him when he suggested moving them all into his secure keep: first the council members, and then the rest.

Unfortunately, he couldn't just order it; every major decision required a vote. And wasn't that a damn shame. But then again, he had an ace up his sleeve that guaranteed the vote would go in his favor.

21

ANDREW

"What do you think?" Andrew's boss leaned over his shoulder to look at the photos attached to the file Andrew was reading.

"Apparently, business is booming in Maldives, judging by the sudden increase in visitors from that country over the last couple of weeks."

Arriving within days of each other, three groups of "businessmen" from that tiny country had entered the United States through the Los Angeles International Airport.

His boss tapped the top row of photos. "What alerted security, beyond Maldives being a godforsaken bunch of insignificant islands with no industry to speak of, was that each group consisted of four young male members. Too young to be businessmen, and too heavily muscled. Besides, these bushy beards are an excellent disguise. They will be unrecognizable once they shave them off."

Airport security had used this oddity as an excuse to forward the information to their department without the risk of being accused of profiling. Looking at the security camera photos of the twelve young men, Andrew grimaced. Businessmen. What kind of businessmen looked like that? None that he had ever met. Not that he had met that many.

Be that as it may, it was a shame that airport security needed an excuse to report characters that would've raised the suspicion of anyone with half a brain. In his opinion, outlawing profiling was a perfect example of political correctness gone too far.

The vast majority of terrorists were young men between the ages of eighteen to twenty-five. In fact, most violent crimes were perpetrated by the male members of this age group. Seventy-year-old grandmothers and five-year-old girls posed a very remote security risk, so did families with small children. By considering everyone an equal opportunity threat, Homeland Security was wasting its limited resources and increasing the risk of missing the real thing.

Like these boys.

"I wonder what kind of trouble they are up to." His boss straightened and pulled his pants up over his hefty belly. It was hard to believe that once upon a time the guy had been a warrior in an elite unit.

Andrew smirked. "The bunch wouldn't have raised suspicion if Maldives were happening to compete in an international pro-wrestling tournament, and these impressive specimens were the team members."

The men exuded health and vitality, the kind that came from strenuous physical activity, and their straight and sure postures were those of well-trained soldiers.

The boss was of the same opinion. "They look like Marines."

The guys were all tall and seemed to be of several different ethnicities. One was Asian, a tough-looking fellow. Two looked like they were of Scandinavian descent, handsome, blond, blue-eyed devils. They kind of reminded Andrew of his Special Ops buddies and the way the motley bunch had looked coming back from a mission with their suntanned faces covered by several weeks' worth of growth.

"Find out where they are staying and what they are doing. The report mentions three different hotels the men listed for their stay."

"I'll follow up on this tomorrow and see if they ever checked in."

The boss clapped him on the shoulder. "You do that. Now get your ass out of here and go home."

As was his habit, Andrew was the last one in the office. The other agents had families to go home to, but there was no one waiting for him at his house. Tonight, though, he had plans; a date with his sparring partner down at the gym, and if she was in the mood, a romp later on.

Susanna was another *analyst* in his department, which meant that she still went on missions abroad same as he. What had started as an easy camaraderie, had quickly turned into a "friends with benefits" arrangement.

At first, he had been wary of taking their friendship to the next level. According to conventional wisdom, a workplace fling was a disaster waiting to happen. But it had worked out fine. Neither had any expectations or treated it as an exclusive arrangement. They were just scratching each other's itch.

Andrew couldn't allow for anything more and neither could she. Not as long as they were still going on active missions. For him, the party was going to end soon. He was about to hit the dreaded forty. Susanna still had time before the powers that be chained her to a desk.

When he got down to the gym, Susanna was the only one there.

"You're late," she said from behind the punching bag she was practicing her kicks on. The woman was one hell of a martial arts enthusiast.

"Sorry about that. I just had another file dropped on my desk. The boss wanted me to take a quick look at it."

She delivered a punch and followed it with a kick. "Anything interesting?"

"I don't know yet. Tomorrow, I'll know more. It might be nothing, just a bunch of kids touring the States."

She slanted him a knowing look. "But you have a hunch they are up to something."

Andrew rubbed his neck. "Yeah, a gut feeling. By the look of them, they are either athletes or soldiers, but I'm betting on the second one. Their postures give them away. Put uniforms on them and they can easily impersonate Marines."

She chuckled. "You mean they look like they have sticks up their butts?"

Andrew narrowed his eyes at her. "Watch it. I was a Marine once."

Susanna executed a series of quick jabs. "And how long did it take you to lose that posture so it wouldn't give you away?"

Andrew snorted. "Months. I don't know why they bother to recruit from the Marines when they want guys who can blend in."

"I guess because of the training and the stamina." Susanna took off her gloves and sauntered up to him. "Talking about stamina, how about we skip the workout and check out what you've got?"

Andrew grinned and wrapped his arm around her muscular shoulders. "I'm all for it."

"I thought you would be."

22

KIAN

A little after eight, Kian closed the file on a property in Maui he'd been trying to read for the past half an hour and walked out of his home office.

"Do you have my robe ready?" he asked Okidu.

"It is freshly ironed and hanging on a hook by the front door. Let me get it for you, Master."

"Thank you."

As Okidu handed him the robe, Kian draped it over his shoulders and headed for the underground complex.

Once he reached the Grand Council Hall, Kian flicked on the lights and took a good look around. He hadn't seen the amphitheater-style auditorium since he'd inspected the newly completed building four years ago.

The room's opulence and grand size was reminiscent of a bygone era of indulgence, representing Kian's largest splurge on the clan's headquarters. Working from what he'd remembered of his mother's descriptions, he'd tried to replicate the gods' council chamber as best he could.

Semicircle rows of comfortable red-velvet seats formed a horseshoe pattern, and large columns held graceful arches with murals and plaster reliefs depicting mythical scenes. Exquisite detailing adorned mosaic-inlayed marble floors, and the staircase leading to the second-floor balcony featured elaborate plaster moldings and brass rails.

At four hundred seats, the council hall could accommodate all of his clan's American members with room to spare. And just to be on the safe side, the currently unfurnished second-floor balcony could house an additional two hundred seats if needed.

Kian had no idea what had possessed him to build it on such a grand scale. Between his two hundred and eighty-three, Sari's one hundred and ninety-six, and his mother's seventy-two, the whole clan numbered five hundred fifty-one members. What were the chances of all of them gracing his keep at the same time?

Probably none.

But he liked to plan big and prepare for all conceivable contingencies. Perhaps in the future a monumental event, hopefully a celebration, would require the presence of each and every clan member.

The chamber had turned out exactly as he had envisioned it. Well, with the exception of the council members' seats that were still just as ugly as the first time he had seen them, and were proof that contrary to what everyone thought of him, he had the capacity for compromise.

Sitting on the raised platform, arranged in an arc to face the audience, the thirteen throne-like monstrosities had been Amanda's choice. She'd somehow managed to convince Ingrid, the interior designer, to back her up, and so despite his protests the ostentatious gaudy things had stayed.

Some battles were just not worth fighting.

Still, as he sat on his regent seat, stretching his long legs and bracing his arms on the heavy armrests, Kian had to admit that the thing, albeit an eyesore, was comfortable. His seat was in the center, with the six council members to his right and the six Guardians to his left. Onegus, as chief guardian, sat on the council side.

Glancing behind him, he made sure that the two large movable screens at the back of the stage were at the optimal angle for teleconferencing Mark's service. After he had talked it over with his mother and Sari, it had been agreed that tomorrow night all members of the clan would take part in the ceremony.

Satisfied with the screens, he shifted his focus to the multiple rows of plush seats. Damn, the room was huge. Too big for the small council meeting he'd called for.

Reaching under the robe's voluminous folds into his pants pocket, he pulled out his phone and called his secretary. "Shai, we need a smaller room for future council meetings. Call Ingrid, have her choose a suitably sized room and prepare a design for it. I want it on my desk by tomorrow morning."

"It shall be done." Shai clicked off.

With a sigh, Kian pushed to his feet and walked over to the six light switches located near the entry doors. Flipping each one on and off, he eventually figured which one controlled what and turned off the lights over the audience section, plunging it back into the shadows.

Walking back to his seat, it suddenly dawned on him that he was micromanaging everything.

Did he really care how the new small council room would look? He should delegate the whole thing to Ingrid and give her free rein to do as she pleased, trusting her to do it right.

Yeah, like those goddamn awful chairs.

Except, this was the whole point, wasn't it. If he wanted to free up any of his time, he'd have to deal with these kinds of insignificant petty annoyances. His obsessive need to control each and every detail had worked in simpler times. Now it was hindering his performance.

He had to rethink the way he was doing things.

Some of his workload would have to be relinquished to others. Though knowing himself, trusting them to do it well and then living with the consequences would be tough.

Kian planted his ass on his throne and waited in the empty auditorium for his people to arrive—not because anyone was late, but because he'd gotten there early to make sure everything was in order.

Just another example of his OCD...

As if Shai couldn't have done it for him.

Tapping his fingers on the armrests, he watched the door, expecting the Guardians to get there first.

Tradition dictated that the council's meeting place had to be secured and protected prior to the arrival of its distinguished members. Though with safety not being an issue in the bowels of the keep, the men would be upholding the custom more out of respect, or maybe habit. Still, he had no doubt they would be arriving soon.

Other than Kri, the only female Guardian and their most recent addition, the six men were seasoned warriors who'd been serving in this capacity for centuries and were likely to stick to doing things the way they had always been done.

Anandur and Brundar were the oldest, serving with him for over a thousand years. Born of the same mother and two very different sires, they were nothing alike.

Besides both being deadly, that is.

On the surface of things, Anandur appeared charming and easygoing, always ready to jest and pull pranks. But as a stalwart defender of the clan, the guy was a ruthless slayer of its enemies. His tactic of projecting a demonic visage of himself into his opponents' minds and scaring them shitless was his kind of a cruel joke. They either ran for their lives or died believing they were going to hell.

Brundar was still an enigma after all the long years he had been serving as Kian's bodyguard. Besides his brother, no one really knew him, and Kian wondered how well even Anandur did. Brundar was aloof, secretive and somber. Rumors hinted he had a sadistic streak, others that he was a masochist. One had to wonder, though, how someone that couldn't stand being touched could enjoy being at the mercy of another.

Brundar looked like an angel—a vengeful, deadly angel of

wrath. Possessing unparalleled skill and agility, he had perfect aim with any kind of projectile weapon and complete mastery with any kind of blade.

Just as Kian had expected, the brothers made it first, Onegus walking in right behind them.

"Good evening, Kian," Onegus said. The brothers nodded their greeting.

As Brundar climbed the three stairs and took his seat, Anandur stopped for a curtsy, lifting his robe's tails like a lady's gown and batting his red eyelashes at Kian.

The guy just couldn't help his compulsion to clown around, despite it being highly inappropriate considering the circumstances that had brought them here.

Nevertheless, for once Kian was grateful for the comic relief.

Onegus, on the other hand, didn't share his leniency, flicking the top of Anandur's head. "Show some respect!" He pinned the redhead with a hard stare before taking his seat.

It was doubtful Anandur had felt the flick through the cushion of his crinkly hair, but he rubbed at his scalp as he looked at his superior. "It's not my fault that you have no sense of humor."

"Oh, just shut up." Onegus was clearly not in the mood to carry on with the guy, and rightfully so.

What often started with Anandur goofing around, ended up with a sparring match at the gym where the big oaf ruled as an undisputed champion. So unless Onegus wanted to pull rank, he was smart to nip the thing in the bud.

An inch or two shorter than Anandur, Onegus was still quite tall but not as burly, more on the lean, athletic side. With smiling brown eyes, curly blond hair, and a million dollar smile, he claimed to be more of a lover than a fighter, which, of course, was total crap. Still, it was true that he often used that charm as a weapon in his diplomatic capacity on Kian's behalf and to his own benefit with the ladies.

"I'm telling you, the assholes didn't know he was one of us!" Kri's agitated voice turned Kian's attention away from the guys. He glanced at the door as she entered the room while arguing with the stoic Yamanu.

For all intents and purposes, Kri was as good as invisible next to that guy. Yamanu had this effect on people, his startling looks commanding everyone's attention to the exclusion of everything else. Which might have been the reason Yamanu hardly ever left the keep. Except, that raised another important question... How the hell did he manage to get any sex without prowling the clubs and bars?

Not that he would have had to work hard for it, towering as he did at six and a half feet and built like a sculptor's fantasy of how a male body should look. And as if that was not enough, Yamanu wore his shiny, black hair in a straight curtain that fell down to his waist.

His most startling feature, though, were his hypnotic, pale blue eyes, strange and out of place in his dark, angular face.

Yamanu was a master illusionist with an ability as powerful as that of the gods of old. His illusions could alter the perception of reality in thousands of mortal minds, providing a sense of touch, smell, and sound, in addition to sight. On more than one occasion, this unique talent of his had saved the clan from serious trouble.

With hordes of mortals attacking anything in their path, Kian's small force of warriors hadn't stood a chance, and though his people were hard to kill, a sword could sever a mortal's or immortal's head with the same ease. Even worse, the thought of what those savages could've done to the females if they had gotten past his warriors' defenses... and the children...

Hell, he'd better not go there if he wanted his head clear for the meeting.

The last Guardians entering were the somber duo from the Bay Area, Bhathian and Arwel.

The two looked worn out and miserable, but the sad truth was that it hadn't been the recent tragedy that had caused their misery. It had just amplified it.

Bhathian always looked pissed off. If not for the unpleasant vibe emanating from him, the big guy could've been considered handsome. His tall muscular frame and strong face were certainly attractive. As it was though, his angry expression and sheer size made him look more like an ogre. And Arwel, with his out-of-control empathetic ability, was wearing a perpetually tormented expression.

Regardless of their disparate physiques and temperaments, Kian had to admit that the seven Guardians formed an impressive, unified front in their formal ceremonial attire. Onegus's robe as both Guardian and councilman was white with a double edge of black and silver, the others were black with a single silver edge.

Kian's, in his opinion, was ridiculous. Made of blood-red velvet and edged in black, silver, and white it looked like a glitzy monarch's costume. The despotic getup was only missing a crown and scepter. But be that as it may, he had no intention of arguing with his mother over her choice of formal robes. Not that it would've done him any good.

The doors pushed open again as Shai and the four council members he was escorting entered the room. Acting as if he'd designed the place himself, Shai flicked all the lights back on. Pointing proudly, he explained the chamber's features and decor, "...we have four hundred seats down here, and two hundred more can be added on the balcony. The room is decorated in the Neo-Grecian style..."

Kian tuned Shai out, focusing on the council members instead.

Bridget, the local clan's only MD, had her medical and research facilities located in the building's underground, and they bumped into each other on occasion.

Kian liked and respected the pretty redhead, with her pleasant and unassuming demeanor. It never ceased to amaze him that a woman so petite could break and reset badly fused broken bones with ease. It was one of the few things a near-immortal needed medical care for; delivering babies and sewing up the more serious wounds being the other two. All were rare occurrences, which left Bridget with plenty of time to research their kind's unique biology.

Edna, a brilliant attorney and an expert on clan law, oversaw the legal aspects of their business transactions and presided over clan members' trials.

Besides her sharp mind, Edna was a tough cookie, which was the main reason Kian had chosen her as his replacement in case something happened to him. He could trust her to handle the job. That didn't mean that the rest of the clan would be happy with her at the helm. She was known as a harsh and unforgiving judge, and though respected, wasn't well liked.

Kian couldn't remember seeing the woman ever smiling, and her looks matched her austere attitude. Edna didn't bother with making herself pretty. If anything, the opposite was true. It must have been a deliberate effort for her to look so plain. Her brown hair was tied in a severe knot on her nape, she wore no makeup, and the ceremonial robe was a big improvement over her daily wardrobe of ill-fitting pantsuits.

Edna's one saving grace was her eyes. They shone with intelligence and the kind of understanding that delved into the most hidden places of her victims' souls, reaching behind their mental shields and baring all of their nasty secrets. It was quite unnerving, as Kian remembered from personal experience. It was also a rare ability. Normally, immortals couldn't penetrate each other's minds, only those of humans. Annani could, but then she was a full-blooded goddess.

Because of her unique talent, Edna was nicknamed the Alien Probe.

William, the Science Guy as everyone called him, was the opposite. Good-natured and bubbly, he looked like a chubby bear, proving that even superior genes couldn't combat the consequences of a big appetite. William liked to eat a lot, while sitting in front of the computer, or the television, or with company. He was the go-to guy for all things technological—one of the few smart enough to translate and comprehend the technical information contained in the ancient gods' tablet.

Walking between Edna and William, the suave Brandon stood

out like a peacock amongst ducks. In charge of culture and media, his job was to promote books, movies, TV shows, and magazine stories; advocating the gods' social agenda—starting with democracy, through equal rights, to education and research—the list was long.

By portraying the desired state as an expressed ideal, enacting it in stories, plays, and movies, mortals assimilated the message. To strive for something better, people had to imagine it first to be aware of the possibility.

Understanding this dynamic, oppressive regimes denied their people free access to these sources, fearing the exposure to new and better ideas would promote social unrest. Demonizing the cultures that produced the dangerous materials served as a deterrent to their ignorant and brainwashed masses against seeking the corrupt, immoral, evil, etc. sources of information.

Unfortunately, there was little Kian could do to bring enlightenment to those closed-off regions, and their populations were falling further and further behind the Western world.

He often asked himself what came first—Navuh finding fertile ground for his propaganda in these places, or his propaganda creating the atmosphere in which oppressive regimes could gain power.

The fact remained, though; wherever women were marginalized, considered inferior, and denied rights available to men, the society as a whole lagged behind.

No exceptions.

"Would someone please open for me?" Amanda called for help while kicking the doors.

As Shai rushed over to let her in, she handed him one of the two Starbucks trays she had been carrying. Besides the trays, she also managed to hold onto a paper bag full of bottled drinks, her robe, and her purse.

"Sorry I'm late, everyone. I had to have coffee and stopped at Starbucks, but then figured it would be rude to be the only one with a cappuccino, so I brought some more."

Brandon relieved her of the other tray and the bag, then together with Shai they passed the drinks around.

"Thank you, guys." Amanda put on her robe and took a look around. "Kian, this is so not the place to have a small council meeting in; it's huge! We need a small room, one with a table to put our drinks on." She took the last vacant chair next to Onegus.

Kian shook his head. It was so like Amanda to ignore everyone and everything and just say whatever popped into her head.

"Already on it. Can we begin now?" he asked as he pushed to his feet and turned to face the council.

"Hold for one more second, I'm starting the recording!" Shai called from his command station at the controls of the sophisticated equipment.

Kian waited for the guy to give the thumbs-up before he began again.

"Okay. This is council meeting?" He had forgotten to check the number of the last session.

"Four hundred and twelve!" Shai supplied.

"Thank you." Having a secretary with eidetic memory was definitely convenient.

"This is council meeting four hundred and twelve. All members present." Kian recited the standard opening sentence meant for record keeping.

Taking a deep breath, he addressed the council. "Last night, Mark son of Micah, was murdered by the DOOM Brotherhood in his own home." Kian paused for a moment, waiting for everyone's shocked responses of disbelief and sorrow to settle down.

"We were dealt a monumental blow. Beyond losing a beloved family member, the loss of his incredible talent will hinder our progress in developing the software that could potentially save the world by disabling the weapons meant for its destruction." Looking at their worried and pained expressions, he added in a softer tone, "Bhathian and Arwel brought his body home, and the service in his honor will be held tomorrow at midnight." Kian looked at their faces as each member gave him a somber nod of agreement.

His next request wouldn't meet with such easy acquiescence. Bracing for the inevitable argument, Kian gripped the lapels of his robe and fixed the council with a hard stare.

"Until the level of threat is ascertained, I move to seclude all council members in our secure building. We can't afford to lose any of you, and we don't have enough Guardians to provide each member with a security detail. You'll have to cancel any appointments you had scheduled for the time being. I'm sorry for the inconvenience, but I see no other option."

"I don't know how anybody can find us among the mortals, there is nothing pointing to us," Brandon protested. "We can't be prisoners in your glass tower; you know we need to consort with mortals for obvious reasons."

Kian had been expecting someone to raise that objection. "At this point, we don't know how much the Doomers know. Mark's laptop and sat-phone are missing. We can only hope they don't have anyone capable enough to break through his firewalls. And besides, there might have been other clues at his house that can lead to us. I'm not willing to take unnecessary risks. As to being prisoners, you can still go to clubs, bars, restaurants, and whatever random places you like. I just don't want you anywhere near your habitual meeting or workplaces."

"If they try to break into his laptop, it will self-corrupt all info. Same for the phone, I'm not worried," William offered.

"What if they have someone of Mark's caliber?" Kian kept playing the devil's advocate.

William snorted. "Then we're screwed, but they don't. No one has."

"Did you inform Mother and Sari?" Amanda looked at Kian with her big, sad eyes, ignoring the whole seclusion discussion. She'd already expressed her opinion about this idea earlier. Hopefully, she wouldn't stir things up and embarrass him in front of the entire council.

"I called them shortly after Arwel delivered the news. Tomorrow during the service both of them, together with their people, will be with us via teleconferencing. The whole clan will take part in Mark's final journey."

"Thank you," she said in a small voice.

He was glad she hadn't argued with him about the seclusion, but it pained him to see Amanda's usually animated face look defeated as she sank back into her chair.

"I think you're being overly cautious, but let's vote on it!" Edna went straight to the point, probably under the assumption that the council would vote against Kian.

But he had an ace up his sleeve.

"As this is a security issue, the Guardians will take part in the vote."

This was another advantage of keeping the council members in the dark about the subject of this meeting. Edna hadn't thought to check the emergency bylaws. Not that she could've done anything to stop him if she had known. The council members had no chance; they were as good as tied and locked.

The Guardians always voted with Kian.

"Let's see then. All in favor of seclusion, raise your hands!" he called.

The Seven Guardians and Kian all raised their hands, and so did Bridget. Not a big surprise since she already lived in the keep. Defeated, William and Edna joined the show of hands.

That left two.

Brandon shrugged. "Well, what do you know, vacation time for me! I'll finally get to see all the *Battlestar Galactica* episodes."

Kian glanced at Amanda, expecting her to argue, but she didn't. Evidently, the experience at the lab had scared her into compliance.

23

SYSSI

The nightmare was back.

Terrified, Syssi was running away from a pack of snarling wolves. With the moon obscured by dark clouds and the dense canopy of tall trees, the barely visible trail was illuminated only by a darting speck of light. Following it, Syssi prayed she wouldn't stumble and fall.

All alone in the foreboding darkness, the huge monsters' red glowing eyes and sharp fangs never far behind, she was defenseless.

Soon, she wouldn't be able to run anymore, and they'd get her. Rip her apart.

How did I get here?

Why are they chasing me?

Desperate tears streaming down her cheeks, Syssi kept running, when up ahead in the distance she glimpsed something that gave her a glimmer of hope. Hidden under the dark shadows cast by the thick limbs of a tree was a silhouette of what looked like a tall man.

"Help me!" Syssi called to him.

There was no response.

Was he even real? Or was her mind playing tricks on her?

Desperately searching for a pattern in what was nothing more than rocks and bushes loosely resembling a human form?

But what choice did she have?

It was either find help or die a horrific death.

She had nothing to lose by changing direction and running toward him. If there was nothing there, she would just keep on running. Until she could run no more.

But as she got closer, and it became apparent that the man wasn't a figment of her imagination, hope and relief bloomed in Syssi's chest.

"Help!" she yelled again. But he ignored her, his gaze fixed on the pursuing red eyes.

"Help me! Damn you!" Syssi shook his arm, forcing him to look at her.

Finally he turned, shifting his intense eyes to her. "No need to yell, Syssi. Get behind me." He turned back to stare at the rapidly approaching wolves.

How did he know her name? Did she know him? She would've remembered someone like him. The man was stunningly beautiful.

What a strange thing to notice at a time like this.

Never mind. He is going to help me.

Hiding behind his large frame, she watched the wolves burst out of the tree line and circle them, snarling; their horrid yellow fangs dripping with fetid saliva.

The man raised his hands and snarled back at the wolves, exposing a pair of huge, acid-dripping fangs.

Acid?

What made her think it was acid?

Oh, right, the dirt sizzled where drops of it fell.

The wolves began backing away with their tails curled under their bellies, still snarling and drooling at her rescuer as they made their retreat.

"Run! You mangy cowardly dogs! Not so brave now, are you?" she taunted the wolves from her safe spot behind the guy's back.

The wolves turned and ran into the thicket, leaving her alone with the stranger.

"Thank you. You saved my life. I don't want to think what would've happened if you weren't here to help me." Syssi smiled at him. The guy was so tall that she had to crank her neck way up to look at him.

"You should keep on running, Syssi. There is a reason the wolves fear me, I'm a monster too." He flashed his fangs.

Was he trying to scare her off? She wasn't afraid of him.

"Why aren't you running?" he asked when she didn't budge.

"How can you say that? You're not a monster. You're a hero!" Syssi stretched up on her toes and kissed him on the lips.

"Are you crazy? What are you doing? You'll get burned by the acid!" The man brought his thumb to her lips and wiped them vigorously.

"Your acid is harmful only to the demon wolves. It tastes good to me." She licked her lips and smiled, coyly inviting another kiss.

"You have no idea what you're asking for," he growled, looking at her menacingly and flashing his sharp fangs again.

But then a small, terrible smile curled his lips, and his lids dropped halfway over his eyes. "Do you want these fangs piercing the skin of your neck? Do you want me to bite you?" It sounded more like a promise than a threat.

"Will it hurt?" Syssi asked in a small voice.

"Yes, it will. But it will also bring you intense pleasure. Do you feel adventurous?" He dipped his head and brought his lips to the base of her neck. Not touching. Threatening.

"Then I want you to," Syssi whispered, brushing her hair away to give him better access. And yet, despite her brave words her heart began beating faster and she closed her eyes, her excitement tinged by fear.

"Why?" he whispered in her ear, brushing his lips lightly against her neck.

Shocking herself, Syssi blurted throatily, "Because I want you to make love to me."

Hey, it's my dream...

Yes, she realized—this was only a dream.

Good. Inside her own head, she could be as brazen as she wanted to.

"Would you?" she asked.

"I don't know how." He turned away from her.

Incredulous, Syssi gasped. "Have you never done it before?" There was no way a man like him wasn't constantly propositioned by women. His celibacy could only be explained by religious prohibition, perhaps priesthood. Or maybe he was a monk. Except, he didn't seem like either.

"It was so long ago, I forgot how." He sounded dejected.

At least he wasn't a virgin. But she was curious about his decision to abstain. "Did you take a vow of celibacy? Join a monastery?"

But then, as she thought more about it—

Wait! There could be another explanation. What if he can't? What if he has a condition, and I'm making it so much worse for him?

Talk about putting one's foot in one's mouth.

With a sinister smile on his beautiful face, he dipped his head to look into her eyes. "No, I didn't abstain, I had plenty of sex, just not the kind that qualifies as lovemaking," he said sarcastically.

"Oh..." What was she supposed to say to that? Suspecting she knew the answer, she asked anyway. "What's the difference?"

The way his expression turned predatory seemed familiar for some reason. Had they met before? She would have remembered him. Really not the kind of guy she could've ever forgotten.

"One is the gentle lovey-dovey kind a girl like you likes, the kind you have with someone you care about. The other is just a fuck, rough and intense, so much so that it sometimes hurts. But you don't give a damn because it hurts so good. Not something a good girl like you knows anything about or wants." He gave her a haughty, condescending look.

Who did he think he was? Assuming things about her? Even if they were true? Still, he had no right.

"How would you know? You know nothing about me," she protested. "Don't presume what I know or what I want."

"Fair enough, although I'm in your head, so I should know. But I'll ask anyway; what do you want, Syssi?"

Now, wasn't that the million dollar question. What did she want?

Thinking, she bit down on her bottom lip and looked down at her feet, when out of nowhere a memory surfaced, flooding her with intense desire.

Syssi remembered being pressed against a wall, a man's hand fisting her hair, pulling just hard enough to provide the smidgen of pain that was driving her wild. He was kissing her, grinding himself against her, his ferocity and intensity making her wet and needy. She'd urged him to do more, but he'd withdrawn, leaving her unsatisfied.

It had been him! The same guy...

Why couldn't she remember his name?

Was it Cain? Kaen?

"I remember you. You kissed me. It was exactly like you said; rough, intense, a little painful. It was an amazing kiss and I was desperate for more. But you stopped and left me hanging. Except, you looked as if you regretted letting me go. And I know that you cared."

Wow, who was that woman that possessed her and spoke out of her mouth so blatantly?

Cain, or whatever his name was, eyed her like a tasty treat, smiling and flashing his fangs. "So, you like a little pain with your pleasure, don't you, naughty girl?"

Syssi paused to think. "I guess it's like sprinkling spice on a dish that is otherwise bland... I don't like bland food."

Okay, saved by a metaphor; no way she was spelling it out for him. Not even in a dream.

"That is something we have in common. I don't like bland food either."

Was he mocking her? She glanced up, checking his expression.

No, he wasn't. If possible, he looked even hungrier for her. And his blatant lust ignited a fire within her.

Syssi felt herself grow wet, dizzy, dimly aware that she'd never understood what swooning was all about before experiencing it herself.

As her legs nearly went out from under her, he saved her from falling by grabbing onto her waist and holding her against his body in a tight embrace. For a long moment, he just looked into her eyes, his gaze so hungry and yet unsure, his lips so close and yet out of reach.

She'd die if he didn't kiss her.

Or scratch his eyes out for teasing her like this.

One of the two.

"Don't you dare…" she started.

Misinterpreting her words, he pulled his head away.

"Kiss me!" she commanded.

A small smirk brightened his fearsome expression. "Make up your mind, sweet girl. Do you want to be kissed or not?"

"Don't you dare not kiss me."

His brows lifted and he grinned. His long fangs on full display, he looked absolutely evil. She should've been frightened, but she wasn't. If anything, the sight of them sent a blast of desire down into her core.

He inhaled, his eyelids dropping over his eyes for a moment as if he'd just smelled something delicious. "Lustful little thing, aren't you? And so demanding."

Oh, for heaven's sake, was he going to make her beg?

Whatever, it was just a dream, right? No one would ever know if she did.

"Please, kiss me…," she breathed and parted her lips in invitation.

His arm still wrapped securely around her, he tangled his free hand in her hair. Grabbing a fistful, he held her in place and lowered his lips to hers.

Time slowed down as Syssi watched him close the distance in

slow motion. Breathing was impossible, and her heart felt like it had stopped beating. She was going to die. Right here, right now, in this dream. But she didn't care. Besides this man and the way he was making her feel, nothing mattered. She needed him more than her next breath. Or her next heartbeat.

When their lips finally touched, the relief was so profound that she felt dizzy with it. Though the part of her that was still capable of thought suggested that it might've been the lack of oxygen in her lungs.

At first, his touch was gentle as he took possession of her mouth, even unexpectedly sweet, but it lasted no more than a second.

She felt, rather than heard, the hungry growl that started deep in his throat. And as he let it loose, his restraint snapped and he attacked—his tongue invading her mouth, the hand fisting her hair tightening, pulling at the roots, and the fingers of the other one digging deep into her flesh. It should've been painful, uncomfortable, but her body was somehow transforming it into erotic heat.

Syssi's eyes rolled back and the husky moan that escaped her mouth was like no sound she'd ever made before. It should've been embarrassing, but she couldn't care less.

Her dark stranger was turning her into a mindless puddle of need.

"I'd better finish what I've started then. It'd be very ungentlemanly of me to leave a lady hanging, wouldn't you agree?" he whispered as he lowered her to the ground... laying her... on a bed?

Oh, the wonders of dreamscape.

Propped on his elbow, he loomed above her, looking into her eyes as his hand snaked under her shirt, finding her achy nipple and circling it slowly with his thumb.

Syssi arched her back, her shirt and bra performing a magical disappearing act as she offered him more.

Holding his eyes locked on hers, he dipped his head and took the offering in his lips, suckling gently as he moved his thumb to rim her other nipple.

The pleasure was so intense, she felt as if a tight coil was winding inside her, and at any moment it would spring with an explosive force.

Syssi was panting, her hips undulating, her juices flowing. *More,* she begged soundlessly, *I need more.*

As if to answer her silent plea, she felt his teeth graze the bud he was suckling, and then gently close around it. And yet, no alarm bells sounded in her head; there was no fear. She trusted her dream lover not to hurt her...well, that wasn't entirely true... she trusted him to hurt her just right.

Applying light pressure to her achy nipple with his blunt teeth, he pinched her other one between his thumb and forefinger and tugged.

She whimpered, the zing of pain opening the floodgates down below. She couldn't remember ever being so wet—her panties soaked through and her juices running down her thighs. And yet, there was no embarrassment, no anxiety.

Instead, unexpectedly, there was joy.

The joy of discovering that she was capable of experiencing such pleasure, that there was someone, even if only in a dream, who knew the secret code to unlocking her hidden desires.

Looking at her with hooded eyes, he kept the pressure steady, then began gradually increasing it until it became too much...

Exploding, Syssi screamed, her hips arching off the bed, her climax rippling powerfully, shaking her whole body.

When the tremors subsided, she reached for Kian, trying to bring him down to cover her trembling body with his warmth and his strength.

To connect.

Kian, that was his name. She remembered it now.

"Shh... it's okay." He resisted her pull, caressing and licking her tender nipples, easing the hurt away.

As he lifted his head, the hard planes of his face looked softer, his gaze appreciative. Stroking her damp hair, he bent down and kissed her lips softly, sweetly. "You're a treasure, beautiful girl," he said, his features blurring, dissipating...

"Wait! Don't go!" Syssi panicked. "Don't leave me alone... I want to give you pleasure too..."

He was almost gone now...

"You did, my sweet Syssi..."

She woke up gasping, her face flushed, her body sweaty, her panties soaking wet.

It had been just a dream.

It hadn't been real.

As a deep sense of loss and disappointment enveloped her, Syssi curled upon herself, hugging her knees.

The most amazing sex she'd ever experienced had been nothing but a dream, a fantasy.

God, if the foreplay had been enough to bring about such a reality-altering orgasm, what would the actual act have been like?

Could she even imagine it?

Dream it?

Probably not.

How could she?

Without experiencing this little taste of how it could be, she wouldn't have known to yearn even for this, let alone more.

Was it even attainable in the real world?

She would never know, would she?

Heavens, how she longed for her fantasy lover—the man from her dream.

If she were lucky, she would dream of him again. It was the most she could hope for.

24

KIAN

Back at his apartment, Kian dropped the ceremonial robe on one of the kitchen counter stools and walked over to the bar. Too wired to go to bed, he poured himself a drink and took it outside to the terrace. Getting comfortable on a lounger, he pulled out a cigarette from the pack he had left there, lit it, and inhaled gratefully.

As he watched the smoke curl up and dissipate into the dark sky, his thoughts wandered to Syssi. Her innocent, hopeful expression when he had first seen her face emerge from behind the curtain of her wild hair. The way her body had felt tucked against his when she'd slept in the car, her cheek resting on his chest.

That kiss...

After spending such a short time with Syssi, getting a taste for her, her absence already felt like something vital was missing from his life, and he had an inkling that he could never go back to the numb state of existence he had been living in for so long.

Except, what choice did he have? He had to stay away and somehow try to forget her. Unfortunately, it wasn't going to be as easy for him as it had been for her. After all, he couldn't thrall away his own memories.

With a sigh, he took another drag from his cigarette and

wondered if she was still sleeping, and if she was, was she dreaming about him?

As memories could never be truly erased, just pushed below the barrier separating the conscious mind from the unconscious, she might remember him in her dreams. Or maybe conjure him in her fantasies. He hoped she would.

He'd be thinking and dreaming about her. Of that, he was certain.

Sometime later, Kian woke up miserably cold and achingly hard. Apparently, he had fallen asleep on the lounger outside.

It was one hell of a dream.

The way she flew apart from so little...

Only in your dreams, buddy... you're not that good, he chuckled.

But it had felt so real...

She had felt so real...

So good.

The girl was haunting him even in his dreams.

He needed to get rid of this obsession with a woman he could never see again. If he wanted to retain a shred of self-respect and one untainted spot on his dark soul, he would stay away from her.

Damn, sometimes it seemed like the cost of doing the right thing was too steep. Except, to succumb to his craving and take her would be the equivalent of a hit and run. Or more accurately, a fuck and run.

He had enough on his guilty conscience as it was.

Hell, he had enough guilt to fill up a lake.

Kian hung his head and let out a sigh, his breath misting in the cold air. If only Syssi weren't so sweet and naive, if she were one of those girls who went out looking for hookups in the nightclubs he frequented, he would've taken her without a second thought and then forgotten about her the next day. But then, that sweetness and that naiveté were exactly what made her so irresistible to a man like him.

A dark-souled killer.

Heaven knew how many had breathed their last breath at his hands. And it didn't matter that he had killed only to protect his family.

At first he'd had nightmares, but with each subsequent kill another part of his soul had shriveled and died, until one day he'd realized that ending a life no longer bothered him—it left him indifferent.

There was a dark void in his soul that craved Syssi's light. Trouble was, the vacuum was so big that it would've devoured her whole and still hungered for more, long after depleting all that she had to give.

He couldn't do it.

Syssi was a forbidden fruit.

A fresh, sweet, succulent fruit.

He'd better stick to the somewhat overripe, often even rotten variety he was used to. Not as tasty, but with less guilt attached.

Except a glance at his watch revealed it was four twenty in the morning; too late to go prowling for sex in bars or clubs.

Resigned, he made his way inside, not looking forward to the cold shower he was about to take.

25

DALHU

"I'm sorry, sir. I've done the best I could. These Guardians were invincible. I've never seen anyone fight like this. I would've stayed and fought to the death, but I thought you would like to know what happened." The guy was about to piss himself, and rightfully so.

In the failed attempt to grab the professor, Dalhu had lost two out of the three men he had sent to retrieve her. And the worthless coward who had managed to escape and come back to report the fiasco was still alive only because Dalhu was down to ten warriors including himself, and he couldn't afford to lose one more.

"You've done well. Dismissed." He managed to get the words out without his rage spilling out, then waved the worthless piece of shit away.

He should've sent more men. Hell, he should've gone himself.

If you want something done, do it yourself; as the saying went.

Three men should've been more than enough to abduct one female.

One very beautiful, immortal female...

Dalhu lifted the framed article that his men had found at the programmer's home. Staring at the professor's stunning face, he commended the scientific journal's editor for choosing to dedicate most of the page to her beautiful image and only a few paragraphs to describe her research. Smart man.

The fact that she'd autographed her picture with "To my darling Mark" had tipped off Dalhu that Dr. Dokani might be another immortal. A quick Internet search had yielded only a few references to the little-known scientist and her specialized and not that popular field of study, proving that Dr. Amanda Dokani wasn't some famous celebrity. Which had led Dalhu to believe that the woman must've been someone important to the guy. Otherwise, it made no sense for the programmer to value the autographed article enough to frame it and place it on his desk, where he would have been staring at it whenever he'd sat down to work. And as the bastard had been gay, it sure as shit hadn't been his girlfriend or a case of infatuation with a pretty face.

The professor was family.

Besides, encountering Guardians at her lab had been a nasty surprise, but it had served as proof positive that his hunch had been right. Dr. Dokani was an immortal female of Annani's clan. Not only that, but to warrant the protection of Guardians, she was someone of vital importance.

Fuck! He should have gone himself.

With the bitter taste of failure souring his exuberant mood over yesterday's victory, Dalhu's face contorted in a nasty grimace. If he had better fighters at his disposal, she would have been in his possession now. But the inferior stock he had to work with had been no match for the superior warriors protecting her.

Well, fuck it.

It wasn't as if anyone else had ever succeeded in snatching one of the clan's females. Being such a priceless commodity, they were fiercely guarded by their males, and as they were also almost impossible to detect, none had ever been captured by the Order.

Nonetheless, it felt like such a failure. A once in a lifetime opportunity squandered.

Absconding with the professor would've been the ultimate coup...

Fuck!

Dalhu felt his anger gain momentum, bubbling up from the churning fire always on a low simmer in his gut. Damn it, he had to douse it before it exploded into a full-out rage, pushing logic and reason out and turning him into a mindless beast.

With a curse, he slammed the seat cushion beside him, his fist tearing into the fabric. Taking several deep breaths, he fought the overwhelming urge to strike again.

Breathe in through the nose, breathe out through the mouth, in and out... He counted to ten, focusing on his breathing as he made a deliberate effort to unclench his fists.

Calm down, identify the problem, think of a solution, he recited the three steps of anger management that he'd learned from an Internet course. It had taken a couple of minutes, but eventually the red haze of rage began to recede, and a semblance of logic returned. His mind was taking the slow road back to sanity.

It didn't matter. It wasn't even a setback.

As it was, this mission had turned out to be far more successful than he had expected it to be. What had begun as a simple retaliation strike, designed to cripple the Americans' progress in their war on weapons of mass destruction in the hands of Navuh's protégés, had given the Order their first clan hit in centuries.

Taking that immortal programmer out had been a sheer stroke of luck.

It was Dalhu's triumph.

His kill.

It had happened on his watch.

Dalhu's position in the Brotherhood of the Devout Order of Mortdh was about to get a serious boost.

With smug satisfaction, he reclined on the elaborately carved sofa and propped his booted feet on the dainty coffee table. He could already taste Navuh's praise, even though it irked him that he was craving it from the lying, manipulative son of a bitch.

Stretching his arms and lacing his fingers behind his head, Dalhu pushed out his chest, filling it with so much air it was a wonder his shirt buttons didn't pop. With the pendulum of his emotions back on the upswing, he was once again soaring on the wings of his success.

Man, it feels good to be top dog.

Taking a satisfied look at the elegant room he was in, Dalhu no longer felt like an interloper in all that opulence. The Beverly Hills mansion he had rented for this mission was spectacularly plush; Persian rugs in every room, impressive reproductions of famous art, and fake, dainty French antiques that were covered in miscellaneous shit. Definitely not the right scale for his massive body. But he liked it nonetheless. He could get used to that; a king of his own castle.

It was a nice change from the training facilities and battlefields he was accustomed to. Regrettably, the lavish accommodations were temporary.

Not that their current home base was lacking in any way... If he could disregard the fucking lack of privacy, and that besides his clothes and his weapons nothing really belonged to him.

Navuh provided for his army of mercenaries well. They were well paid, well housed, well fed, and well fucked.

The small tropical island, indistinct from the many other tiny land pieces scattered throughout the Indian Ocean, provided them with a perfect setup. Its thick jungle canopy hid the training grounds from view of passing aircraft and satellites, and with their quarters as well as the rest of their facilities built underground, no one suspected that thousands of immortal warriors called it their home.

Steep, rocky cliffs prevented approaching their side of the island by boat, and the jungle made landing an aircraft there near impossible. The only way in or out of their base was a secret tunnel road connecting it to the island's other side.

The underground passage terminated in a small airport that was operated by mortals. It served the men leaving for or returning from missions, as well as the oblivious tourists visiting the other side.

For obvious reasons, the mortal pilots were thralled within an inch of their lives, and Dalhu often wondered how safe flying with them really was.

The planes shuttling people and cargo on and off the island had no windows, and apart from the pilots flying them, no one other than Navuh and his sons knew the island's exact location.

The secret was safe with the flyers. The compulsion they were under was so strong that there was no chance in hell they would talk. No matter what was done to them.

Given enough pressure, their brains would just blow a fuse, and they'd either end up brain dead, or dead period.

It was just the way it needed to be. For the island to serve its dual purposes, its location had to be extremely well guarded.

Known to the select few as Passion Island, the other side was home to a very exclusive and luxurious brothel. Young and beautiful prostitutes, junkies, and runaways were abducted from all over the world and brought to serve the rich, famous, and depraved... as well as Navuh's men.

It was pure genius.

Navuh made shitloads of money out of the girls while providing an in-house brothel for his army's needs.

Dalhu hated to admit it, but the son of a god was a brilliant businessman.

To make the place the success it was, its money-generating assets were well taken care of. Good food, good medical care, supervised drug and alcohol use, plus careful monitoring, in all likelihood prolonged the girls' otherwise compromised life expectancy.

But it was slavery nonetheless.

The only alternative the girls had to prostitution was to serve as maids, waitresses, or cooks. The only way off the island was a one-way ticket to either heaven or hell, leaving their corporeal bodies behind.

Given the choice between manual work and prostitution, most opted to work on their backs; lured by the nice private rooms and the patron gifts that paid for their drugs and their drinks and other small luxuries.

The service personnel, on the other hand, got only the basics, worked twelve-hour shifts, six days a week, and slept four to a room.

Between the illusion of having a choice, the promise of rewards, and the fear of punishment, the girls did their best to provide outstanding service, earning them a reputation for being the best money could buy.

Navuh was a master at the art of motivation, or rather manipulation.

Come to think of it, the soldiers didn't fare much better than the whores. Probably worse, as their servitude was indefinite. The only way out was the same as the girls'. Except, final exit options for immortals were limited by the nature of their near indestructibility.

The fastest way for a Doomer to die was to get blacklisted by Navuh and executed, either fighting to the death gladiator style, with a lethal dose of venom, or a beheading.

Dalhu couldn't remember anyone actually choosing to end things that way. Although over the years, he had witnessed enough pitiful bastards succumb to that fate.

Hell, they all knew they lived or died at their Exalted Leader's whim.

It was what it was. As long as they served Navuh well and kept their heads down, the soldiers had nothing to worry about.

And nothing to show for it either.

Looking back to his own nearly eight hundred years of service, his compensation had been mainly room and board and the use of prostitutes.

As he saw it, his rewards were the ones he had given himself. The things he had accomplished. The things he had learned. He had done it all without any guidance or help. Even literacy had been something he had accomplished on his own, teaching himself to read and write not that long ago.

For most of his life, Dalhu had lived in ignorance.

But not anymore.

To most Doomers, the money they were paid for their services seemed great, but Dalhu was smarter than that. Although his account in the Order's bank held millions, he knew the amount was meaningless. He could never take it out.

He charged his expenses to the Brotherhood's American Express that was covered by his account, but as it was routinely monitored, all he could use it for was to buy himself fancy shit and pay for his use of the island's whores. Cash withdrawals were limited to no more than five thousand dollars at a time, and only when going on missions. A detailed account of what he spent it on was required upon his return.

To most of Navuh's fighters, it was more than enough. The simple-minded, brainwashed morons couldn't conceive of using the money for anything else.

Navuh's system was brilliant.

He paid his soldiers well so they felt rewarded and stayed loyal. But by limiting their access to their own money, he ensured they always had to come back. If they didn't, they were presumed dead and the money reverted to him.

Win-win for Navuh.

Dalhu lifted his hand and stared at the Patek Philippe watch on his wrist and the five-carat diamond ring on his index finger. Just these two pieces alone were worth in excess of one hundred and fifty thousand dollars. He had another Patek Philippe and two Rolexes, each in the hundred thousand range.

Strutting around and showing off the stuff, he pretended to be a consummate connoisseur of fine jewelry... Dalhu couldn't have cared less for the ostentatious shit.

But it provided the means to an exit in case he needed one.

Like a cunning mistress to a rich man, he was accumulating a wealth of marketable goods under the guise of vanity. He had to be smart about it, though, waiting years between each purchase to avoid suspicion. Navuh executed men at a mere hint of sedition or suspected desertion.

It wasn't much, and Dalhu wasn't planning anything yet. But he liked to be prepared as best he could for anything life might throw at him, be it an unforeseen calamity or a great opportunity.

One never knew what tomorrow might bring.

"Sir, we are ready to place the call." Edward, his second, bowed politely, jarring Dalhu from his thoughts.

Pushing off the couch, he stretched his big body, then jutted his chest out and his chin up. Dalhu was ready for his reward—the rare praise from Navuh.

As he entered the mansion's sophisticated media room, Dalhu nodded to the assembled men and walked over to the equipment, making sure the wiring had been set up correctly for the scheduled teleconference.

'Inspect, don't expect' was a good piece of advice for any leader, more so if one had morons for underlings.

The equipment worked fine and everything else was ready as well. His men had already cleared a large carpeted area in front of the screen by pushing the overstuffed recliners all the way against the side walls, and were now taking their places on their knees in a compulsory show of respect and devotion to their master, Lord Navuh.

Dalhu took hold of the keyboard and knelt facing the screen with his men at his back, watching the electronic clock on the side of the screen. He made the call at the precise time it had been scheduled for, sending the request and waiting for it to be acknowledged.

Several long minutes passed before the face of Navuh's secretary finally appeared. "Greetings, warriors, please get in position for his Excellency, Lord Navuh."

The men prostrated themselves with their foreheads touching the floor and their hands beside their heads, palms down.

"Our exalted leader, Lord Navuh," the secretary announced, signaling they could begin the devotion.

Ten strong voices sounded the chant.

Glory to Lord Navuh the wise and the just
In his guidance and mercy we put our trust
With his bounty we thrive
By his will we live and we die
We are all brothers in
the Devout Order of Mortdh
In his name we wage this Holy War

As always, the devotion was repeated three times. When it was done, the men held their position while Dalhu pushed up to his knees and faced his leader.

"Was your mission successful, warrior?" Navuh asked.

Addressing Dalhu by the generic term probably meant that Navuh hadn't bothered to learn his name. Anger flared, but he managed to keep his expression impassive and his tone respectful.

"It was, my lord, an unparalleled success. We infiltrated the enemies' secret organization and took out their number one asset, effectively halting any further progress their technological mastery could produce for the foreseeable future. But the victory was even greater than the one we set out to win. The programmer we killed was an immortal. At long last we succeeded, taking out one of our true adversaries. I believe we are closer than ever to uncovering the hornet's nest. It would be a great honor for my team and myself if your lordship would allow us to stay and hunt them down." Dalhu bowed his head, touching his forehead to the carpet as he anxiously awaited the praise that was his due.

"You have done well, as is befitting of my scions. It is a great victory in our ancient war against the corruption and depravity of our mortal enemies. You are to be commended for your bravery and your loyalty to the Holy War. May Mortdh strengthen your hands and harden your hearts to go forth and deliver his vengeance to the vile and the wicked."

Basking in Navuh's lavish praise, Dalhu and his men commenced the devotion.

Glory to Lord Navuh the wise and the just
In his guidance and mercy we put our trust
With his bounty we thrive
By his will we live and we die
We are all brothers in
the Devout Order of Mortdh
In his name we wage this Holy War

As the screen went blank the men rose to their feet, embraced, and clapped each other's backs.

Dalhu joined in reluctantly. As their leader, it was unavoidable, even though he didn't share in their revelry. He was already thinking and planning ahead, something the simpletons were incapable of doing.

It was the Doomer way. A commander was the brain and his underlings were his feet and his arms. He led and they followed. He wasn't one of them, not in his heart or his mind. They were beneath him. His to use or dispose of.

Navuh had not asked about casualties, and Dalhu hadn't volunteered the information. It wasn't important. No one cared. But he was short on fighters if he was to go on a hunt for immortals.

Their kind was notoriously hard to find.

In close proximity, an immortal male was relatively easy to detect by the tingling awareness that alerted the males to each other's presence—a built-in warning mechanism that competition was near.

A female, on the other hand, was nearly impossible to discern.

Dalhu had never met one. He'd heard rumors, though. Supposedly, when aroused, an immortal female emitted a unique scent that was distinctly different from the one produced by mortal women. But that necessitated that he found her while she happened to be in that state, and what were the chances of that?

No wonder one had never been caught.

How was he going to do it? Where would he start looking?

He had deduced already that the enemy had a presence in California, in the Bay Area as well as in Los Angeles. The programmer and the professor had to be part of a larger nest. But both areas were huge and densely populated by millions of mortals.

He needed more clues.

Tomorrow, he would go and check out the professor's lab himself. Not that Dalhu was expecting to find her there. Spooked by the failed abduction attempt, the professor wouldn't dare come back to the university. But others would, and he could ask them some questions. Perhaps someone knew where she lived.

If they knew nothing, he would check with human resources. The university must have a physical address for her, not the post office box listed everywhere else he'd checked.

26

SYSSI

The morning came all too soon for Syssi.

Tossing and turning for hours after waking from that dream in the middle of the night, she had finally fallen asleep when the sun had come up. Her alarm had gone off in what seemed like only a few minutes later.

She felt groggy.

The headache that had begun in the lab must've developed into a full-blown migraine, complete with the symptomatic confusion that accompanied it. As hard as she tried Syssi couldn't remember how she had gotten home.

There was a vague memory of Amanda driving her, and she must've collapsed on her bed straight away because she was still wearing the clothes from the day before.

Shuffling to the bathroom, Syssi took them off and dropped them in a dirty pile on the tiled floor, then stepped into the shower. With her head hung low, she let the water soak her hair.

What the hell is wrong with me?

That numbness refused to wash away. Feeling as flat as the two curtains of dripping wet hair at the sides of her face, Syssi found it a strain even to reach for the shampoo. Going through the motions, she worked it into her scalp and watched the foaming clumps wash down the drain. The laborious process of shampooing her mane had to be done twice, then came the conditioning, once, then soap, then towel.

Blow-drying all of that hair was exhausting as well. She loved her luxurious mane, but sometimes it was just too much work. Chopping it off would have made her life so much easier.

Right. Like there was a chance in hell she'd ever do it. It was the one feature that she was positive was beautiful. The rest? It depended on her mood. Some days she thought she looked pretty good; others? Not so much.

Her deflated mood meant that today was going to be one of the "not so much." Not a big deal, she was fine with being just okay and not spectacular.

Like Amanda.

Syssi wouldn't have wanted it. Amanda's beauty was a burden. It was too much, too intimidating, too restrictive, too isolating. With her confidence and her dramatic flair, Amanda carried it well, but Syssi could have never pulled it off. The stares alone would have sent her running for shelter.

Syssi shivered. How was Amanda dealing with all that leering, the envy? How did she feel about intimidating the hell out of everyone she came in contact with?

Being somewhere on the spectrum between okay to pretty was exactly where Syssi was comfortable.

Eyeing the pile of jeans, she grimaced—too constricting. Shifting her gaze to the comfy yoga pants, she grabbed them instead. Not exactly stylish or appropriate for work, but whatever, she had no energy for anything tight.

Finishing her unprofessional attire with a plain T-shirt, Syssi plodded barefoot to the stretch of counter that was her kitchen and made herself coffee.

As she sat at her dining table, still feeling lethargic from the lack of sleep, the prospect of leaving the house and walking to work seemed daunting. She couldn't bring herself to get going. For some reason, there was an unpleasant feeling churning in her gut, warning her to stay away from the lab.

It had something to do with Amanda. Maybe it was about her boss's bitchy mood yesterday. The prospect of spending another work day with a grumpy tyrant was not appealing.

Still, it might not be about work at all. The sense of loss that had come on the heels of her dream still clung to her, weighing her down like a wet, sticky sludge.

Except, it couldn't explain the foreboding. The only thing that made sense to her was that it had something to do with her premonition about Amanda.

Her phone rang, and Syssi jumped, answering without bothering to check the caller ID. "Hello?"

"Syssi, darling, I wanted to tell you that I'm not coming to the lab today." Amanda produced a very fake sounding cough. "I must've caught something. I need you to take over my test subjects for me. I'll email you the schedule." Another fake cough.

"Sure, no problem. I hope you'll get well soon."

"Thank you, darling. Me too. Hopefully by Monday, I'll be as good as new. A weekend in bed will surely help. Thank God it's Friday, right?"

Syssi laughed. "Absolutely. Feel better and don't forget to stay hydrated."

"Of course. Love you, darling. Have a good one."

"Love you too."

Amanda had been faking it big time. One of the odd things Syssi had noticed about her boss was that she never got sick. Heck, the woman never got tired. She was a work horse. The last flu epidemic had the entire lab surviving on Dayquil and cough drops, but not Amanda. She'd attributed her resilience to the flu shot she'd gotten, but so had everyone else at the lab.

Her boss was probably arranging a long weekend for herself. Except, why did she feel the need to lie to Syssi about it?

It had to be guilt. She was leaving Syssi to deal with a double load of test subjects. Not a big deal, she could handle it. But not before she had another cup of coffee, or two.

Sipping on the fresh cup she'd poured, Syssi popped open her laptop and started going through her emails, when images from the dream tried to push their way into the forefront of her mind. She pushed them back. It was best to ignore them. What was the point of dwelling on something that could never be? The fantasy was better forgotten; else real life would always pale by comparison.

That erotic dream had come out of nowhere, shaking her conviction that she wasn't all that sexual.

Syssi sighed, she couldn't remember the last time she'd felt even a spark of desire for a man. Was it possible that she had been repressing her needs while subconsciously yearning to be touched?

Oh, well, she didn't have time for all that self-analytical nonsense. She needed to get going or else she'd be late.

Reluctantly, Syssi closed her laptop and pushed up from her chair. She rinsed out her mug in the sink and then headed to her closet for shoes. But as she reached for a pair, she froze, suddenly seized by an overwhelming sense of dread.

Something dark and dangerous was looming out there. But what?

What the hell? Her heart started pounding a crazy beat against her ribcage.

Trying to overcome her panic attack, she looked for a reasonable explanation for what might've triggered it. The wolves chasing her in the dream, the grueling workday she had yesterday, the headache...

But all along Syssi knew that none of these were the real reason. That kind of panic had seized her only once before.

On the night her brother Jacob had died.

She had been living in the dorms at the time. Jennifer, her roommate, and Gregg had been there when the panic attack had struck.

Syssi still remembered that when her phone rung, she'd had her head down between her knees struggling to breathe. Knowing with complete certainty that nothing would ever be the same once she answered that call, she'd let it ring, trying to postpone the inevitable.

Eventually, Jen had answered it for her…

"Syssi, sweetheart, it's your brother..." Jen handed her the phone.

Andrew's voice was pained... "It's Jacob...," he managed to croak through his choked-up throat. "That damned motorcycle... he was killed on the spot..."

Syssi sat there, frozen, not really listening to the rest of his words. Her eyes staring into nothing, she felt like her life force was draining out of her, and the cold was spreading from the center of her heart to the rest of her shaking body.

She was going into shock.

It had happened over four years ago, and she had spent most of the first two crying.

It still hurt like hell. Heaving a sigh, Syssi wiped away the few tears that escaped her tightly squeezed eyes.

If it hadn't been for Gregg, she wouldn't have made it. He had been wonderful throughout that ordeal, a real lifesaver. Syssi shivered as she imagined going through all that pain without his help. He had held her for hours while she'd cried, had arranged for someone to take notes at the classes she'd missed, had fed her, had talked to her, and somehow had managed to pull her out of the dark vortex she had been sucked into.

She wondered if it hadn't been too much for him to bear at such a young age. Maybe the erosion in their relationship had started then. Could she really blame him? What twenty-year-old wanted a girlfriend who was perpetually sad? Was it possible that he had stayed as long as he had out of pity? Or some misplaced sense of guilt?

Be that as it may, she would forever be grateful to him for standing by her side in her time of need.

This was what Andrew failed to understand when he'd accused

her of being a softie. After the breakup, she'd been so down that her brother had been convinced Gregg was the worst kind of scumbag. Syssi had no doubt that Andrew would've gone after Gregg had she not warned him to leave him alone. But contrary to what Andrew believed, she'd done it not because she was a pushover, but because when it had really mattered, Gregg had been there for her. Everything else that hadn't worked between them, all her grievances, paled in comparison.

So yeah, he'd been a jerk at times, and his behavior had left her with some emotional scars. But those weren't the kind that wouldn't eventually heal.

She knew they would. They were there only because she had let them form in the first place. If she'd been stronger, Gregg's petty jerkiness would've bounced off her.

Forgiveness hadn't come easy, and it hadn't happened right away. This wisdom had taken her a long time to acquire.

She'd been angry for months.

But letting go of all that anger had been one of the best things she had done for herself. It had been therapeutic. And realizing that Gregg had earned her forgiveness in the best possible way had been instrumental in that healing.

Syssi wished him nothing but happiness.

Hopefully, one day he would find his perfect someone, and when he did, she hoped he would invite her to his wedding. And she would go, gladly, and celebrate with him. After all, they'd shared each other's lives for four years and parted on good terms. Syssi no longer harbored resentment toward him, and she believed that the same was true for him also.

Would she invite him to her wedding? Maybe.

Syssi wasn't sure Gregg had reached enlightenment the same way she had.

To be angry was poisonous to the soul, and forgiveness wasn't easy. But she'd found a way to do it, and not only with Gregg.

Often, there was at least one good thing or quality that

deserved gratitude. Finding this one thing and focusing on it was helpful, it allowed letting go of resentment with ease.

Syssi chuckled. This was another thing she should be grateful to Gregg for. If not for him, she wouldn't have learned this valuable lesson.

She had a feeling that she would have to put this technique to the test again. Letting go of anger was something she would have to deal with in the future.

Unfortunately, it wasn't a philosophical conclusion. More like a premonition.

Great.

Plopping down on the couch, Syssi covered her eyes with her hands, and taking a deep breath, thought back to all of her other premonitions—big and small. There were none she could remember that in one way or another hadn't come to pass.

Pushing up to her feet, she walked over to the kitchen counter and snatched the phone off its cradle.

"What's wrong?" Andrew answered right away.

It was such a relief to hear his voice that she plopped back on the couch. "Nothing yet. I had a bad feeling and wanted to check that you were all right."

"Phew, you got me scared. A call from you this early, I thought you heard something from Mom and Dad."

"No, but I'm going to call them next. Are you at work already?"

"Yes. Why?"

"Are you going to be there all day?"

"Yes."

"Good. Call me before you head home. Will you remember?"

"No problem. Can you do me a favor and text me after you talk with Mom and Dad?"

"I will."

Next, she called her father's sat phone. Everything was fine over there. They were getting ready for bed. And no, they had no plans to visit anytime soon. She texted the update to Andrew.

Okay, who else?

Amanda?

The premonition must've been about her. She was probably going on some last minute romantic getaway with one of her boy-toys, and something was going to happen to her. Syssi needed to call Amanda back, caution her again, and hope her boss would heed the warning.

"Yes, darling," Amanda answered, all traces of her pretend sickness gone from her voice.

"I just wanted to remind you to be careful. Remember that bad feeling I had? I was just hit with another wave of it."

Amanda was silent for a few seconds, and when she answered, she no longer sounded as cheerful. "Staying in bed over the weekend seems like a good strategy to avoid risk, don't you think?"

"If that is what you're really going to do."

"I don't plan on going anywhere."

"Promise?"

"Yes."

"Okay. Stay safe, and get well."

"I will."

The good news was that the panic had eased. Whatever Amanda had decided to do following Syssi's call would keep her safe.

Otherwise, Syssi knew the panic would not have ebbed.

27

AMANDA

Amanda ended the call and put her phone back in her purse. Syssi's premonition must've been about what had happened in the lab yesterday. And the bad feeling persisted because of the traumatic experience.

She hadn't spoken with Kian since leaving him alone with Syssi yesterday, but Amanda was sure he'd thralled the girl before sending her home with Okidu.

Syssi's conscious mind didn't remember what had happened, but her body and her subconscious did. It took time until the elevated levels of hormones released during fight-or-flight went back to normal.

She should question Okidu about Syssi's state of mind when he'd taken her home. It was possible that the girl's powerful mind had helped her resist the thrall. Kian might have been able to submerge her memories of him and what had happened in the lab, but perhaps not as deeply as he thought he had.

Pulling on a pair of leggings under her sleep shirt, Amanda didn't bother with shoes before padding across the vestibule to Kian's penthouse, and she didn't knock before entering either.

If he wanted her so close under his nose, she would make sure that it tickled.

There was no one in the living room or the kitchen, but she knew Kian was home. His office was the last room at the end of the long hallway, but even though she couldn't hear him, she sensed his presence.

Except, she wasn't looking for her brother. Not yet.

"Okidu, dear, where are you?"

One of the doors along the hallway opened, and the butler hurried out to greet her.

"Mistress Amanda, how can I be of service?"

Good question. It wasn't as if Okidu could describe Syssi's emotional state.

"When you took Syssi home yesterday, did she say anything to you on the way?"

"Master Kian took Mistress Syssi home. I offered to save him the trouble, but he said it was his pleasure to drive her himself."

Oh, this was good. Amanda smiled. Very, very good. Kian never bothered getting his thralled partners back home, he sent Okidu, same way she did with hers, having Onidu take care of getting them back safely, either to their home or to the club where she'd picked them up.

Kian must've felt something for the girl.

"Do you know if he thralled her before taking her home?"

"No, Mistress, he certainly did not. I must assume he did it later at her place of residence."

Fantastic.

Amanda should thank the Doomers for helping her plans along. Without their surprise visit, Kian would not have been forced to spend time with Syssi.

What surprised her, though, was that Syssi had gotten under Kian's skin in such a short time, and that was without doing a single thing to encourage him or even show him that she was interested. Not that it hadn't been obvious.

Amanda wanted to dance a victory dance around Kian's living room.

But there was another piece of information she needed before she could celebrate. "Okidu, could you tell me what time it was when Kian took Syssi home, and then when he returned?" The Odu had an internal clock that recorded everything. He could provide her with the exact timing of anything he'd witnessed.

"Certainly. Master Kian left at six twenty-four and returned at seven fifteen."

Amanda tapped a finger on her lips. Not enough time for a hookup, but possibly some kissing. She had to find out. If Kian had managed not to touch Syssi at all, she would have to reconsider her assessment of their compatibility.

Him driving her home was a good start, but something along the lines of not being able to keep their hands off each other would've been better.

According to her mother, truelove mates were always desperate for each other—more so than other horny, run of the mill immortal couples.

But she was getting ahead of herself. Kian would've said that she was letting her romantic fantasies cloud her good judgment. There was no guarantee Syssi was even a Dormant, let alone Kian's true love mate.

"Thank you, Okidu. That will be all." She dismissed him before heading down the corridor.

He rushed after her. "Mistress Amanda, Master Kian is working with Master Shai, he asked not to be disturbed."

She put a hand on his shoulder. "Thank you, Okidu. But it doesn't apply to me."

"Yes, Mistress." Okidu bowed.

Kian's closed door didn't even slow her down. Amanda pushed the handle and entered.

"Good morning, gentlemen."

Kian looked over her attire, or lack thereof, and grimaced. "Go back to your place and put something on, Amanda."

There were two chairs in front of Kian's desk. Shai occupied one, and Amanda took the other while casting them both haughty glances. "What's the matter, don't you like my fashion statement?"

Keeping a straight face while watching their confused expressions was a struggle. They didn't know if she was being sarcastic or serious.

Smart man that he was, Kian knew when he was out of his element and changed the subject. "What can I do for you, Amanda?"

She smiled. "I wanted to talk to you about your date with Syssi yesterday."

Shai's head snapped around, and he gaped at Kian. "A date?"

Kian waved his hand. "There was no date. It's just Amanda's twisted sense of humor. Would you excuse us for a few moments, Shai? I'll call you when I'm done."

His voice had sounded cultured and polite, but both she and Shai had heard the menacing undertones. The difference was, Shai got scared and scurried away, while Amanda smiled sweetly and got ready to spar with her brother.

Let the games begin.

She was going to get details out of him, and she wasn't going to stop until she did. Kian had no idea what he'd brought upon himself by insisting she move into the keep.

When the door closed behind Shai, Kian dropped the polite mask and growled, "I don't care what fashion statement you're trying to make, but this is a working office. You will dress appropriately when you come in here during working hours. Is that clear?"

She batted her eyelashes. "Of course. But you'll need to post a schedule on the door. As far as I know, it's always working hours for you."

Kian's lips lifted in a little smirk. "Then I guess you always need to dress appropriately when you come in here."

"I don't know what your problem is, Kian. There is no one here that is not family. Why should you or anyone else care what I wear?"

"According to your logic, I can spend my workdays in boxer shorts, or better yet, naked."

Amanda couldn't help the snort that escaped her throat. Imagining her stuck-up brother working in the nude was just too much. "Okay, I agree."

Kian lifted his hands. "Hallelujah. For once, I win an argument with you."

Let him think that. It would put him in a more compliant mood. "You see? I can be reasoned with. By the way, how did it go with Syssi yesterday?"

Immediately, his expression closed off. "Fine."

Damn, she would have to pull it out of him one crumb at a time.

"Did she stay long after I left?"

"No."

"What did you guys talk about?"

"Nothing. I took her home a few minutes later."

Ugh. "Why did you take her home yourself instead of letting Okidu do it?"

"Where are all these questions leading, Amanda? I have work to do and you're wasting my time."

Well, if he wanted her to get to the point she would. "Did you like her?"

A shade of melancholy flitted over Kian's harsh features. His eyes were trained on her, but there was a faraway look in them. Amanda held her breath. Kian wouldn't lie to her, but he was perfectly capable of refusing to answer and kicking her out.

"Yes, I did." He pushed his hair back, raking his fingers through it. "I erased myself from her memory along with everything that happened in the lab and after." He sighed. "I wish I could do the same for myself. She will be difficult to forget."

Poor Kian. He was drawn to Syssi but fighting it with all he had. And for what? For some misguided sense of honor? For upholding a definition of right and wrong that he himself had written?

Or was the formidable Regent afraid of feeling something after nearly two millennia of feeling nothing—of burying himself in work and duty while clinging to a code of honor in an effort to anchor himself to something and not disappear completely?

The task she'd undertaken was going to be even tougher than she'd anticipated. Both Syssi and Kian had built themselves an armor made out of routine and habit. Feeling safe and at home inside the little bleak cubicles they had crawled into, they were terrified of venturing out.

There were only two ways to force them to change. Blow up their safe zone, or tempt them with something they couldn't resist.

28

DALHU

So this was what a university looked like.

Dalhu strolled along the winding pathways between grassy lawns and flower beds, observing the small groups of young humans sprawled on the grass. Books open, laptops propped on upturned knees, they were socializing more than studying.

A ping of envy coursed through him. He'd never had the opportunity to devote time to learning, or to socializing for that matter. He didn't know how to relate to people other than as soldier to commander or commander to soldier. He knew how to take orders and issue them, but not how to conduct a conversation.

Not entirely true.

The other thing he was an expert on was seduction. Lucky for him it didn't involve much talking. His kind exuded powerful pheromones females found difficult to resist. He didn't know it for a fact, but it made sense. Otherwise the ease with which he entrapped women would have been hard to explain.

Even here, in the open air, he could scent the surge of lust his appearance induced in the young females he was passing by. Perhaps after he was done with what he came here to do, he would pick up one of them and take her home with him.

No, this was a really bad idea. He would take her to a hotel instead. Bringing a lone girl into a house full of horny immortal males was asking for trouble. Human females were fragile. They could barely satiate one immortal male and survive it. Even hookers had trouble keeping up. If he ever brought a woman to the Beverly Hills mansion, he would make sure to bring one for every one of his men as well.

Hire a whole damned whorehouse for a night.

"Excuse me." He forced a smile for the girl he'd stopped. "Could you please point me toward Dr. Amanda Dokani's laboratory?"

The girl pushed her glasses up her nose as she looked up at him. Way up. He tried to smile again.

"Are you volunteering for her extrasensory tests?"

"Yeah, that is exactly what I'm here for."

"What's your talent?"

Killing. He was really good at that, but as far as he knew he had no other talents. "I don't have any."

She shrugged. "Oh, well, you never know. Anyway, you see that gray building over there?" She pointed.

He nodded.

"The labs are on the lower level. There should be a directory near the entrance."

"Thank you, miss." Dalhu bowed his head.

She cast him a perplexed look. "You're welcome."

He'd messed up again. To humans, he looked no older than a man in his early thirties. He should pay better attention to how they interacted with each other, and make sure he was responding the way someone his perceived age should. Tonight, he was going to watch American television and absorb their contemporary culture. Apparently, the movies he'd watched in preparation for this mission were outdated.

When he got to Professor Dokani's laboratory, Dalhu found it underwhelming. It wasn't big, or fancy looking, and it was one of many. The entire basement level of the building was comprised of various labs, and the place was teeming with activity. There was a lot of research going on in the neuroscience department, and Dr. Dokani was just one of many other researchers.

"Can I help you?" A chubby girl with a pretty face gave him the once-over. He did one of his own. It was hard to estimate her height from behind the desk she was sitting at, but she wasn't short. A big plus. Dalhu liked his women tall, and had no problems with generous curves either. On the contrary. Perhaps she was the one he would take with him after he was done with his investigation.

"I'm looking for Professor Amanda Dokani."

"I'm sorry, she is not in today. Is there anything I can do for you? I'm Hannah, her research assistant." She offered him her hand and he shook it, holding on as he gazed into her eyes.

"Do you know where she lives?"

Caught in his thrall, the girl's pupils dilated, but she was fighting it. Hannah shook her head and pulled her hand out of his grip. "I don't. You may want to check with Human Resources."

He looked at her with new appreciation. The girl was both pretty and smart. Only those with powerful minds could resist his thrall.

Still, he couldn't leave without erasing her memory of him. Bracing his hands on her desk, he leaned forward, putting his face very close to hers.

"You are a very pretty girl, Hannah. But I need to tell you something." He leaned even closer. "Your hair is messy." Dalhu smiled as he pushed full force into her mind.

Hannah's hand shot to her head and she finger-combed her chin-length curls.

"You need to go to the bathroom and brush it."

With her pupils completely dilated, Hannah's eyes turned almost all black, only a thin brown border remaining. "Excuse me, I need to go brush my hair." She reached for the strap of her purse, lifting it from where it hung on the back of her chair, and pushed up to her feet.

In a few minutes, she would have one hell of a headache. His thrall had been forceful and not exactly surgical. There would be more than just him missing from her memory.

Alone in the lab, he walked over to the small office he'd noticed on the other side. Several framed diplomas hung on the walls. Among them, was an enlarged copy of the article his men had found at the programmer's home.

Dalhu stood transfixed in front of the professor's picture, unable to pull his eyes away from her. She was so beautiful that it hurt. His hand went to his chest and he rubbed at his sternum.

"Excuse me, you're not supposed to be in here."

Dalhu tore his gaze away from the framed article and pivoted on his heel.

A petite blonde, with a thick mane of hair like that of a lion, was standing with her hands on her hips and glaring at him with a pair of blue-green eyes. She wasn't fooling him with her bravado, though, he could hear her heartbeat thundering behind her ribcage. She was scared of him. As she should be, and not only because he towered more than a foot over her.

"I'm sorry. I was looking for Professor Amanda Dokani, and I thought I would find her here. Then I got stuck reading this article." He pointed at the wall.

She followed his eyes and smirked. "Yeah, I'm sure it was the article."

Dalhu flashed her what he hoped looked like a bashful smile. "Okay, you caught me. I was staring at the picture. She is very beautiful."

Her heartbeat slowed as she relaxed and smiled back. "That she is. But she is not here today. You can try again on Monday."

Dalhu stepped out of the professor's office and leaned against the wall, sliding down so he could look into the girl's eyes. "Do you know where she lives?"

She frowned. "Why? Are you a friend of hers?"

What was it with the kids in this place? Were they all brainiacs? This one seemed even more resistant to thralling than Hannah.

"Yes, I am. What's your name?" He tried a different approach. If he primed her with questions she didn't find suspicious she might relax her resistance.

"Syssi."

"Have you been working here long?"

"No, it's my second week. Why?"

"No reason. Just being friendly. Would you like to have a cup of coffee with me?" He wasn't really interested. Not because she wasn't pretty, the girl was beautiful in her own way, but she was too small. Dalhu preferred his women tall. Besides, she was blond when he craved a brunette. A very particular brunette. After gazing at the professor's face, no other woman could compare.

He extended his hand but she didn't even look at it. Her pupils were dilated, and she couldn't move her eyes away even though he could see she struggled to. "No, thank you, I can't," she whispered her refusal.

It seemed he couldn't compel her to do as he said, but maybe he could compel her to tell the truth.

"Why?"

"Because you scare the crap out of me." Her eyes widened in horror and she slapped a hand over her mouth. "I'm sorry. I don't know what came over me," she mumbled behind her fingers.

Dalhu laughed. "It's okay. I scare a lot of people. It's the size." He waved a hand over his body.

Syssi shook her head. "Maybe. Do you want me to tell Amanda that you stopped by? What's your name?"

"No, I want to surprise her. I'll come back Monday. It was nice meeting you, Syssi." Again he offered her his hand, and this time she took it. Holding on, he repeated what he'd done with Hannah.

Rubbing her temples, the girl was still standing in the same spot Dalhu had left her when he closed the lab's door behind him.

"Could you please point me in the direction of Human Resources?" he asked the first guy he saw in the corridor.

"Sure. I'll show you where it is."

The young man walked with him all the way to the building housing the department he was looking for.

“Thank you. I appreciate it.”

“No problem, dude.”

In the office, Dalhu found an elderly woman whom he thralled easily to search the database for the professor’s address.

“Here you go, dear.” She handed him the scrap of paper she’d scribbled it on.

“Thank you.” He thralled her again to forget he was ever there.

29

SYSSI

Syssi held up a card, the picture side facing her and the back facing her test subject. "What am I looking at?"

"A rabbit." Michael didn't hesitate before guessing correctly.

She picked another card from the stack and lifted it up. "Okay. What am I looking at now?"

"A locomotive. Can we stop now? I think I've proven my telepathic ability many times over. I'm bored."

She couldn't blame him. Michael was a powerful telepath, but the purpose of this experiment was to find out if his ability diminished over time.

With most talents it did, as Syssi could attest from her own experience. She could guess the first ten coin tosses correctly, but her accuracy diminished with each subsequent toss until after the hundredth she was no better than someone with no paranormal talent at all.

"Let's keep going until you start making mistakes. I want to find out at what point you start losing concentration."

"Okay, shoot."

She lifted another card.

"House."

It was a flower. Syssi rolled her eyes. "I know you're doing it on purpose. Come on, Michael, you are getting paid by the hour and you are mine for the next thirty-five minutes."

Michael waggled his brows. "I can think of more pleasant ways to spend those minutes."

He was such a flirt. Michael was cute and he knew it, but he was just a kid. A twenty-year-old business major who also played on the football team and had the muscles to show for it.

"Me too, but I'm getting paid by the hour as well." She lifted another card.

"A man's face."

After another fifteen cards Michael started making mistakes, real ones, and after another ten he wasn't getting any of them right.

"Okay, I think you're done." Syssi glanced at her watch. Michael still owed her fifteen minutes, but he was useless at this point.

He leaned back in his chair and stretched his long legs. "When are we going to try real thoughts? I'm tired of the pictures."

There was a sequence she needed to follow, but Michael was spent. "We have a few minutes left, but I doubt you'll be able to do anything. Your brain is fried."

"Try me."

Syssi closed her eyes and thought about coffee. She was tired, had a headache, and wanted to go home and take a nap. But with Amanda missing in action, she had to stay. And later on she had another obligation.

"You want to take a break and go have a cup of coffee with me."

"Close. I was thinking about coffee but not about having one with you."

Syssi frowned.

Something bothered her about this exchange and it wasn't Michael's flirting. She had a weird sense of déjà vu, as if she'd had the same conversation with someone else today. An image flitted through her mind. A giant of a man, dark, scary, smiling at her and asking her out.

Syssi shook her head. She was losing her mind. As if the dreams weren't enough, she was now having waking hallucinations. Maybe it was the headache's fault. She'd been having a lot of those lately. She should get it checked out.

Or maybe she just needed to start getting out more, preferably to do something outdoorsy. The two things she was short on were guys and fresh air. Combining the two sounded like a plan.

"You know what? Why not? Let me invite you to a cup of cappuccino."

Michael's eyes widened in surprise. "Really? You're not just saying it?"

Syssi smiled. "Nope. How do you like it? Lots of milk or lots of foam?"

He looked confused. "Are you going to order it?"

"I'm going to make it. We have a cappuccino machine in the kitchenette. So, how do you like it?"

"However you make it is fine." The disappointed look on his handsome face tugged at her heart. She shouldn't have teased him like that. But they were playing a game. It wasn't as if Michael believed she would ever say yes.

"Come on, you can watch me prepare it."

Making her way to the kitchen, she stopped by Hannah's desk. The postdoc was slumped in her chair, eyes closed, rubbing at her temples.

"You have a headache too?"

Hannah nodded.

"We need to call maintenance and have them check the ventilation in here. I've been getting way too many of those lately."

Hannah opened her eyes. "I think you're right. I never get headaches, and this one came out of nowhere. It was right after that guy left."

Syssi narrowed her eyes. "What guy?"

Hannah frowned. "I don't remember. Now that I think about it, there was no one here. I must've imagined it."

Syssi got an uncomfortable feeling in her gut. "Was your imaginary guy huge?"

"How did you know?"

That uncomfortable feeling had just gotten worse. "A lucky guess."

Syssi continued to the kitchen with Michael following closely behind. "What's going on, Syssi?"

She waved her hand dismissively. "Nothing." This was too weird even for a place that dealt with paranormal phenomena and extrasensory perception.

Michael put a hand on her shoulder. "I can sense your feelings, Syssi. You can't hide it from me. You're worried about something. Spit it out. There is nothing that would freak me out at this point."

She was tempted. After all, as a fellow talent, he wasn't going to think she was crazy or make fun of her. And it wasn't as if she had many opportunities to talk about her premonitions with others.

"It might be a coincidence, but I don't think it is. If it were only me, I would've blamed lack of sleep or poor ventilation. But both Hannah and I have a headache, and we both have a vague impression of a huge guy visiting the lab but can't remember it. The more I try to focus on that fleeting image, the more it dissipates."

Michael closed his eyes, his forehead furrowed in concentration.

"What are you doing?" she asked after long moments had passed and he didn't even twitch.

"Feeling." He opened his eyes and sighed. "Sometimes, I can sense a residual of intentions. There is something here, I can feel it. But it could've been left by anyone, even you or Hannah or Professor Dokani. Not David, I can always feel his imprint clearly and it doesn't belong to him. That guy is genuinely full of himself. None of his posturing is a front."

"What is it, then?"

"A powerful yearning."

"Yearning for what?"

Michael shrugged. "I don't know. It just feels like a need. It's kind of sad. Lonely."

Shit, was it her?

It wasn't Amanda's, that was for sure. Most of the time the woman was upbeat and cheerful. It couldn't have been Hannah either. The postdoc was a social animal with tons of girlfriends and more guys chasing after her than she knew what to do with. And it wasn't David, who thought he was all that. So it had to be either one of the test subjects, or the mysterious visitor who had or hadn't been there.

Or maybe it was her.

Syssi had thought she'd managed to get over the melancholy that had assailed her this morning. But maybe, the yearning she'd felt for her dream lover hadn't gone anywhere.

30

DALHU

Dalhu couldn't believe how easy it had been to obtain the professor's address.

Too easy.

For centuries, the clan had been hiding from Navuh's vengeance, keeping their existence secret and leaving no trail that could lead back to them. Until this recent stroke of luck with the programmer, the Brotherhood hadn't been able to locate any of their hideouts.

It would have been careless of the professor to have her address recorded in a database that was so easily accessible. Then again, the programmer had been easy enough to find. As long as their true nature remained hidden, Annani's clan members could live and work among the humans, trusting that their anonymity would keep them safe.

His gut churning with anticipation, Dalhu parked his rented Mercedes in front of the Santa Monica condominium complex. It looked exactly like a type of place a wealthy clan member would choose. Only a few blocks away from the ocean, the luxurious complex was gated, and there was a guard on duty.

A weak thrall sufficed for the guy to let Dalhu inside the complex grounds.

The door to the professor's residence was naturally locked, and as far as he could tell there was no one inside. Perhaps the professor had gone out.

He could wait for her to come back.

The problem was how to enter without breaking the door or the door knob. He needed her to enter her home without suspecting anything was wrong. Any sign of trouble would send her running.

Dalhu circled around, jumping the six foot gate leading to the condominium's backyard with ease. First, he checked for alarm sensors in the windows. There was no wiring in the screens, but it didn't mean that there were no sensors on the window frames. His best bet was to find a fixed window. It wouldn't have a sensor, and if it wasn't visible from the front door, he could break the glass to get in and still have the element of surprise.

From the back, the only access was a sliding door that for sure had a sensor on it. He found what he needed on the wall facing the side yard. One of the bedrooms had a window that was made of three panels, with only the one in the center openable. The two on the side were fixed glass and although narrow, they were big enough for him to slide through.

Picking up a good-sized rock, he tapped the glass with it, counting on the heavy drapery hanging on the inside to absorb the sound of the falling shards.

The window cracked. When no alarm sounded, he took care of the rest of the glass with a few more taps. The opening was low, and Dalhu stepped over the sill, careful around the jagged edges protruding from the frame.

As Dalhu pushed the drapery aside, he found that the bedroom he stepped into was vacant. No furniture at all. The next room over was the same, and when he reached the living room, Dalhu had to concede defeat.

The professor hadn't been careless, she'd been smart. She might've owned the condominium, but she obviously didn't live there.

He needed to go back to that lab and search Dr. Dokani's office until he found something. Anything. A receipt from the dry cleaner or a car mechanic was all he needed to find her real residential address. Chances were that the professor had her laundry delivered home and her car picked up for service and returned.

Tonight, he would send men to search the lab and go over every piece of paper they could find.

31

SYSSI

At four o'clock, Syssi collected her purse and waved to the postdoc. "Bye, Hannah, have a great weekend."

"How is your headache?" Hannah asked.

"Better, but it's still there. How about you?"

She shrugged. "I'll live. Are you going to the old people's house?"

"Of course. It's Friday, and my girls are waiting for me."

The *girls* ranged in age from late eighties to mid-nineties, and yet she often thought of them more as girlfriends than grannies.

Syssi chuckled. They sure as hell didn't behave like anyone's grandma.

Toward the end of her life, her Nana had lost her eyesight, and Syssi had been reading to her whenever she'd visited. Her Nana's three friends had soon joined, and Syssi had found herself reading to the four of them. With few exceptions, she'd been visiting the *Golden Age Retirement Home* every Friday afternoon for the past three years, even after her Nana had passed away.

The three had become her substitute grandmas. Hattie was the oldest and fully blind, but she didn't let her disability slow her down and was the ringleader of the group. A gutsy and spunky

Holocaust survivor, she had enough stories to fill the pages of at least twenty books.

Clara was the youngest. She could see well enough to move around but not to read or even watch television. Leonora was sweet and motherly and could see just fine, but she loved hearing Syssi read even though she was partially deaf. Which meant that Syssi had to be really loud.

Embarrassing as hell, given the types of books the three loved to hear her read—raunchy romances with lots of explicit sex scenes.

They'd even made her read *Fifty Shades of Grey* to them.

All three books.

She had to admit that it had been fun, though. The old girls had laughed so hard she'd feared for their lives, and eventually she'd loosened up and laughed with them.

It was easy to forget that two generations separated her from the three. Sitting in one of the girls' rooms, door closed, Syssi often felt like she was in a college dorm, having a good time with her friends.

"Hello, ladies." She tried to peek at the book Leonora was holding in her lap. "What are you hiding in there?" Not that anything could be worse reading out loud than *Fifty Shades*. Other than straight up erotica, that is. Hopefully the old loons wouldn't go that far.

"Sit down, girl, and tell us about your week first," Clara said, patting a spot beside her on Hattie's bed.

Syssi dropped her purse on the night stand and with a sigh flopped down next to Clara. Sometimes she suspected the girls were looking forward to this part of their get together more than the reading. Nosy busybodies.

"Nothing special. The new job is exciting and challenging. I'm learning new things every day."

"How is that boss of yours treating you? Is she nice?" Hattie asked. Out of the three, it seemed she had taken Syssi's Nana's dying wish most seriously; looking after Amelia's granddaughter as if she was her own.

"I have no complaints. Most of the time she makes me feel like I'm her darling. There was this one day, though, that I saw another side of Amanda. When someone pisses her off, she can get bitchy as hell."

Clara patted her knee. "Everyone gets moody from time to time. What you need to keep in mind is that it is probably not about you, and there is no reason for you to get upset. The best thing you can do is to get out of the line of fire. You don't want to get hit just because you are there and make an easy target."

"Amen to that," Leonora said.

"I know, and I didn't take it personally. It was just such a departure from her usually upbeat, cheerful personality."

Clara sighed. "Don't be fooled by appearances, girl. Lots of folks put on a happy face to cover a sad heart."

"Mm-hmm." Hattie nodded in agreement.

Was Amanda sad? Not likely.

Her boss was too excited and optimistic about her research, too busy being dramatic, and too sexed up to have an inclination toward melancholy.

"I don't think she is a sad person. She just got mad over something. Not a big deal."

As Leonora leaned closer and smiled, Syssi knew what was coming next.

"Now that we've covered work, we want to know if you met a nice young man, or even better, a naughty one." Leonora winked, an exaggerated one complete with a twisted mouth like some character from an old gangster movie.

"Someone to get your heart pounding and your blood pumping?" Clara added and waggled her brows.

Syssi shook her head.

"Anyone at all?" Hattie asked.

She was going to disappoint them the same way she did every Friday since she'd broken up with Gregg. "No."

In unison, the three let out a sigh and sagged.

Leonora shook her head. "I was so sure that this week you were going to meet someone and finally end your self-imposed celibacy. In my day, a girl had to get married if she wanted some action between the sheets. But women today have the pill and all the other contraptions to keep them from getting nasty surprises. Get out there and have fun, girl. It is time." Last Friday, Leonora had read Syssi's future in her tarot cards, like she had been doing every other week or so, and had decided Syssi was about to meet someone. "All three cards were there. You had the lovers, the two of cups, and the ten of cups."

Syssi had agreed to Lenora's readings for the fun of it, not because she really believed that cards could predict her future. But evidently Leonora felt differently. Still, arguing the point with a ninety-year-old was not only futile but potentially hazardous to the woman's health. It was much better to just roll with it. "Maybe the timing was wrong, or maybe I met him but didn't realize that he was the one. And besides, the week isn't over yet."

That seemed to mollify Leonora, who was holding her hand over her heart as if she was experiencing chest pains. The old woman crossed her arms over her ample bosom. "That must be it. My cards don't lie."

Syssi glanced at the others, expecting them to snicker at Leonora's proclamation, but found the two nodding solemnly. She loved them, but they were all loony.

"Are you sure no handsome boy made your heart flutter?" Clara asked, flapping her old hands up and down.

Did a dream flutter count?

Whatever, she could make them happy with that one. If the old bats believed in tarots, chances were that they also believed in dreams. She would just skip the parts that were not so innocent.

"I kind of met a handsome guy, but he wasn't real. I dreamt of him."

Hattie snickered. "What kind of a dream?"

For once the blush that crept up Syssi's cheeks didn't embarrass her. Not only were two of the women vision-impaired, but she didn't mind even if they could've seen it. During their long lives the three had experienced more than she could ever dream of or imagine. Her naughty dream would have amused them. Not that she was going to give up any details.

"I don't remember much," she lied. "It was a nightmare, and I was running away from a pack of wolves. The guy who helped me chase them off was very handsome."

The three smiled knowingly.

Syssi stifled a relieved sigh. Now that she'd given them something to be happy about, they would stop asking about her nonexistent love life.

Pulling out the book that had been lost in between the folds of her skirt, Leonora handed it to Syssi. "I'm sure you had enough of us old crows pecking at you. How about you read to us now?"

As Syssi lifted the book, her breath caught. On the cover, a couple was kissing passionately against a dark and ominous background. A pale moonlight cast light on the tall man and the petite woman, while the tree branches encroaching on the small clearing looked like monsters, their gnarled branches tipped with taloned fingers.

The title, though, was what caused goose bumps to rush all over her skin. In bold white letters, it read: *Dreams of a Dark Lover.*

32

KIAN

Kian watched the mourners as they made their way into the clan's large council room, each stopping by Micah, her brother Otto, and their mother. The three were seated on the raised stage next to Mark's beautifully carved sarcophagus.

Wearing their traditional mourning robes made of brown jute, the clan members waited their turn to approach the small grieving family one by one, then kneel beside them, hugging or clasping their hands.

Nothing was said, as there were no words that could ease the pain of Mark's immediate family. It was more about sharing their energy, their warmth, and their love with those who were in desperate need of it.

The overhead screens showed the other clan members in Scotland and Alaska arriving at their respective council rooms and taking their places for the ceremony.

Looking at the screens, Kian waited for Annani and Sari's arrival, grateful for the marvel of modern technology that made it possible for the whole clan to participate, and for his mother to lead the dirge.

The goddess's voice would accompany Mark on his journey to the other side, honoring his memory with her song.

Once everyone was seated and the doors closed in all three chambers, Annani made her grand entrance. And though they all knew her and had seen her before, some still gasped and oohed before a respectful hush fell over them all.

The awe and reverence the clan felt for their matriarch was palpable.

She was small and slender, a mere inch or two over five feet, her delicate, otherworldly beauty misleadingly youthful. But there was no mistaking the awesome presence. Fiery red hair cascaded in thick waves over her shoulders all the way down to her hips, and every bit of her exposed skin radiated with white luminescence. Her big green eyes, so old and so wise, shone tonight with an inner light that was bright enough to illuminate an auditorium and inspire reverence.

Raising her glowing arms, Annani pulled the brown hood of her mourning robe over her head, then tucked her hands inside the robe's sleeves, effectively cutting off her luminescence in a show of respect for the dead.

Lowering her head, she began the lament.

Her voice was angelic, pure and strong. It resonated inside the hearts and souls of her audience, touching their sadness and tugging at its strings. As a chorus of voices joined her, the lament was magnified by the hundreds of voices coming from the sea of brown robes swaying to the mournful sounds.

When Annani reached the last bars of her sad song, Shai activated the hovering platform under the sarcophagus, raising it a couple of inches above the floor.

Kian, together with the seven Guardians, stepped up to the platform. They formed two lines, four on each of its sides, and guided the ornate coffin down the steps. The rest of those present joined the procession behind Mark's family, accompanying him on his final journey to his resting place in the catacombs.

Once there, Shai raised the sarcophagus higher, and the Guardians helped guide it into the niche that had been selected for him in one of the largest chambers. The same artist who'd made the beautiful sarcophagus had been tasked with carving the inscription into the stone right under the niche.

Kian waited until the chamber was filled, and the last of the mourners entered before addressing the crowd.

"Mark will be missed and remembered, not only by his immediate family, but by each and every one of us." He pointed to the plaque. "It says here, 'Mark, beloved son of Micah, nephew of Otto, grandson of Jade, great-grandson of Annani.' But the truth is that Mark is not inside this beautiful sarcophagus. What's left behind is just the vessel that carried Mark's eternal soul for as long as he walked the earth. I hope that his journey to the other side was peaceful and that beyond the veil he found love and joy awaiting him. And yet, even though we must believe Mark's new reality is the mythical heaven, and that he's well, it's of little comfort to those who are left behind. We miss him, and his absence will always feel like a vacuum, an open wound in our hearts that will not heal until the day we join him on the other side. Regrettably, the veil which keeps us apart from him and the others we've lost and miss is impossible to pierce. In the meantime we, the ones on this side of the divide, must draw strength and courage from each other. Our task of providing enlightenment and holding evil and darkness at bay will never be done as long as the Devout Order Of Mortdh Brotherhood is still out there. We are a family, we stand together, and we will not be defeated, for the simple reason that we cannot. Without us, humanity's future is doomed to eternal darkness."

As his people responded with grim nods and quiet murmurs of approval, Kian demonstrated by embracing first Micah, then her mother, and lastly Otto. When the family left the chamber, Kian and the Guardians took their places on both sides of the empty hovering platform and guided it out. A path was cleared for them, and then the procession reformed behind them.

When the last of his people left, Kian removed his robe, folded it and draped it over his arm. Alone in the penthouse's dedicated elevator, he could finally let go of the strong posture and reassuring expression he'd been forced to keep up all evening long. With a sigh, he let his shoulders sag and hung his head.

33

SYSSI

Immersed in the story, Syssi hadn't noticed how long she'd been reading until her sore throat started protesting. A glance at her watch confirmed that it was late. She lifted her head to glance at the window.

It was getting dark.

Any other Friday, she would've paused for a cup of tea and some gossip with her girls and then continued reading for another hour. This time, however, she didn't feel safe driving home alone at night. The uneasy feeling that had been troubling her lately persisted, and it cautioned her to play it safe.

She closed the book and lifted her head. "I'm afraid this will be all for today. It's getting dark and I want to get home before nightfall."

There were some murmurs of disappointment, but none of the women voiced a protest. They didn't like her going home while it was dark outside either.

"You'll have to come back tomorrow, then. I can't wait until next Friday to hear the rest," Hattie said.

Syssi agreed, she didn't want to wait either. The book was amazing, and she was just getting to the good parts. "I know, I'm dying to find out how it ends. I'll come tomorrow morning, but not too early. I like sleeping in on the weekends."

Clara clapped her on the back. "Don't worry about it. It's not like we are going anywhere. And take the book with you. You can finish it tonight."

Syssi was tempted. It wasn't as if she had anything else planned, and reading beat watching the tube any day. "But it's not fair to you girls. You'll have to wait until tomorrow." She offered the book to Leonora.

The woman pushed it back into Syssi's hand. "It's okay, child, we know how the story ends." She winked. "And they lived happily ever after. That's the beauty of romances—predictable endings that are always happy."

True, that was why Syssi liked them too. It was light, feel-good reading, and God knew she needed it given the dark clouds always looming on her horizon.

"Thank you." She kissed Leonora's cheek, then Hattie's, and lastly Clara's. "I'll see you tomorrow. Good night."

Twenty-five minutes later, Syssi parked her car in front of her landlady's house. It wasn't completely dark yet, but it was getting close. Clutching her keys in one hand and the book in the other, Syssi rushed down the long driveway to the guesthouse. She opened the door and locked it immediately after getting in, securing the chain.

The thing was a joke, she knew that—a strong kick and the chain would detach from the wood it was screwed to—but it made her feel just a little bit safer.

Her dinner consisted of a bag of mixed greens topped with stir-fried tofu, and she washed it down with a Coke Zero, which was the only poison she allowed herself in her otherwise healthy diet.

Being good about every little thing was boring. A girl needed to be bad about something.

Giddy with anticipation, she got ready for bed and crawled under the blanket with her book. Pathetic, really, that this was what got her excited these days.

But whatever, it wasn't as if she had anything to prove to anyone. Living an adventure by immersing herself in the pages of a romance novel was much safer than going for real thrills, and it suited her just fine.

Two-thirds into it, her eyelids started drooping and she fell asleep without finding out if the lovers found a way to be together.

Her brain supplied an alternative ending all of its own.

The woods were as dark as they always were in her nightmares, but no wolves were chasing her this time. Unafraid, Syssi strolled leisurely along the familiar path, her eyes trained on the massive tree in the distance. Her lover awaited her there, and she was safe because he would never let anything happen to her. She was precious to him.

He'd told her so.

Feeling the soft fabric of her long white dress caress her thighs and her calves as she walked, Syssi felt sexy, desirable. On her feet, she had simple, flat sandals, but in her dream her modest height didn't bother her. She felt confident even without the benefit of heels making her taller. Her lover found her beautiful as she was.

With a frown, she tried to recall his name, but even though it felt as if it was on the tip of her tongue, it kept slipping away. She remembered figuring it out the other night, so why for heaven's sake was it eluding her now?

How was she going to greet him? Hello, my dream lover?

Syssi chuckled as funnier ideas flitted through her mind. She could call him her handsome dude, or hunky hunk hunk. Or she could borrow Amanda's lingo and just call him darling, or sweetheart, or honey. Men did it all the time when they couldn't remember a woman's name. She could do it too.

But it felt distasteful.

She had every intention of continuing what they had started the other night—with a man whose name she didn't know.

Bad girl, Syssi. Shame on you.

When she got closer, she saw him standing in exactly the same position as the other night. Unmoving, he was looking at something in the direction she was going, but she couldn't see what it was.

"Hi." Now that she was so close to him that she could smell him, her confidence faltered and her voice quivered. The man smelled absolutely delicious. Fresh pine and something wild yet safe.

He turned, his intense blue eyes mesmerizing her. "Hello, beautiful. How come you're here? Did I summon you?"

This was embarrassing. Hadn't he been waiting for her?

"Are you disappointed that I came?"

Faster than she thought possible, his arm looped around her and he pulled her against his big, hard body. "No. I'm glad you're here. You're braver than me. I was afraid to come for you."

Him? Afraid? Impossible. He was so big and so strong. He made her feel safe.

Lifting her face up, she brought a hand to his cheek and cupped it gently. "I can't imagine what can scare a man like you."

He lowered his lips to hers and kissed her lightly. "You do."

Her eyes widened. "Me? No one is scared of me. I'm a nice person. I would never harm anyone."

"I know, sweet girl. Not intentionally. But you are very dangerous. I'm afraid that you're going to tear out my heart from my chest and hold it in the palm of your hand—my life at your mercy."

Ugh, not romantic. Not at all.

"That sounds awful."

He smiled, his fangs not as long or terrifying as they'd been the other night. "You see? I'm bad at this. I don't know the right things to say."

So that was what scared a big guy like him. He wasn't big on words. Well, what she wanted from him didn't require a lot of talking. He might feel more confident with the doing.

Good thing it was a dream and she wasn't encumbered by her overpowering shyness. It was such a good feeling, to just say what was on her mind. Get it out.

"Make love to me. You're good at that."

He chuckled. "That, I am."

The bed appeared out of nowhere, a four poster monstrosity covered with white fluffy pillows and a white down comforter that looked like it was a foot thick.

Should she climb on top of it?

It wouldn't be graceful. The mattress was at least three feet off the ground, and Syssi would have to either hop or scramble to get there. Neither of which could be done in a sexy or alluring manner.

As dreams went, she wasn't doing a good job at creating the right environment for a romantic atmosphere.

He solved her dilemma, swinging her up into his strong arms in one fluid motion, and sitting on the bed while still holding her tight.

Not sure what to do next, Syssi brought her hands to the row of small buttons at the front of her dress and started fumbling with the first one.

He grasped her hands and brought them to his lips for a kiss. "Let me, sweet girl, you keep your hands down by your sides."

The unmistakable tone of command in his voice did something to her. Syssi felt her nipples draw tight and her panties grow damp. A flush bloomed on her face and on her chest, the white dress contrasting and accentuating the redness. But it wasn't embarrassment that had caused it. It was the heat of excitement.

The only other time Syssi had felt passion that intense had been the night before. With the same man—her dream lover.

She should ask him for his name.

Later.

Done with the top portion of the buttons, he parted the two halves of her dress, stealing her ability to think let alone talk or ask questions.

Her back arched of its own volition, thrusting her chest up. She couldn't wait to feel his big hands on her naked breasts. What a shame she was wearing a bra. Unlike the other dream, though, she didn't dispense with it with a thought. She wanted him to do it at his own pace. Having him in charge of her pleasure was exactly how she wanted it.

In a dream, social conventions and her own ideas of how a woman should act were of no consequence.

This was about pure pleasure.

She couldn't help a frustrated whimper as his fingers brushed lightly over her lacy bra, barely touching her stiff peaks.

With eyes that were smoldering with passion, he went back to the buttons, opening each and every one until the two halves of her dress slid open. Her body was fully on display for him, with nothing other than a sheer white lacy bra and matching panties.

"You're beautiful," he whispered, placing his palm over her soft tummy. Fingers splayed, his palm spanned the entire width of her.

A thought drifted through her mind that a man that big would be proportionally endowed. It gave her pause. What if she was too small?

She had a thing for tall guys, but this man was exceptionally tall. Maybe the disparity was too much?

Except, this was a dream. Her dream. And she could make sure that everything fit perfectly.

The hand on her tummy moved lower, and Syssi held her breath in anticipation. She was burning with desire, clutching her teeth together to stifle the needy whimpers that threatened to escape her mouth. When his palm finally made contact with her heated center, engulfing it in its entirety, she closed her eyes and let her head fall back.

"Look at me, sweet girl," he commanded. "Watch me pleasure you."

Lifting her lids halfway, she obeyed, watching his hand as he pushed her panties aside and slid his fingers over her engorged folds.

"You're so wet for me," he hissed out, and the smoldering look in his eyes turned luminescent.

He was casting light on her.

She'd seen something like that before. Amanda's eyes were the same. Maybe that was where her brain had taken the idea from.

The last vestiges of her lucidity flew away when she felt the tip of his finger press against her opening. Gently, he gathered moisture before pushing his finger a little farther, then retreated to do it again.

He treated her like a virgin, and in a way she was. It had been so long that she might as well have turned back into one.

Slowly, maddeningly slowly, he was getting her accustomed to his touch. Not expecting such gentleness and consideration from a man as dominant as him, Syssi felt her heart swell with gratitude.

Hell, it was more than that.

Her heart was swelling with love for her dream lover.

A man she'd conjured in her mind.

And how devastatingly sad was that?

34

AMANDA

Amanda's phone was dancing the jig on her kitchen counter, buzzing and chiming at the same time. Reaching for it, she smiled at Onidu's quirky face on the screen.

The picture had been taken during last year's trip to Hawaii, capturing perfectly his look of repugnance at the shorts and T-shirt she had insisted he should wear in place of his habitual suit. It was the best picture she had of him; with his expression so close to the real thing, she could almost believe it was genuine.

"Yes, darling."

"I have grave news, Mistress. It seems your laboratory has been ransacked by vandals. All is in disarray, with pieces of equipment strewn about and loose wires dangling precariously from what is left standing. Every last drawer has been pulled out of its place and its contents lie torn to pieces, littering the floor. But the worst are the disgraceful, hateful words—which I am too much of a gentleman to repeat—scribbled all over the walls. It is terrible! What should I do, Mistress?"

Onidu sounded truly distraught, and Amanda had to remind herself that it was nothing more than his programming providing the appropriate tone for the situation at hand.

"Onidu, sweetie, can you record what you see with your phone and send it to me?" Amanda knew it was no use trying to persuade him to recite the graffiti. His programming prevented the use of profanities; her mother's work no doubt.

"Yes, Mistress, right away."

WHORE, SLUT, HARLOT, TART, DIE... were some of the endearments scribbled with a black sharpie on the walls, and a sloppy drawing of the Doomers' emblem ensured she knew whom the message was from.

Very creative boys. Nice vocab. Amanda's face tightened with distaste as she turned off the phone and dropped it on the granite counter. Shaking her head, she crossed the kitchen to pour herself more brew. But then, as she lifted the carafe, she froze with the thing suspended in midair.

What if she had left something behind? The thought sent a cold shiver of unease up her spine. What if the Doomers had found something?

Chewing on her lower lip, she tried to remember if there had been anything left in the lab that the Doomers could use. The test results from her pet project were safely stored on her laptop, which she remembered taking with her. And the small notebook with her hastily jotted ideas and random thoughts was always in her purse, ready for whenever and wherever inspiration struck...

That uneasy feeling gaining sudden momentum, Amanda raced to her bedroom and started rummaging through the multitude of pockets in her purse. Getting frustrated, she upended it, emptying the whole thing on her bed.

The notebook wasn't there.

Running back to the living room, she repeated the routine with her laptop case.

It wasn't there either.

Oh, shit, shit, shit... Amanda raced back to the kitchen for her phone.

"Kian, we've got a big problem," she said the moment he answered.

"What's going on?" He tensed, picking up on her urgency.

"I left something behind in the lab, and if the minions-of-all-that-is-evil have found it, we are in deep shit!" She relayed Onidu's report, telling Kian about the break-in and the graffiti.

Kian wasn't interested in the details. "What did you leave in the lab, Amanda?"

"Look, I'm sorry! I thought I had it in my purse, but I didn't... I must have left it somewhere." She was on the verge of tears.

"Just tell me what the fuck it is, Amanda!" Obviously, Kian had lost his patience.

"I can't find my notebook, the one with all my great ideas and all the other stuff I like to keep handy. The thing is, I wrote in it the first names and cell phone numbers of all my paranormal test subjects." She sighed. "And the rankings I assigned to them. Most are between one and three, Syssi is a ten, and there is one boy who's an eight. If the Doomers have half a brain between them, they'll go after these two, but if they are all morons, they might go after each person on that list."

Amanda paused, waiting for Kian to explode. When all she heard was his heavy breathing she continued, offering what she believed was a slight glimmer of hope. "It's only first names and phone numbers, maybe it's not enough for the Doomers to go by?"

"Oh, that's plenty enough. It may take them some time and some cash to find someone to dig through the phone records, but when they do, it will be child's play for them to zero in on your subjects' cellular signal and locate them. We are probably out of time already. Call Syssi and tell her not to leave her home. I'm going to pick her up myself. Text me the info for the boy. I'll send Guardians for him as well."

The line went dead.

"Damn." Amanda searched for Syssi's contact, pressing call before it crossed her mind that the girl was probably still sleeping. Six o'clock on a Saturday morning was too early to call a human.

Syssi picked up after several rings. "Hello?" As Amanda had expected, her voice was groggy from sleep.

"Good morning, sweetie. I'm so sorry to wake you. I wanted

you to do something for me and didn't realize how early it was. Are you planning on going anywhere in the next couple of hours?"

"No. But later I'm going to the retirement home. Why? What do you need?"

Explaining the whole mess to Syssi while she didn't remember a thing was too much. Better leave it up to Kian. Shit, she wouldn't remember who he was either.

"I'll call you later, after you've had a few cups of coffee. I know you don't function before your third one."

Syssi yawned. "Thanks."

35

KIAN

"Meet me down in the garage, and bring your weapons," Kian barked into his phone, then shoved it in his back pocket as he rushed out the door.

It had never crossed his mind that the Doomers might pose a threat to Syssi. The only one he'd been concerned about was Amanda. Frantic with worry for the girl, he punched the button for the elevator over and over again, and when he finally stepped inside, he couldn't wait for it to descend fast enough.

His body pulsing with pent-up aggression, Kian wasn't surprised at what he saw when he caught his reflection in the mirror. He looked like a killer. Eyes glowing and fangs protruding over his lower lip, the face staring back at him didn't look even remotely human—the vicious expression reflecting his murderous intent.

Damn, he would have to calm down before showing up at Syssi's doorstep. One look at him and the girl would drop in a dead faint. Which could actually work to his advantage. She wouldn't resist when he picked her up in his arms and took off with her.

Not the best way to go about it, but Kian doubted that he'd be able to calm down enough to pass for a human during the short drive to her place, leaving him no other choice.

As he raced through the parking level toward the Lexus, Anandur's and Brundar's heavy boots pounding behind him, he was inundated with gruesome images of Syssi in the hands of his enemies. Like snippets out of a nightmare, they were flashing in his mind, each one worse than the next.

"What's going on, boss?" Anandur called from behind him.

"The Doomers have Amanda's list of paranormals. They will go after at least two of them. We are picking up her assistant, Syssi. She tops the damn list."

Snarling, his lips peeling away from his elongated fangs, he vowed that if anything happened to her, if the sick fucks laid a finger on her, hell hath not known the fury he'd unleash on them.

As he turned on the ignition, Amanda's text came in, reassuring him that Syssi was home and wasn't planning on leaving anytime soon. It did little to calm him down. He wouldn't relax until he had her in the safety of his keep.

Ranting and cursing at LA's goddamned traffic, Kian drove recklessly, speeding and weaving in between cars. It was a miracle he hadn't gotten pulled over yet. He prayed his luck would hold, not because he was concerned with getting a ticket, but because of the delay it would introduce.

With his anxiety for Syssi growing worse with each passing moment, constricting his chest and twisting his gut, the pain he was feeling was more than physical—the unfamiliar sensation one he'd hoped never to feel again.

Shaken by the ferocity of his reaction, Kian was forced to admit that she'd awoken in him something he believed had been long dead. Feelings that he had sworn off long ago because experience had taught him that they were nothing but a prelude to disaster.

Kian had loved once.

It had been so long ago that the memory of the actual events had faded, but he still remembered the pain of it ending.

Her name was Lavena, a beautiful seventeen-year-old mortal girl. He had just turned nineteen. Too young and too inexperienced to know better, he fell head over heels in love with her. And as the young often do, he believed himself invincible; there were no obstacles he couldn't overcome, no difficulties great enough to deter him from his beloved.

Disregarding his mother's dictum, he ran away and married the girl. They loved each other passionately, and as he tended to the small farm he'd bought for them, and she to their modest home, for a short time they lived in simple bliss.

Slowly, though, Lavena's mind began showing the effects of the frequent thralls he was forced to subject her to. Even as impetuous as he was, he knew he had to make sure she never found out what he was.

Lavena grew distraught, believing she was losing her mind; finding herself time and again spacing out and forgetting where she was or what she was doing.

In his effort to lessen the damage, Kian refined his thralling technique to a level of fine art, doing his best to keep it minimal, but the episodes kept coming. By the time he realized the fairy tale had to end, it was too late. They were expecting a child.

Their life together became a nightmare.

At first, he tried to abstain as much as he could. When it became clear he couldn't hold back his raging immortal hormones, he resorted to the use of prostitutes.

Kian hated himself, hated what he was doing to the girl he loved, hated the kind of twisted life he was forced to live.

Lavena became distant and mistrustful. No longer blinded by her adoration, she began noticing that he never got sick and that his scrapes and bruises would disappear just as soon as he got them. She began to fear him, believing he wielded some kind of dark magic.

He had to leave.

It was easy to fake his own death. All it took to convince Lavena and the rest of the villagers that he had been mauled by wild beasts was for his torn, bloodstained tunic to be found in the woods. With no body to bury, his wife buried that shirt.

Shrouding himself, he watched from a distance as Lavena mourned his death, as she delivered their beautiful, healthy daughter, as she got better, as she married a widower with four kids of his own.

Kian kept coming back. He watched his child get married and have children of her own. He watched them live their lives, get old and die, while he remained unchanged; their lifetimes but a blink of an eye on the horizon of his own.

Years upon years of gut-wrenching sorrow and regret.

Kian had vowed never to be that stupid or careless again.

He had kept that vow for nineteen hundred and seventy-six years.

36

SYSSI

Syssi cursed, burying her face in a pillow. Amanda's call had woken her up from the most amazing dream way before she'd been ready for it to be over. Heck, if it were up to her, she would've been happy staying in that dream world with her dream lover forever.

Like the other night, he'd brought her to an earth-shattering climax, moments before the dream had abruptly ended. This time, by an annoying ringing.

Worse, she had no name to go with the memory of his gorgeous face.

And yet, the big difference was that this morning she wasn't consumed by melancholy. The thing that kept the sadness at bay was hope that she would dream of him again. Two nights in a row was the beginning of a pattern.

As she showered and dressed, Syssi wondered what brought on the dreams. Last night it had obviously been the paranormal romance novel she'd been reading. It could explain the fangs. Except, the leading guy's, or rather vampire's, description didn't match that of her dream lover. Besides, the book couldn't explain the night before. Nothing could. Except perhaps for her subconscious trying to tell her the same thing as the three wise old ladies, that it was time to end her self-imposed celibacy and take a chance on life.

Trouble was, just thinking about it made her anxious.

She wasn't ready for the dating world. Hell, she had never been ready. Syssi hated the whole process of sifting through numerous guys in the hopes that one of them would turn out to be the one. She hated the awkward dates and having to say it was nice, but no thank you.

Out of nowhere, an image of a huge and scary man flitted through her mind. Vaguely, she remembered someone like that asking her out, but it didn't feel like an actual memory, more like a dream. Not a good one, though. Perhaps she'd dreamt it before dreaming of her imaginary lover.

Except, she had a nagging suspicion that there was more to it. Not a premonition, not exactly, but a gut feeling that something dark and dangerous was lurking outside, waiting for her to make the wrong move. It was the same feeling that had prompted her to leave the retirement home early and avoid driving in the dark. And she was pretty sure it was somehow connected to her premonition about Amanda.

Great, now she was anxious, and feeding off her thoughts the fear was gathering momentum. She needed a distraction before it turned into a full blown panic attack.

Syssi turned on the television and made herself a fresh cup of coffee, spiking it with Kahlua to help calm her down.

After two more spiked coffees and an old episode of *Friends,* she felt her anxiety ebb.

Until the startling screech of tires brought it back.

Syssi ran up to the window to see if anyone was hurt.

Trouble was, her guesthouse was all the way at the end of the driveway in the back of the lot, and only a small section of the street was visible from where she was standing and peeking from behind the curtain. The main house was blocking the rest.

She didn't see a car, but clearing the side of the main house were three large men. One rushed down her driveway, leaving the other two at the curb.

What was going on?

Fear gripping her, she let the curtain drop back into place, taking a step sideways to get out of his line of sight. As he kept getting closer, the sound of his pounding boots thundering in the quiet of the peaceful morning, her fear morphed into panic.

Tall and muscular, the guy looked like a menacing predator closing in for the kill—that is, until his beautiful face came into focus.

Recognizing him, Syssi's hand flew to her mouth and she gasped.

It couldn't be. Backing away from the window, she lifted her hand to her forehead.

Was it possible the dream had been a premonition? Or had all that Kahlua addled her brain and she was seeing things; superimposing the face of her dream lover on that of a stranger?

Not sure she had the guts to find out, Syssi took another step back.

The man must've seen her backing away and figured he was frightening her. Slowing down, he stopped several feet away from her front door.

"Syssi, it's me, Kian...," he called out. "Amanda's brother. Don't be afraid. Please open the door."

With her hand on her heaving chest, Syssi moved back to the window and pushed the curtain aside to take a better look.

Kian? Amanda's brother?

Her frantic heartbeat had slowed down a bit, but her hands were still clammy and shaky.

What was Amanda's brother doing in my dream? What is he doing here? Is Amanda okay? Why didn't she mention him when she called?

Suddenly worried about her friend, Syssi rushed to open the door. "What happened? Is Amanda okay?"

"Amanda is fine. I'm sorry to have given you a fright, but we have a bit of a situation. Everything is under control, no need to panic, but I do need to talk to you. May I come in?" he asked and stepped closer.

Now that he was standing right in front of her, she could appreciate how really tall he was. To look at his strikingly beautiful face, she had to crane her neck way up. But even though her worry for Amanda had been assuaged, and she was feeling calmer, she was still scared of this man. Or rather of what his appearance on her doorstep at six thirty in the morning could mean.

Syssi swallowed nervously.

Amanda's brother was even more intimidating than her conjured dream lover. With all those muscles coiled and ready to pounce, he looked like a killer—the tension and menace radiating from him a sure sign that the situation was not as trivial as he'd tried to make it sound.

God, all this gorgeous maleness was turning her head into mush.

He was gazing at her intently as if expecting her to say something.

Oh, that's right, she was supposed to invite him to come in. Damn, Syssi felt her cheeks redden. Not only was she acting like a moonstruck teenager, but her place wasn't as tidy as she would've liked when inviting someone like him inside. There was nothing that she could do about it, though. She couldn't just leave him standing outside when he'd so politely asked if he could come in.

"Yes, of course, please." Syssi smiled a tight little smile, gesturing for him to follow her while doing her best to pretend as if he wasn't making her nervous and awkward as heck.

The stranger that wasn't a stranger...

Following her, he walked in and closed the door. Her place seemed to shrink with him in it, and suddenly she felt trapped, struggling to get air into her lungs as if Kian had somehow consumed all of the breathable air. And yet, as she felt the heat rolling off him at her back, a rush of awareness coursed through her body, tightening it all over in some places, while loosening it in others. She had to take a breath if only to inhale his scent.

Unable to bear the tension, she whipped around only to find herself a fraction of an inch from his solid chest. Afraid of what she might see, she hesitated a moment before looking up at his face.

Syssi inhaled sharply. His eyes were the most intense shade of blue she had ever seen. She felt enthralled by them. Hypnotized.

Wow, waking up must have been a dream within a dream, and she was still sleeping, still dreaming, and conjuring this gorgeous man, those amazing eyes.

She wondered if he would feel real if she touched him. Except, remembering how very real he had felt in her dream... well, that obviously offered no proof one way or the other.

Syssi waited for him to say something, or at least kiss her senseless, but he did neither. Instead, he was boring into her eyes, holding her captive.

It felt as if he was pushing at some mental barrier inside her head, the pressure at her temples getting progressively worse until the barrier shattered and a flood of submerged memories came barging to the forefront of her mind.

As Syssi struggled to process and assimilate the influx, she was aware of Kian's hard eyes watching her intently.

At first, Syssi felt as if her head was about to explode from the tremendous pressure, but as it eased and the memories rushed in, she was certain she was losing her freaking mind.

Kian at the lab, the danger, rushing to the car, the penthouse, that kiss, the dreams.

What was real?

What was a dream?

Searching his eyes for answers, Syssi found her own burning desire mirrored. Except, his seemed more like a predatory hunger, one she'd experienced before. She remembered him standing in this exact spot, looking at her with the same ravenous expression on his handsome face.

This hadn't been part of her dream. It had happened.

Overwhelmed, she took a step back.

Kian looked so intimidating as he loomed over her like a mountain of a sex-starved man. And yet, curiously, now that she remembered him, she was no longer afraid. Excited, anxious, needy, awkward... yes... but not afraid. For some reason, she felt she could trust him. Kian would protect her.

Syssi had no reason to question her infallible instinct. It had never steered her wrong before.

Which brought back the issue of what the heck he needed to protect her from, and what really was going on?

"What...?" she began.

Kian cut her off, gesturing for her to stop.

Clearing his throat as if trying to bring some moisture into his dried-out mouth, his voice came out sounding like gravel. "I need you to pack a bag, you're coming with me," he commanded and then waited for her to do as she was told.

"Really? Just like that?" Syssi cocked an eyebrow.

"I'll explain everything on the way. The situation I mentioned before makes it dangerous for you to stay here. We need to get out of here, ASAP. Please hurry up and pack only what you'll need for a couple of days." Kian took hold of her shoulders and turned her around toward the bedroom, playfully smacking her butt as if to hasten her on her way.

Taken by surprise, Syssi jerked her head back, giving him the what-the-hell-do-you-think-you're-doing look before strutting to the bedroom.

But as soon as her face was turned away, she smiled.

What was it about this man that she would allow him to do that? Delivered by his hand, a move that she would've found offensive coming from anyone else had brought her a delicious tingle of arousal.

He had a lot of nerve, though—playing around as if they were an item and as if nothing was going on, without bothering to explain what the hell it was.

Rushing, she opened drawers and threw items of clothing on the bed. Yesterday's bizarre events and this morning's panic attack were enough to convince her that she needed to get away. But from whom or what?

She'd soon find out. Kian had promised he'd explain.

Pulling her overnight bag from under the bed, Syssi thought about her strange memory loss and its sudden return. She shook her head. At least one mystery had been solved. The erotic dreams hadn't come out of nowhere. They had been the result of her attraction to Kian. She hadn't remembered him consciously, but her subconscious had done a marvelous job of choosing this incredibly handsome man to star in her sexy dreams.

She had a feeling Kian had something to do with her memory loss. But what? Had he hypnotized her? And if he had: when? How? Why?

Could she trust him if he had?

Was she a complete idiot if she did trust him?

Syssi was packed and ready to go in a matter of minutes, hurrying to brush her hair, apply a little eyeliner, and step into her platform slides. She was ready to step out of her bedroom when her eyes fell on the romance book lying face down on her nightstand. Unzipping her bag, she added it to the few things she was taking with her.

Five inches taller, with her hair falling in thick, shiny waves down her back, she left her bedroom more confident in her looks, but less so in the soundness of her mind.

That extra minute spent had been so worth it.

As she walked back into the room with her duffle bag slung over her shoulder, Kian's eyes widened, and the heat in them made her feel feminine and powerful.

Sexy.

Wanted.

Walking toward him, she even swayed her hips a little. But then her confidence faltered, and she searched his eyes, hesitantly gauging his reaction.

As if guessing what she was looking for, Kian gave her an

appreciative once-over, his hooded gaze letting her know how much he liked what he saw.

She smiled, wordlessly thanking him for his mute admiration. But then she lost her nerve and lowered her eyes, her momentary bravado replaced by an embarrassed blush.

In two quick strides, Kian closed the distance between them and reached for the duffle bag. Slinging it over his shoulder, he wrapped his arm around her waist and pulled her close against his side.

Syssi stiffened momentarily, not sure what to make of the possessive move. It definitely wasn't the casual type between friends. It was something more. And though she didn't want to read too much into it, it felt incredibly good just to go along and lean into him as if it was the most natural thing for her to do.

As they walked out the door with their arms around each other, she sensed it was a new beginning. But of what? And as they kept going down the long driveway, the feeling intensified, shaping into a strong premonition that she was never coming back.

She didn't know the why or how of it, or if it was good or bad.

Regrettably, it was in the nature of premonitions to be vague, revealing only a hint of an outcome and very little if any of the particulars.

Syssi wondered if there was anything she would terribly miss. The furniture belonged to her landlady, all her photos were safely stored on her laptop, and the rest of her stuff could be replaced with as little as a thousand bucks. Except her Precious, of course.

Her BMW convertible was the only luxury she had accepted from her parents, and she loved that car. Precious would go wherever she went. Leaving it unattended on the street was out of the question.

"What about my car?" She turned to Kian.

By then they had reached the curb, joining the two imposing men standing guard. One was a huge redhead, the other a slightly smaller, gorgeous blond. Both were looking her over with unabashed male curiosity and appreciation.

Tucking her closer against his side, Kian tightened his hold. "Give me the keys." He held out his palm, staring daggers at his companions.

Puzzled by his abrasiveness, she lifted her eyes to look at his angry face. "Aren't you going to introduce us?"

Pointing dismissively at the men, he barked, "The big red oaf's name is Anandur, and Rapunzel's name is Brundar." Partially blocking their view of her with his body, he finished the introduction. "And this is Syssi, Amanda's assistant."

Sidestepping Kian, the one named Anandur smiled and brought his lips down to her offered hand for a kiss. "Enchanted."

Was she imagining it, or did Kian just hiss?

Brundar bowed his head without saying a thing, but his lips curled up slightly, suggesting he was suppressing a smile.

This time, there was no hiss.

"Which one is yours?" Kian asked, closing his fingers over her keys.

"The blue BMW over there." She pointed.

He tossed the keys to Anandur, who caught the dangling thing midair, and mock-saluting Kian walked over to her car.

"Brundar, you're driving," Kian ordered and opened the SUV's back passenger door for Syssi. Motioning for her to scoot over, he joined her in the back seat, and settling close to her, placed a proprietary hand on her thigh.

With the thick curtain of her hair hiding her face, Syssi smirked. She wasn't sure what to make of Kian's behavior. He was acting like a jealous boyfriend.

On the other hand, it was entirely possible that he was always rude to these guys, or that the animosity between them lingered from something that had happened before. In either case, it had nothing to do with her.

Still, whatever the reason, Syssi didn't mind the feel of his body pressed against her side, or his fingers closing around her knee. On the contrary, it felt nice. It had been so long since she had enjoyed this kind of closeness.

Suddenly overcome by an intense yearning for it, her gut twisted with a sense of loss as she realized how improbable it was for something meaningful to develop between them.

She was such an idiot.

One hot kiss and two erotic dreams didn't constitute a relationship or even a fling.

What was she thinking?

Syssi sighed. Wishing for it wasn't going to make it so.

But in the meantime, she could pretend a little and enjoy the warmth of togetherness. Even if it was all an illusion. For the duration of this adventure, she decided she would let it unfold and deal with the consequences later.

37

KIAN

Holding Syssi close, Kian savored the feel of her. Still worried about how haggard she had looked when he had first gotten to her place, he glanced down, but her face was hidden behind her hair.

Damn! The girl had looked ashen as if she had been sick or tired from a sleepless night, and her pretty face had been pinched with worry and fear.

It was his fault.

He must've harmed her somehow with his thrall the other night, and this morning had scared her out of her mind, galloping down that driveway the way he had. The fact that he had no choice did nothing to ease his guilt.

He wanted to make that tired look go away, to enfold her in the shelter of his arms and ease her fears and worries, to cocoon her in safety and warmth and undo whatever damage he had unwittingly done.

But this was not the right time for this. And besides, he would probably freak her out. As it was, his body didn't get the message that it was okay to power down yet, and with the way he was still primed for a fight, he could just imagine how threatening he must seem to her.

Forcing in a deep breath, Kian tried to relax his coiled muscles.

He was so grateful that he had made it in time. His original plan had been to thrall Syssi again to get her to cooperate, but he was glad he had decided against it and had restored her memory instead. It had confused the hell out of her, but at least he hadn't compounded the damage to her brain.

Yeah, keep telling yourself that.

The truth was, he wanted Syssi to remember him; and all other plans had flown out the window once he had seen her again and his hormones had taken over, doing his thinking for him.

Kian smirked, remembering how following her inside, he had zeroed in on that shapely behind of hers.

Lucky for him, she hadn't caught him ogling it.

But oh, boy, those form-fitting leggings she was wearing outlined her ass so perfectly and left so very little to the imagination, he'd had to fight the urge to cup them with his hands, and after giving them a nice squeeze, run his fingers along that center seam all the way down to her core.

When she had turned around and found him almost pressed against her, he had wanted to kiss her, badly. It was good that he had learned some restraint over the years because with the way she had gazed at him, wanting him to do just that, he had to remind himself that there was no time and that he had to restore her memories and get her out of there first. The kissing had to wait. Though he had managed to get away with that little slap on her delicious ass, thankfully, without getting in trouble.

She might've even liked it.

Perfect, the girl was absolutely perfect.

Sexy, sweet, beautiful.

His.

Sitting next to Syssi, feeling her warmth radiate through their clothes, smelling her delicious scent, Kian wondered what it was about her that stirred these unfamiliar cravings in him. The lust was to be expected; Syssi was beautiful and sexy and it was in his nature to want her body. But the possessiveness, the protectiveness, the tenderness he felt toward her, these were new.

He hugged her closer and caressed her knee lightly, reluctant to spoil the moment and upset her with the explanation he had promised. But it needed to be done.

Taking a deep breath, he shifted so he could look into her eyes and took her hand, squeezing it gently.

"Remember the people we were trying to avoid the other day in the lab?" Kian used the most reassuring tone he could muster, hating that he had to scare her again. "They came back last night and ransacked the lab—wrote hateful things on the walls."

Syssi's hand flew to her chest and the color drained from her face. "Oh my God! Poor Amanda, she must be so upset!"

Fuck, that hadn't worked as well as he had planned; the girl had turned as pale as a ghost.

And he hadn't even gotten to the punch line yet.

"She is distraught, but not over the damage. That is easily fixed... Amanda had a notebook. Among other things, it contained a list of all her paranormal subjects by their first name, phone number, and the ranking she assigned them. That notebook is missing, and we believe the vandals got it and may try to harm those on the list."

"Why?" Syssi kept rubbing her chest as the bad news kept piling.

"Why do they do all the evil deeds they do? Hate, fear, ignorance, greed, envy. Take your pick. They may believe special abilities are evil, the mark of the devil or some other nonsense like that. The why doesn't matter, just know that they will. You are the highest ranked on Amanda's list, which makes you their number one target."

Just talking about it had blown his hard-won composure away. The idea of anyone or anything posing a threat to Syssi had him seething with rage. "Can I have your cell phone? We need to get rid of it. The fuckers can track you by its signal." He held out his palm. "Don't worry. I'll buy you a new one."

Syssi handed him the device and scooted away, putting some distance between them. Kian knew he'd sounded vehement delivering his little speech, and with her already being scared, his dark mood must've added a layer of anxiety.

Pulling her back to him, he plastered her against his side and squeezed her shoulders reassuringly, tightening his fingers on her cold, sweaty hand. "Don't worry, sweet girl. I'd never let anything happen to you. I'd rip to shreds each and every one of those bastards with my own bare hands before I let anyone lay a finger on you. You are safe with me." Kian finished his gruesome pledge with a kiss to the top of her head.

Except, it didn't seem to help with her anxiety. The poor girl remained silent and rigid.

Way to go calming her nerves, moron.

At this point, she must've been as scared of him as she was of the looming threat.

Opening the window just a crack, he sent her phone flying straight into a construction curbside trash bin.

Now the fuckers could follow it to the dump.

38

SYSSI

"You could stumble and twist your ankle wearing these insane shoes," Kian bit out as Syssi wavered and gripped his bicep for support.

Walking from the car to the elevators, she felt a little lightheaded. Was it the Kahlua? Perhaps. Though it also could've been whatever Kian had done to her head. But then, being scared out of her freaking mind might've had something to do with it as well.

"It's not the shoes, they're actually pretty sturdy. I'm just a little dizzy. I might still be tipsy from all the Kahlua I had this morning. Or, what's more likely, the weakness and lack of balance are the results of all the excitement. I was so scared..." Embarrassed, she glanced his way before looking down at her feet.

Some of the dark shadows had lifted off his handsome face, and he no longer looked as frightening as he had in the car. Though judging by his stiff posture, he was still tense.

"Tipsy? Before lunch? Somehow you don't strike me as the type." A smile tugged at his lips as he wrapped his arm around her waist, propping her against his side so she was almost floating, her feet barely touching the ground.

"No, I'm not, I hardly ever drink. I've been feeling anxious for the past few days. The bad feeling was so strong that I couldn't shake it off." Syssi looked up at Kian with a sad smile, deciding to tell him the truth about herself. After all, Amanda had probably already told him all about her and her questionable talent. "I've learned from experience to listen to that cursed foresight of mine and not disregard it as nothing. When I feel something bad is going to happen it almost always does. So anyway, long story short, I spiked my coffee with some Kahlua to soothe my rattled nerves."

Kian kissed the top of her head and squeezed her shoulder. "I'm grateful for your foresight, and you should be too. It's a good warning mechanism that might've saved you from something very nasty. But enough of that, I don't want you thinking about it anymore. You're safe now."

Parting ways with Brundar at the elevators, they stepped into the one going up to the penthouse.

"How many of those spiked cups did you have?" Kian asked as the doors opened to the vestibule.

"Three, but there wasn't that much alcohol in them. It's just that I'm a really lightweight drinker." She grimaced. "Half a glass of wine makes me woozy."

"You'll feel better after you eat. This dizziness is probably the result of stress combined with alcohol and an empty stomach. I'll have Okidu whip up something." Kian dropped her duffle bag by the entry and headed for the kitchen.

Hesitating, Syssi wasn't sure if she was to follow him or wait by the door. Looking around and twisting her hands as she reacquainted herself with the place, she wondered if Kian planned for her to stay with him.

She should've thought of asking him to drop her off at Andrew's.

Truth be told, though, she'd let him lead her like a goose and hadn't been thinking at all. It seemed that her brain took a hiatus whenever Kian was near, mistakenly assuming they were an item and letting him take care of her as if she was his. Except she wasn't, which explained why she felt so awkward and displaced coming home with him. Besides, she was an independent woman who didn't need anyone to take care of her. Except until recently, it had meant earning a decent income and paying her own bills.

Defending herself from crazy cult members wasn't something she'd ever anticipated dealing with.

Syssi wasn't a warrior, she had never even taken a self-defense class, and she had a feeling calling the police wouldn't have done her any good. She needed someone like Kian or her brother to keep her safe from them. Posturing her independence and insisting on staying home would've been just stupid. Sometimes, a girl needed to acknowledge her limitations and accept help.

Taking a deep breath, she put one foot in front of the other and followed Kian to the kitchen.

39

KIAN

The sound of Okidu chopping vegetables greeted Kian as soon as he opened his front door. The thing was, the speed at which his butler was performing the simple task would've seemed unnatural even for an experienced sushi chef. He hurried to the kitchen and put a hand on Okidu's shoulder. "Good, I'm hungry, and so is Syssi," he said, letting Okidu know that they had company he should be mindful of.

The speed slowed immediately.

"It seems we both skipped breakfast." He turned around and motioned for Syssi to join them in the kitchen, then reached under the counter and pulled out a stool for her.

Okidu paused his chopping and turned around with a big welcoming smile already plastered on his face. "Of course, Master, and good day to you and the lovely lady. It is a pleasure to see you again, madam." He wiped his hands on a dish towel and bowed.

"May I serve breakfast in the dining room, Master?" He intercepted Kian as he was about to pull out another stool for himself.

"Yes, good idea, the dining room..." Kian pushed back the stool and redirected Syssi toward the formal dining room.

Good save.

Thankful for Okidu's intervention, Kian shook his head. As ridiculous as it was for someone his age, he didn't have much practice at being a host. Besides the Guardians, he never had guests over—not that the guys qualified as such or required special treatment.

If not for his butler, it would've never crossed Kian's mind that there was anything wrong with inviting Syssi to eat brunch at the kitchen counter. Not that there was, necessarily, but she deserved a little courtesy, and the truth was that he wanted to impress her.

Never mind that what Okidu had been programmed to consider as proper etiquette no longer applied to this day and age. Kian, however, was a product of a different era.

Damn, it had been such a long time since he had treated a woman like a real lady. Problem was, he would've been laughed at if he tried it with any of the mortal women he typically interacted with—in any capacity.

Kian grimaced as it crossed his mind that his mother would've been appalled to see him behave like this. If she ever decided to grace his home with her presence, he'd have to brush up on the good manners she had attempted to instill in him all those centuries ago.

Regrettably, he didn't have much use for even a fraction of those manners with the kind of company he kept. Curiously, though, it hadn't bothered him before. His nightly prowls required little if any effort or finesse on his part. He'd show up, zero in on his chosen prey, and the females usually took it from there.

Easy...

He had never brought any of them home.

If he hadn't fucked them against a wall in a dark alley or some other secluded corner, he would bring them to one of the timeshare apartments on the lower levels, or a hotel. Later, Okidu would make sure that Kian's thralled and confused partners found their way back safely.

He had never spent the night with any of them.

"I don't mind eating at the kitchen counter," she said in a small voice.

Kian leaned to whisper in her ear, "I don't mind either, but it will upset Okidu to no end, and he'll act pissy for the rest of the day. I'd rather humor him." He was such a rotten liar. But Syssi looked uncomfortable and he wanted to put her at ease.

She smiled. "I wouldn't want to upset the poor guy. Lead the way."

Walking her toward the dining room, Kian put his hand on the small of her back—his touch eliciting a slight shiver. Syssi was attracted to him, but so were most of the women he came in contact with. He wanted more from her even though he shouldn't. There could be nothing between them other than some harmless flirting, and he was pushing the limits of that too.

As he pulled a chair out for Syssi, he was acutely aware of how different she was from his nightly fare.

The women who tended to take his bait were the hardened, disillusioned types frequenting the bars and clubs, looking for some good times. Just like him.

No questions asked and no expectations.

Most times he hadn't even asked for their names.

Syssi seemed so innocent and fragile in contrast, sitting there like a proper lady with her back straight and her hands in her lap, looking nervous.

Her eyes darting around, she looked at everything and anything in the room just to avoid meeting his eyes.

So shy... so reserved... so sweet...

She wouldn't make it easy on him. She would expect him to woo her, be romantic.

Kian's brows drew tight as it dawned on him that he didn't know how to do that. He had never felt the need to make that kind of an effort before.

Living the way he did, and with hardly the time or patience to watch or read anything romantic, he didn't even have the benefit of learning by example from fiction.

Yeah, he had the finesse of a bulldog and was just as charming.

He would have to improvise, and hopefully, manage not to blunder too much. Because even though he expected to have Syssi for only a few days, he wanted those days to be special, different.

40

SYSSI

Kian was acting like the perfect gentleman. It started with him pulling the chair out for her, then waiting for her to be seated before gently pushing it toward the table. When Okidu brought a pitcher of orange juice, Kian insisted on pouring it into her glass, and when the salad arrived, he loaded her plate himself.

No guy had ever doted on her like this. In fact, she'd only seen such manners in a period movie, or read about it in a historical romance novel. Although Kian looked to be in his early thirties, he was old-fashioned like a man at least double his age.

Which reminded her.

"I forgot to ask Anandur to bring me the keys to my car. Could you please call him?" She glanced at her watch. "I have an appointment later today that I can't miss."

Kian frowned. "Could you reschedule?"

Syssi shook her head. "I could, but I would hate to do it. I promised three dear old friends that I'd come back and finish reading a book to them today. They'll be very disappointed if I don't. We were just getting to the good parts yesterday, but it was getting late, and I didn't want to drive home at night."

He looked doubtful. "Is this some new thing? Friends reading together?"

Syssi chuckled. "No. The three were my grandmother's friends. Toward the end of her life she lost her eyesight, so I read to her whenever I came to visit, which was every Friday afternoon. Her friends always joined us, and after she passed away, I didn't have the heart to stop the visits. They kind of adopted me as their granddaughter. Besides, I enjoy their company. They are lots of fun."

As she thought about the kinds of books the ladies had her read, Syssi felt a blush creeping up. After all this time, she should've been cured of the damned blushing. Was it possible that her grandmother's friends sought to help her get over it by making her uncomfortable on purpose?

If they did, then it wasn't working. The bane of her existence was incurable.

Perhaps she should use a heavy foundation, the kind actors used on stage. Because nothing else could cover it up. It was such an embarrassment to have her feelings show when she would've preferred to keep them to herself.

For a private person like her, it felt awful to be exposed like that. It had gotten to the point that she avoided talking about anything that might cause her discomfort, which unfortunately included talking with guys she was interested in. Not that there had been many. But there had been one or two instances when she would've liked to start a conversation but hadn't out of fear that her flaming cheeks would advertise her interest.

Kian was no exception. The only difference was that she was stuck with him and had nowhere to run.

He clasped her hand. "That's very nice of you."

She tried to shrug it off. "It's nothing. As I said, it's not a big sacrifice. I enjoy doing it."

Kian nodded. "I'll have one of my guys drive you."

"I would hate to inconvenience anyone. I have a car and no one knows I visit the Golden Age Retirement home. I'll be perfectly safe."

"Perhaps. But I'll be going out of my mind with worry. I'll feel so much better knowing you have someone to protect you in case of trouble."

Syssi narrowed her eyes at Kian. He was a sneaky one, guilting her into agreeing. "I know what you're doing."

He smirked. "Is it working?"

"What do you think?"

"Good. It's a huge relief. I meant every word of it." He sounded sincere. "When do you need to be there and how far away is it?"

"I didn't tell them an exact time, but I think ten will be perfect. The drive there shouldn't take more than twenty to twenty-five minutes."

Kian seemed happy with that. "Excellent. That means we have plenty of time to have coffee out on the terrace. It's a beautiful sunny day and it would be a shame to spend all of it inside."

"I would love that."

Okidu prepared a tray and Kian carried it outside despite the butler's protests.

"He is awfully bossy, isn't he?" Syssi said as they stepped outside.

Kian lowered the tray onto a mosaic-inlaid bistro table. "It's not that he is bossy, it's that he is programmed to assume responsibility over all domestic duties, and whenever I do something that he considers as his domain, he gets rattled."

Syssi arched a brow. "Programmed?"

Kian paused in the middle of pouring coffee into one of the small porcelain cups Okidu had put on the tray. "Set in his ways, that was what I meant. We all have habits we cling to. Sugar?"

"Yes, please. One cube."

Kian dropped it in. "Creamer?"

"A little bit… That's enough."

He stirred it all together and handed her the cup. "Any habits that you have and don't like anyone to disturb?" he asked.

Syssi took a sip, relieved that it had come out the way she liked it. "I'm very particular about how I like my coffee. I was gritting my teeth when you did it for me. But it came out good."

"Why didn't you tell me?" Kian poured a cup for himself and didn't add anything to it. "I would've left your coffee alone to fix any way you wanted."

She shrugged. "It would've been rude. But you asked."

"I appreciate the honesty."

She nodded. "It's one of the things I value most about people. I'll take rude and honest over polite and deceitful any day. But I know I'm odd that way. Most people prefer polite even if it involves some white lies."

Kian flinched as if she hurled an insult at him. Did he think she was insinuating that he'd lied about something?

Perhaps he had. But about what?

He seemed to recover fast. "Yeah, most people are too touchy to hear the brutal truth."

That was probably what had caused the flinch. He'd been reminded of hurting someone's feelings. The guy was doing his best, but he seemed like the type who wasn't all that attuned to other people. Under his good manners and sophisticated veneer, she sensed a rough edge. Even danger. Curiously, it didn't scare her. On the contrary, it was titillating.

Syssi shook her head. There must be something wrong with her. She'd never understood the appeal of bad boys, thought herself above such silliness, and yet here she was, pining for a man who was hiding something dangerous just underneath the surface.

The thing was, she also sensed that Kian was a good guy. He wasn't as full of himself as she would've expected from someone so good-looking and successful, but he carried himself with the confidence and self-respect of an honorable man. A decent man. The whole package was quite irresistible. Except, he could loosen up a little; the guy was too serious, too somber. She wanted to see him smile more.

"I wasn't completely honest before." She smirked.

Kian arched a brow. "Oh, yeah? How so?"

"If you ever see a huge zit on my nose, and I ask you if it looks horrible, I expect you to lie and say that nothing can detract from my beauty." She made a face, scrunching her nose and forcing her eyes to cross.

Kian didn't laugh, not even a chuckle. Instead, he leaned back in his chair and pinned her with a stare that was hard to read. "I'll remember that. But I wouldn't be lying."

"Oh, you're smooth, very smooth."

He seemed offended again. "That's the honest truth. You could be covered in pimples and still look beautiful to me."

Aaand… the blush was back.

What was she supposed to say to that?

Silly girl, just say thank you. Hattie's voice sounded in her head.

"Thank you, that's very sweet."

Kian chuckled. "Believe me, Syssi, there is nothing sweet about me."

41

KIAN

Kian wanted to kick himself. Syssi looked like she wanted to hide under the table and it was all his fault. It had been going so well, she was loosening up and smiling more around him, and then he had to throw in that last remark, flustering her again.

She was so easy to read. A pretty blush would be the first indicator that she was feeling uncomfortable, then she would dip her head and let her long hair fall forward to hide her face.

She had done both after his last remark.

A change of subject was needed. Something neutral. "How are you enjoying working at the lab?"

Syssi shrugged, still not looking at him. "I like the research and I like working with Amanda, but this is temporary, just until I find another internship."

"You studied architecture, right?"

She nodded, finally lifting her eyes to his and smiling a little.

It was progress. "I know a thing or two about it. Not from the design side, but from the development and construction sides. Our family owns several development companies. In fact, most of the high rises on this street are ours." Why the hell was he telling her that?

It would be just another thing he would need to erase from her memory once it was safe for her to return to the old converted garage she called home. He needed to have a talk with Amanda about the wages she was paying the girl. As far as he could remember, the budget for her research assistant's salary was generous. Syssi should be able to afford a decent apartment.

"I didn't have a chance to get a good look, but from what I've seen so far your building is gorgeous. Who's the architect? Anyone well known?"

Kian chuckled. "Not really. She is a cousin of ours. I can ask if she has a need for an intern." Amanda was going to kill him if he helped Syssi get away from her, but he would be doing them all a favor. The girl had a knack for messing with Amanda's and his heads.

Syssi blushed again. "I wasn't fishing for a job recommendation. Besides, I'm more into designing single family homes and would like to intern with someone that does that."

"I'll ask around. I'm sure an internship will pay more than what my sister is paying you." It was so unlike Amanda to take advantage of the girl and pay her less than the job had been budgeted for, just because she hadn't been trained in neuroscience.

A quiet snort escaped Syssi's throat. "I doubt that. Amanda pays me very well. I'm going to have to settle for much less as an intern."

So why the hell was she living the way she did? Kian ran his fingers through his hair. It could be that she was burdened with student loans. He'd read an article about it last weekend. It said that the cost of tuition had doubled in the last ten years and students were drowning in debt. Or maybe she didn't want to make any adjustments to her lifestyle because this well-paying job was temporary.

"It could be a good idea for you to stay at the lab longer and pay down some of your student loans before taking an internship with lower pay."

She cast him a puzzled glance. "I don't have any. My parents paid for my schooling."

Her parents must've been well to do. That would explain the expensive car. He'd wondered how she could afford it while living so modestly.

"In that case you can save up some money for when the budget gets tighter."

Kian knew the exact moment she realized the reason for his suggestions.

Syssi's ears turned crimson and she lowered her head. She didn't look at him, and if his hearing weren't as good as it was, he would not have heard what she said. "My place is close to the university and offers privacy. That's why I rent it. I don't need anything fancy. I prefer putting money in the bank rather than spending all I make."

He was such an ass, making her uncomfortable again.

Fuck and double fuck, he needed to fix it. "Of course, I understand perfectly. It's very wise of you."

Lifting her head a little, she glanced at him from behind the curtain of her hair. He must've passed her scrutiny because her head went all the way up and she thrust her chin out. "I'm glad you think so. Most people think I'm stingy, and I'm so tired of defending my choices. There is nothing wrong with being frugal. It brings me peace of mind."

Kian couldn't help reaching for her hand. "I admire your financial acumen. A rare quality for someone as young as you. More than that, I admire you for sticking to your wise decisions even though they are unpopular. It requires guts."

That brought a real smile to her beautiful face. "Thank you." It was like someone had flipped a light inside her and she shone like a brilliant star—her inner beauty even brighter than the physical one.

Kian wanted to kiss her so bad that it hurt. Hell, he wanted to do much more than kissing. But he'd promised himself he wouldn't do it again. The taste of that one kiss he'd allowed himself when he'd thought he would never see Syssi again had been his undoing. One more and he would be forever lost.

This beautiful girl, this amazing person, could never be his, not even for one night of passion. Morality aside, he knew that one time with her could never be enough.

He'd better get out of there before his control snapped.

"I need to go and take care of some business, but I'll send up one of my guys to escort you to the retirement home. Will you be okay here by yourself for a few minutes?"

"Yes, of course. I don't want to take any more of your time."

She was disappointed, he could smell it, but he needed to put some distance between them. Fast. "I'll see you when you come back." He squeezed her hand lightly before getting up.

"Thank you, Kian. I appreciate all that you're doing for me. But I don't want to impose. I can stay with my brother, or at a hotel."

"We'll discuss it later. I need to run." He forced a tight smile and walked away, pulling his phone out of his pocket the moment he closed the door behind him.

There was no way he was letting her go anywhere. She wasn't safe out there. But he'd fight this battle later when he was better composed.

Thinking of who to assign as her bodyguard, he immediately ruled out Anandur. The guy was a flirt and a ladies' man. Alone with Syssi, he would seduce her in no time. Brundar was a safer choice. Kian made the call.

"Yes, boss."

"I need you to escort Syssi to an appointment. She is waiting for you out on the terrace. She'll give you the details when you get there."

"No problem. When?"

"Now."

"I'm on my way."

Kian pushed the phone back in his pocket and wondered what to do with himself next. There was always paperwork that needed attention—reports to go over, profit analysis of acquiring new properties to read, the list was long. In fact, it was endless, and he was in no mood to tackle any of it. Besides, the files were in his home office. His other option was to go down to Shai's office in the basement. His assistant kept copies of everything.

Easier said than done.

The fifty feet or so separating him from Syssi already felt like too far. Kian rubbed his sternum. It felt as if his heart was made out of a magnet, and it was pulling him toward the one in Syssi's chest. The difference was that instead of the pull weakening, the farther away he got, the stronger it became.

Damn. He didn't want her going out without him, and it had nothing to do with her safety. Brundar was an army of one and a much better fighter than Kian.

A true master.

Kian just wanted to be near her. Keeping it platonic would be hell, but he was discovering that staying away from her was worse.

He was losing his fucking mind.

42

SYSSI

Syssi took another sip of her cold coffee and nibbled on a biscuit. She was glad that Kian was too busy to accompany her. Imagining him listening to her read that romance book to the ladies was enough to send her running the other way. She wouldn't have agreed to go on with it, and the girls would've been disappointed.

Besides, what did she expect? That he would be her driver? Her bodyguard? He had people on payroll for that.

Kian felt responsible for her because of Amanda, and he was being a gracious host, but that didn't mean he wanted to spend any more time with her than he absolutely had to.

A high caliber businessman, Kian was a very busy guy.

A guy who for some reason had run off like his tail was on fire, leaving her alone with his butler.

Had she said something to offend him? Had he been under the impression that he'd offended her?

Probably the second one.

Truth be told, she'd been more embarrassed than offended. He was right, she wasn't a student anymore, and that guesthouse was a bit shabby for someone who was making decent money. She should move somewhere nicer.

The thing was, he'd actually done her a favor. Talking about her shitty apartment had been infinitely better than obsessing about Kian's sexy lips and piercing eyes and thinking about how he'd made her feel in her dreams. She would have looked like a freaking tomato.

God, how she wished there was a cure for that awful impediment.

If not for that damn blushing giving her away, she could've pulled off looking cool, sophisticated. She envied those women who could pretend disinterest even when they were internally drooling over a guy. The lack of this elementary ability, one that others took for granted, was causing her endless grief.

Pushing up to her feet, Syssi walked over to the glass railing and glanced at the adjoining buildings, trying to guess which belonged to Kian's family. Two across the street were a similar style, but it was difficult to take a look at those that were on the same side as the one she was in.

"Ready to go?"

Syssi jumped and turned around, bumping into Kian's solid chest. His arms shot around her to keep her from falling. "I'm sorry I startled you."

"How do you do that? Do you have silencers on your shoes or something?" She glanced down, hiding the spike of desire his hands on her body brought about.

He chuckled. "You were just preoccupied. That's why you didn't hear us come in."

Heck, she hadn't even noticed Brundar standing a few feet away, looking like a silent assassin. Syssi shook her head. Sometimes her imagination took flights of fancy, producing the weirdest thoughts.

An assassin? Really?

"Let me just grab my purse." She tried to push out of Kian's arms, but he held on, letting her go a second later.

The man was surely sending mixed signals, and she had no idea what to make of them. One moment he seemed to be attracted to her, the next he was treating her like a random acquaintance. And since the second one was more fitting to their situation, it was safer to assume that this was the extent of his feelings for her. But then he'd do something like he'd done a moment ago; hold her for a second too long like he didn't want to let her go.

The thing was, if Kian was interested in her, what the hell was stopping him from making a move? There was no way a guy like him was shy, and unless he was blind and stupid, which he wasn't, he must've realized she was attracted to him. With all that damned blushing, a twelve-year-old would've already figured that out.

Was he waiting for her to make the first move?

Without an audience, Syssi would've snorted. Kian would be waiting until he grew old because that wasn't going to happen. Not because she didn't want to, but because she couldn't.

With a sigh, Syssi walked over to retrieve the book from her duffle bag, dropping it inside her purse.

"I'm ready." She turned to the two men.

Kian took her elbow. "Let's go."

She cast him a sidelong glance. "Are you escorting me down to the car?" He was taking this host thing too seriously.

"I'm escorting you all the way to your destination and staying until you're done." Kian stopped in front of the elevators and pressed his thumb to the scanner.

Syssi's heart gave a little flutter. "I thought you had work to do."

"I do." He shrugged. "But I'd much rather spend time with you than with my paperwork."

He's done it again. Talk about mixed signals.

A soft ping announced the elevator, and a moment later the doors slid open. As the three of them stepped in, Syssi was grateful for Brundar's stoic presence. Without him there, she might have taken off one of her platform slides and bashed Kian over the head with it for driving her crazy.

Maybe that would've prompted him to do something, shaken him out of whatever was holding him back, and he would've finally made his move. Kissing her, touching her, like he'd done in her dreams.

A quick glance at the mirror confirmed that her cheeks were red and she turned sideways, hiding her face.

Don't think about that. Think disturbing thoughts.

Not a problem, Syssi had plenty of those, but it was a weapon of last resort she dreaded to use. All she had to do was open the floodgates on the bad shit swirling in her head. Earthquakes, wars, famine. This dark vortex was always there in the back of her mind, lurking, waiting to pull her down, and it took a constant, conscious effort to keep these disturbing thoughts at bay.

She hated letting the darkness in, but it was the only thing that could get rid of her blush almost instantly. The difficult part was getting rid of the crap later.

"What's wrong?" Kian's arm wrapped around her and he pulled her into his arms. There was nothing sexual in the gesture. He was comforting her.

How the hell could he have known what she'd been thinking about? Did she look upset?

"Why do you ask?"

"You seemed sad suddenly. Is there anything I can do to help?" His palm was rubbing circles on the small of her back.

Yes, you can keep holding me like this forever.

"It's nothing. I just remembered a sad story I read in the newspaper." Reluctantly, she wiggled out of his embrace and cast a furtive glance at Brundar.

Motionless, his stare fixed on the elevator's doors, the guy looked like he was made from stone—so unobtrusive that it was easy to forget he was even there.

It was the same on the drive. Brundar sat in the back, silent and watchful, while Kian and Syssi talked.

"Before meeting Amanda, had you tried to research your paranormal abilities?" Kian asked.

Had she ever. "Naturally. I've read anything and everything I could find about the subject."

"Anything interesting?"

"Lots of things, but very little that is substantiated by solid research."

"Tell me about it."

Thinking back to the books she'd read, she searched her mind for something he would find interesting. "Do you know that some dogs have a telepathic connection to their owners?"

He cast her a sidelong glance. "No, I didn't know that."

"There was an experiment conducted where owners left their dogs in a care facility and were told to come visit them at random times. The dogs would start getting excited as soon as the owners were on their way. Some even before that. They sensed their owners were coming for a visit as soon as the people made the decision, before they even got in a vehicle."

"Fascinating. Any other animals with special abilities?"

"Parrots. In one instance a talking parrot was able to tell what his owner was looking at in another room."

"What about people?"

"Amanda can probably tell you more about this than I can. We ran all kinds of experiments. Like the random shapes guessing, which I hate. She once had me do it for two hours straight. I felt I would go insane if I had to look at another square or triangle or circle."

He winced. "Sounds boring."

"It is."

Kian turned into the retirement home parking lot, and a few minutes later the three of them were standing in front of the reception desk.

"Hi, Syssi, who are your friends?" Gilda, the receptionist, had her eyes glued to Kian and was practically drooling. Fred, one of the orderlies, was eyeing Brundar.

Syssi made the introductions. "Can we go in?"

Gilda shook her head. "You can go in. But not the men. I'll have to call Leonora and ask her if it's okay to bring male visitors into her room."

Kian leaned over the counter and smiled at her. "I'm sure the ladies will be fine with us visiting them. Syssi's friends are always welcome."

Gilda's eyes glazed over and she nodded. "Of course. Syssi's friends are always welcomed."

What was that? Did he just hypnotize the woman? Had he done the same to her to make her forget about what had happened in the lab?

As soon as they were buzzed in and the door closed behind them, Syssi whispered, "What have you done to her? And don't tell me nothing, because Gilda would've never allowed someone new inside without checking who they were."

Kian shrugged, but his shoulders remained tense. "A little mental suggestion, that's all."

"Like hypnotism?"

"Yeah, exactly like that."

"Where did you learn how to do it? And did you use it on me?"

He winced. "It's a useful trick, that's all. I figured you'd sleep better if you forgot all about those lunatics. I thought that that was the end of it. But evidently I was wrong."

They'd reached Leonora's room and Syssi knocked.

"Come in!" Hattie answered.

Syssi opened the door just a crack and peeked in. "I have two guys with me. I think it would be better if you ladies came out and met us at the salon."

The door swung open and Leonora filled the frame. She looked Kian and Brundar over, top to bottom and then back up. "Well, hello, handsome boys." She turned around. "I wish you could see them, Hattie. Mm-hmm, gorgeous!"

"I'm sorry about that," Syssi whispered. "After a certain age it seems that people think they have the right to say whatever is on their minds."

Kian chuckled and patted her on the back. "It's quite alright. They are having some harmless fun. Brundar and I are more than happy to be the objects of their excitement and give the old girls something to talk about. Am I right, Brundar?" Kian clapped his friend on the back.

Brundar responded with a grunt.

Leonora's room wasn't big enough for all of them, especially the two tall guys, but they managed. Brundar went back out to the hallway and brought two more chairs.

Hattie got up and bee-lined straight for Kian as if her eyesight was perfectly fine. "I'm blind, but I can see with my hands. Do you mind if I touch you?"

"Not at all, go ahead." He took her hand and brought it to his face. Hattie cupped his cheek then added her other hand to the exploration.

She nodded. "I approve."

Kian chuckled softly. "I'm glad I passed your test, my lady."

"Ooh, he called you a lady." Clara clapped her hands. "Such a polite young man."

Brundar shifted in his chair, and Syssi caught him frowning before he quickly schooled his face into its usual stoic mask.

"Brundar is very handsome as well, Hattie. Don't you want to see him too?"

Kian looked like he was barely stifling a laugh. "Yes, Lady Hattie. You should check him out."

Hattie shook her head and waved a finger at Kian as if he was a naughty boy. Shuffling back to her chair, she stopped by Brundar and gave his shoulder a light pat. "You don't like to be touched, son, I understand."

How the hell could she have known that about him?

Syssi cast a quick glance at Brundar. Hattie was right. The guy looked relieved to be spared a touching session. She had misunderstood his frown. It wasn't that he'd felt left out, he'd been afraid of getting included.

Leonora poured everyone tea and handed each of them a small porcelain cup. "Did you bring the book, dear?"

Syssi pulled it out of her purse and handed it to Leonora. "I don't think I'll be reading to you today. The guys will be bored by a silly romance novel."

"Let me take a look." Kian snatched the book from Leonora's hands. "*Dreams of a Dark Lover,* a vampire romance novel. Sounds fascinating. I would love to hear it. How about you, Brundar?"

The guy shrugged.

"It's decided then." Kian thrust the book at Syssi's hands. "Everyone wants to hear you read."

She was going to die.

"I can't. It's too embarrassing. Have you ever read a romance novel?"

"Can't say that I have. That's why I'm curious. But if it's too difficult for you, I can read it instead."

That would be infinitely better. "You're my hero," she blurted before thinking how it would sound. "I mean, thank you. I appreciate it." She rolled her eyes. "More than you can imagine."

With a big grin splitting his face, Kian flipped the book open to the page with the folded corner. "My pleasure."

43

KIAN

Two chapters into the story Brundar had excused himself, preferring to wait outside. Five chapters into it, Kian had to cross his legs to hide a massive hard-on.

"As Bernard's fingers skimmed Vivian's breasts, a bolt of desire hit her core, the heat spreading over her trembling body—"

He had no idea how explicit the story would be. Reading about hot sex between a vampire and a human was half the trouble, though. What was killing him, minute by excruciating minute, was the scent of Syssi's arousal. If not for the ironclad control he'd honed over centuries, he would've pounced on her and taken her on the bed she was sitting on—audience and all.

Given the satisfied expressions on their wrinkled faces, the three crones weren't oblivious to what was going on. He'd caught them stealing glances at Syssi and him, smirking and nodding to each other as if this was all some grand scheme they had orchestrated between them and were overjoyed to see it come to fruition.

Thankfully, the last few chapters were dedicated to a big wedding and to tying up miscellaneous loose ends in the plot, giving him a much needed reprieve from all the sexual tension.

Closing the book, he released a puff of breath and forced a tight smile. "Aren't romances supposed to end with and-they-lived-happily-ever-after? I must've missed it." He flipped through several of the final pages, pretending to look for the phrase.

Clara started clapping and the other two joined her. "Bravo, Kian, you've done a marvelous job," she said. "Thank you."

Kian bowed his head. "My pleasure." More like torture.

Leonora patted Syssi's back. "This one is a keeper. You've done well, girl."

Syssi blushed. "Kian and I are just friends. He is my boss's brother."

"Of course, dear," Hattie said in a mocking tone.

Kian pushed up to his feet and handed Leonora the book. "Ladies, thank you for allowing me the privilege of reading to you, but Syssi and I must be on our way."

As Syssi hugged Leonora goodbye, Hattie shuffled up to him and put a hand on his chest. "Take care of this girl, Kian. She is precious to us."

"I will." He clasped her gnarled, small hand, sensing traces of power in her. Unable to resist, he delved into her mind to see what it was, but somehow she was blocking him. The woman was either highly intelligent or suspicious by nature. Most likely both.

Some humans were resistant to thralls, but his was particularly powerful. Kian seldom encountered a human who could block him so quickly and effectively.

It'd taken several more minutes until Syssi and her friends were done hugging and saying their goodbyes, and he had promised to each of them separately that he was going to take good care of Syssi.

Once they were out in the hallway, Kian took Syssi's hand. "Those three are something else." He chuckled.

She dipped her head. "I know. And today they've really outdone themselves. I would've never agreed to you coming in with me if I had known how they were going to behave. I'm sorry if they embarrassed you."

Kian brought her hand up for a kiss. "They didn't. I want to take care of you." He was a masochist, for even holding her hand, let alone kissing it. Every touch was electrifying, and yet he couldn't help himself, needing at least this little contact with her.

She cast him a quizzical look. "What do you mean?"

Damned if he knew. His heart was telling him to take Syssi home with him and never let her go, to do all he could to keep her safe and make her happy. But it was like wishing for the moon. He couldn't keep her because she was a human, and he couldn't make her happy even if he found a way to keep her. What he could do, however, was keep her safe.

"I'm going to make sure that no harm comes to you. And I want to help you find a great internship with an architectural firm that handles the kind of projects you like."

"Thank you, that's very sweet of you." She snorted. "I'm sorry, not sweet, very manly." She deepened her voice, imitating him.

Adorable. Especially when she was like that, playful, not fearful.

Outside, leaning against the Lexus's side, Brundar was watching the front door. "You want me to drive?" he asked as they came out.

Kian tossed him the keys. Sitting in the backseat together with Syssi wasn't a smart idea, but then he had already proven that he was stupid when it came to her. He forced himself to leave some space between them.

For a couple of minutes, they rode in silence.

"Kian." She turned to him. "Could you please take me to Andrew? My brother? I really should be staying with him."

He shook his head. "They will look for you at his place. It's not a stretch to assume that you will run to hide at the home of the only relative you have nearby."

"Not in this case. Andrew works for the government and his address is registered under a different name."

She had no idea how easily the Doomers could get this information. "These people have resources you wouldn't believe."

Her brows lifted. "A group of crazy fanatics?"

"There is more to it than that. It's an international organization and they have massive financial backing."

"How about a hotel, then?"

Brundar nodded as if agreeing that it was a good idea.

Maybe it was. Bringing Syssi to the keep hadn't been the smartest thing to do. He hadn't been thinking straight this morning, the worry and anger clouding his judgment.

It wasn't just the issue of him keeping his hands off her when she was so near. Even if he had Syssi move into Amanda's place, thralling away the memory of an extended stay could be potentially harmful to her. The more memories there were, the more intrusive and widespread the thrall had to be. Especially in the case of a highly intelligent woman like Syssi.

"Fine. Brundar, take us to the Four Seasons."

Her eyes widened in surprise, then in alarm. "Not the Four Seasons. I was thinking along the lines of a Sheraton or a Holiday Inn. I can't afford the Four Seasons."

Kian harrumphed. "Don't be ridiculous. I'm paying for it. We need a two-bedroom suite because I want Brundar to stay with you. I'm not leaving you unprotected. Besides, how did you think to pay for it? With your credit card? You would've led them right to you."

That shut her up, literally. Syssi opened her mouth to say something and then closed it, crossing her arms over her chest and frowning.

Unbelievable, he'd actually won an argument with a woman. His mother and sisters, except perhaps for Sari who was the most reasonable, never conceded this quickly.

He clasped Syssi's hand. "Thank you."

"For what?"

"Not arguing about it."

She chuckled. "That's because I'm still thinking about another solution. I don't like that you're paying for my hotel. I've caused you enough trouble as it is."

"No, you didn't. You are a victim in all of this, and none of it is your fault. If anyone is to blame, it's Amanda. And if it makes you feel better, I can charge the room to her credit card."

"Do you want me to get fired?" Syssi looked horrified by his idea. "And how can it be her fault?"

"If she didn't forget her notebook in the lab, no one would have known about you. But I was joking about charging her. It's not a big deal for me. Can we leave it at that?"

She nodded. "For now."

Good enough.

"What about my things? I left them at your place."

Kian pulled out his phone. "I'll have my butler deliver your luggage. Anything else you need?"

"No, as long as I have my laptop I can keep myself busy."

"Good. By the time we are done eating lunch your things will be there."

Kian texted Shai, asking him to make reservations for the two-bedroom presidential suite and for lunch at *Culina,* the Four Seasons' restaurant.

44

SYSSI

Syssi held the menu in front of her face, hiding as she read through the list for the third time. It wasn't that she was overly picky about what she wanted to eat, she just needed a little time to compose herself.

Surviving the visit to the three evil witches masquerading as nice old ladies was proof that she was much tougher than she thought she was. Between listening to Kian reading sex scenes, with his deep bedroom voice and watching his beautiful lips, while imagining those lips doing things to her that had nothing to do with reading, Syssi had been so close to climaxing that one touch would've sent her flying.

At some point she'd been tempted to follow Brundar's example and excuse herself, but not to wait outside.

A one minute visit to the bathroom would've been all she needed to bring herself release and come back in a much calmer state. The thing was, Syssi had a feeling the witches would have known what she was doing and she would've died from embarrassment.

Even thinking about sad things hadn't done the trick this time. In desperation, she'd closed her eyes, pretending she was testing her precognition with the damn random images projector. After a while, the square, triangle, circle, etc., had done it, and she'd been able to breathe normally. Sort of.

Until she'd gotten in the car with Kian, Syssi had been able to hang onto her composure, but sitting so close to him it had become a desperate struggle. She had to fight her hormonal body all the way from the retirement home to the restaurant. Hopefully, Kian would leave her at the room he'd rented for her, and she could get a cold shower and a change of underwear.

Leaning sideways to peek from behind the menu, she glanced at Kian, and saw him frown. Poor guy, he was probably hungry and she was taking her sweet time. "What do you recommend?"

"Tell me what kinds of foods you like."

"I can't decide. Everything sounds delicious in Italian." Not that she knew the language, but throughout her life she'd spent enough time in Italian restaurants to learn the names of dishes and ingredients. "Between the pera vegana and the pomodoro e basilico, which one is better?"

"If you're not too hungry, the pera vegana. It's a salad, so it's not overly filling."

"Perfect."

As soon as she closed her menu, the waiter rushed over to take their orders. Kian ordered the pasta dish that was her second option, and Brundar ordered the hamburger Italiano with a side of patate prezzemolate.

Syssi wondered what the guy's story was. It was obvious that Kian didn't treat Brundar as an employee, even though he barked commands at him left and right. Besides, there was a vague family resemblance between them. Brundar's face was more delicate, beautiful in an almost feminine way, but not really. He was all man behind his angelic features and long pale hair.

A dangerous man.

"How long have you been working with Kian, Brundar?" she asked to start a conversation.

He cast a sidelong glance at his boss. "Ages."

Syssi laughed. Brundar looked to be about her age. He couldn't have worked with Kian for more than a few years unless he'd started as a kid.

"Brundar and Anandur are my cousins. We've been inseparable since a very young age," Kian solved the puzzle for her.

"That explains it."

When the food arrived, the guys didn't seem in the mood for conversation, and she let them be, watching them eat. Both had impeccable table manners. A rarity for men their age.

After lunch, Kian escorted her up to the fanciest hotel suite she'd ever seen.

"Kian, this must cost a fortune." She wanted to grab her duffle bag, which had been delivered sometime during their lunch, and walk out.

He waved his hand. "If you don't want to share a room with Brundar, we need two bedrooms."

She opened her mouth to say that she didn't mind, but Kian put a finger on her lips. "Let's put it this way. *I* don't want you to share a room with Brundar."

There was no arguing with him. She would stay the one night and check out tomorrow. A suite this big in a hotel this fancy must've cost thousands of dollars. Just thinking about it gave her heart palpitations and not the good kind. If someone wanted to throw around that much money, they should give it to charity instead.

He caressed her cheek. "Just try to enjoy yourself. I wish I could stay, but I need to have some work done today. I'll try to stop by tomorrow morning."

"You work on weekends?"

His chuckle was sad. "I work each and every day. On the weekends I work a little less."

"That's not healthy."

"I know." He leaned down and brushed her lips lightly with a barely there kiss. When he lifted his head, his eyes were closed as if he wanted to savor it, memorize it.

"Goodbye, Syssi." He turned around and marched out of the room.

Brundar sat down on the couch and grabbed the remote, flipping channels until he found a wrestling competition.

Syssi picked her bag up and swung it over her shoulder. "I'm going to take that one." She pointed at one of the doors.

Brundar nodded.

Walking into the bedroom, she continued straight into the adjacent bathroom and dropped her luggage on the floor. After a quick appraisal of the amenities, Syssi decided to forgo the bathtub, even though it was nice and deep, and go into the shower. She needed to cool down first with a splash of cold water.

People did things like that in books and movies, but it had been a remarkably stupid idea. The freezing water had done nothing for her. After all, the mess was in her head and not on her skin. She turned the knob all the way to the other side and waited, shivering, for the hot water to arrive.

Better.

Okay, time to do some thinking.

She was attracted to Kian, big time, and he seemed to be attracted to her, but not as strongly. Which made sense. He was amazing. Not only handsome and smart but also generous and gracious. On a scale of one to ten, he was a twenty.

In comparison, she was an eight. Okay, maybe an eight and a half. She was pretty but not spectacular like Kian. And she was short. At five feet and five inches, she was almost a foot shorter than him. As to smarts, she wanted to believe that they were on an equal footing. She'd always excelled at school. There was the issue of an age difference, but it wasn't huge. Six years at the least and ten at the most.

The biggest divide was the disparity in achievement. She was just starting out, while Kian was managing a multimillion dollar corporation.

Sadly, he was out of her league.

Unless he suddenly showed not only interest but clear intent, she was going to try to play it cool around him.

But what if he actually made the move? Would she go for it, knowing that it could only be a short fling? Syssi shook her head. If she let him in, Kian would break her heart. Not on purpose, of course, he seemed like a decent guy, but because he would regard it as a casual fling and she couldn't. She just wasn't built that way.

Letting him past her defenses was risky.

Having Kian in her dreams, where she could submit to him sexually and yet remain in full control of the situation, was one thing; having him in real life was another. She couldn't allow herself such vulnerability. Besides, no real flesh and blood man could compare to a fantasy, and disappointment was almost guaranteed.

Coward, stop being so cautious. Living means taking chances.

Syssi wished she could borrow some of Amanda's chutzpah. If there was one thing she was envious of, it was her boss's confidence. The woman's beauty was almost a handicap, too much to handle, and money didn't impress Syssi. She liked having it because it provided her with a safety net, but she never wished for the kind of fortune Amanda and Kian had.

Syssi liked being average and attracting as little attention as possible to herself.

God, she was so boring.

45

KIAN

Leaving the hotel had tested the limits of Kian's willpower. Somehow, Syssi had become an addiction, an all-consuming and unhealthy one. It was like an affliction that had taken root in no time. He hadn't even had sex with the girl for heaven's sake.

Maybe that was the problem.

He should get her in bed and get this out of his system.

Fuck, he felt like the worst kind of jerk even considering doing something so dishonorable. It was one thing to seduce women who were looking for a commitment-free hookup and didn't expect anything more from him, and a different thing altogether to seduce a girl that held herself to a different standard and was quite obviously developing feelings for him. Not to mention the dishonesty of it all.

If he made love to her, because with Syssi it wouldn't be just a fuck like with the others, he would be doing Amanda's bidding. He would be sinking his fangs into her and pumping her with his venom, attempting her activation without her consent or even knowledge of the possibility. And it didn't matter that he was convinced nothing would happen. It would still be unethical and immoral.

Allowing this thing between them to drag on was only going to prolong their misery. He would save both of them unnecessary heartache by ripping the Band-Aid off. Getting out and staying out was the right thing to do.

Breaking an addiction was tough, but it had to be done. The only way to sever her mystifying hold on him was to go cold turkey.

Four hours and twenty-two minutes later, Shai closed the file they'd been working on. "I think we should call it a day."

Kian had to agree. He couldn't concentrate because his head was miles away, mulling over a decision that should have been a done deal.

For the first time that he could remember, Shai had to repeat to him the results of a cost analysis. The proposed military-grade drone factory represented an investment in the tens of millions. Not the kind of decision he should be making in his current state of mind. Problem was, Kian suspected that unless he had Syssi sitting right next to him, he wouldn't be able to have any work done anytime soon.

"Yeah, you're right. Let's continue tomorrow."

"No problem." Shai looked relieved.

Kian was well aware that he was using his lack of concentration as an excuse to go back to her. Nonetheless, he found himself calling Anandur.

"Meet me next to the car in ten minutes and bring an overnight bag."

"Oh, thank you, that's so kind of you. Are you taking me on a romantic vacation?" Anandur used a high-pitched valley girl tone.

Kian sighed. "Exactly. You and Brundar and me. Bring a change of clothes for your brother as well."

Unfortunately, protocol demanded that he didn't leave the keep without taking two bodyguards with him, or one when there was no other choice. Kian had already broken the rules by leaving Brundar at the hotel to guard Syssi and returning to the keep by himself.

His punishment was having to bring the ladies-magnet along.

Perhaps he should tell Shai to come too and work with him at the hotel. Maybe he'd be able to get some work done.

Not a bad idea, but Shai had looked so glad to be done that Kian had no heart to call him back. Instead, he collected the files Shai had prepared for him and stuffed them into an antique briefcase that he rarely used. It served more as a decorative piece in his office than as something to carry work in. Fortunately, the metal hinges and latches still worked.

In a way, it was good that Brundar and Anandur would stay in the hotel suite with him and Syssi. Their presence would help him behave and stay away from her bedroom. After all, he wouldn't seduce her with the brothers in the next room.

In his closet, Kian added to his briefcase a change of underwear, a brand new pair of sleep pants he'd never used either, and one of the travel kits of toiletries Okidu kept ready and stocked for Kian's last minute business trips.

"Where are we going, boss?" Anandur said as Kian tossed him the keys.

"The Four Seasons."

Anandur got behind the wheel. "Oh, goodie, so you are taking me on a romantic vacation after all."

"Hardly." Kian got inside and closed the passenger door. "I put Syssi up in a hotel suite and left Brundar to keep her safe."

Anandur lifted a bushy brow. "And you think one Guardian is not enough? Especially Brundar who is an army of one?"

Kian had a hard time explaining it to himself and had no desire to share his reasoning, or lack thereof, with Anandur. "I have my reasons and they are none of your business."

"Aha. So it's like that." Anandur seemed way too happy with himself.

Fuck it, let him think what he would.

For the rest of the drive Kian pretended to work, which kept Anandur's flapping mouth shut.

"Kian?" Brundar opened the presidential suite's door.

"Good evening." Kian pushed by him without answering the implied question of what he was doing there. Mainly because he had no good answer for that.

"Hello, brother." He heard Anandur clap Brundar on the back.

Syssi was nowhere in the living area. "Where is she?" Kian turned to Brundar.

"In her bedroom."

"Sleeping?"

"No."

Kian walked over to where the trail of her scent led and knocked on the door. "Syssi? Are you sleeping?"

"Give me a moment," she answered.

He heard the patter of bare feet and a moment later the clunking of high-heeled shoes on the hardwood floor.

Syssi opened the door. "Kian, I wasn't expecting you back this evening. What happened?"

He would answer her when his tongue unfroze in his mouth. She was stunning. Curiously, she was always more beautiful than his memory of her, surprising him anew each time he saw her again. Instead of the form-fitting leggings she had on before, she'd changed into a pair of jeans that molded to her legs and her hips in the same way the leggings had, and she was wearing a white T-shirt with a deep neckline that exposed the very tops of her breasts.

Mouthwatering.

Kian shrugged, pretending as if she hadn't rendered him momentarily speechless. "I thought I'd come over and keep you company." He leaned closer to whisper in her ear. "Brundar is not much of a conversationalist. Spending time with him is as fascinating as watching paint dry."

Syssi stifled a chuckle. "I see that you brought reinforcements," she said as she saw Anandur sharing the couch with Brundar.

"Yeah. In case I'm not entertaining enough, Anandur is a sure bet. The guy missed his calling; he should've been a comedian." He took her hand and led her toward the dining table where he'd left his briefcase.

She shook her head. "He's too big and too muscular for a comedian. On the other hand, even if he's not that funny, I'm sure he will have an audience. Girls will go wild for him."

Kian barely managed to keep down the growl bubbling up from some primitive place in his gut. If Syssi didn't stop talking about how good looking Anandur was, he was going to lose it.

Oblivious, she kept going. "His brother is also gorgeous. If he smiled a little, the girls would be all over him too. That hard expression on his face is kind of intimidating."

Gritting his teeth, Kian pulled out a chair for her. "My lady?"

"Thank you." She blushed a little.

"Have you eaten already?"

"Yes. I ordered room service for Brundar and myself. The prices they charge here are outrageous. I tried to pick the least expensive items, but Brundar wanted a hamburger and it wasn't like a guy his size could do with an appetizer portion—"

Kian lifted his hand. "Would you stop fretting over costs? Trust me, I can afford it."

Syssi flinched. "Of course, you can. I wasn't implying that you can't."

Damn, he'd sounded too aggressive and impatient, and it had nothing to do with her concern over expenditure and everything to do with the two handsome Guardians.

He turned to them. "I'm going to order dinner, you want anything?"

Anandur lifted a finger. "I ate before we left, but some munchies and a bunch of beers would be much appreciated, boss."

Kian nodded. "Syssi? What about you? Maybe dessert?"

"I would love some ice cream, if they have it. And a cappuccino. There is a coffeemaker in the kitchen and I made myself some, but I didn't like how it tasted."

For some reason, it made him stupidly happy that she'd asked for something, obliterating the anger over her previous remarks. Providing her with what she was craving felt satisfying. Especially since she never asked for anything and balked at every dollar spent.

He ended up ordering two of each appetizer on the menu, beers for the guys, a dinner for himself, and cappuccinos for Syssi and himself. He also ordered each and every flavor of ice cream the restaurant offered.

"Don't you think you overdid it a bit?" Syssi said once he was done with the order.

"Nope. You've seen Brundar eat, and he is nothing compared to that one." He pointed at Anandur. "He can demolish a mountain of food on his own."

She giggled. "Yeah, a big guy like that needs a lot of fuel."

Apparently, the girl wasn't a good judge of character because she was clueless as to what her comments about Anandur were doing to him. Frankly, though, his reaction was totally uncalled for, and she couldn't possibly suspect the kind of jealous monster lurking behind the sophisticated façade he was fronting. Not only that, but he had no right. It wasn't as if he'd done anything to indicate he was interested in her, or had given her the option to encourage him or conversely tell him to go to hell.

The smart thing to do was to steer the conversation to a safer subject. "What have you been doing while I was gone?"

Syssi let out a puff of air. "Amanda gave me a list of neuroscience papers she wanted me to read to get better acquainted with the subject. And let me tell you, scientists are horrible writers. The one I was trying to crack all afternoon was so dense, so obtuse, that I was starting to question my intelligence. In the end, I realized it wasn't as complicated as it seemed. It was just badly written. I made a summary, using clear wording, and I'm going to suggest to Amanda to give her students the summary to read instead of the original paper. It will save them hours upon hours of frustration."

He could watch her talk for hours.

Syssi was so lovely when she got excited and animated. Her eyes sparkling and her hands gesticulating, she let loose of the stiff posture and the guarded look.

If there was a way to get rid of those for good, he would love to know what it was. Despite his efforts to appear polite and agreeable, Syssi was intimidated by him, and he didn't know what else to do to make her comfortable.

Liar, you know perfectly well what she needs.

At his core, Kian was a simple man, with simple solutions and even simpler needs. The sexual tension between them could be relieved only by giving it an outlet.

Problem was, it was out of the question.

46

SYSSI

After Kian had finished his dinner, and Syssi had demolished most of the ice cream, they drank their cappuccinos and talked a little more, while the brothers watched one sports game after the other.

He'd told her about the drone factory he was thinking of building, and she'd told him some more about paranormal phenomena and the prevalent theories concerning it.

It had been a good conversation. She found that talking about interesting subjects and not looking directly into his eyes distracted her from Kian's mesmerizing sex appeal.

Except, she couldn't keep it up forever. She made the mistake of looking at his hands for a second too long, and her imagination went on a wild ride of what those hands could do.

A graceful and prompt retreat was in order.

"I'm sorry, I've blabbered on and on about all these weird subjects. You brought work to do, and I should leave you to it."

Kian grimaced. "I would much rather spend time listening to you talk than deal with this." He tapped his briefcase.

Syssi pushed up to her feet. "We all have to do what we have to do. I need to read at least one more article before going to sleep."

Kian caught her hand. "Bring your laptop out here. We can work together."

Yeah, right. As if she could concentrate on anything with him around. "I'm sorry, but I get easily distracted. I need to work in a quiet place."

Holding on to her hand, Kian pinned her with his intense blue eyes, and it took all she had to pull away and not melt into a puddle at his feet.

"Good night, Kian. Good night, guys." She waved at the brothers and trotted to her bedroom as fast as her high-heeled mules allowed.

Once her door was closed and locked, Syssi collapsed on the bed, face down. Kian was killing her. Except for that one look at the end before she'd gone to her room, he hadn't shown any interest in her as a woman.

He was friendly, and it could've been a pleasure talking to him if not for her out of control hormonal state.

Time for another cold shower?

No, enough of that. Mind over body.

She needed to take control and beat that attraction into submission. Another boring, badly written scientific paper was the hammer she would do it with.

Barely keeping her eyes open, Syssi read page after page of data collected from tests done on monkeys, including the indecipherable math that had been applied to the results. She was good at math, but not this kind. Many of the symbols she hadn't even seen before today. In the end, she surrendered and let her eyes close, promising herself just a few moments of rest.

"What would it be, beautiful?"

Syssi opened her eyes and looked at Kian. He was leaning against her closed door, his arms crossed over his chest. Hadn't she locked it? She thought she had.

"What would be what? I don't understand what you're talking about." She glanced at the floor, looking for her laptop. Was it still on the bed? Syssi patted around but it wasn't there. She wasn't wearing her jeans and T-shirt either.

Instead, what she had on was a white, spaghetti-strapped satin nightgown. Problem was, Syssi didn't own anything like that.

"I'm dreaming again, ain't I?"

Dream Kian nodded. "So what would it be? Do you want me to make love to you or not?"

"You know I do. You're the one who's sending mixed signals, not me."

"I'm not the kind of lover you're used to."

She snorted. "God, I hope not."

He uncrossed his arms and sauntered toward the bed. "Are you sure?" He tugged on the blanket, pulling it off her an inch at a time.

"Yes." Syssi flung it to the side, exposing herself in one fluid motion.

Kian chuckled. "Tsk, tsk. So impatient."

"You think? I've been waiting for this for far too long."

He crawled on top of her, his lips almost touching hers as he held himself up and away from her body. "I need to make it good to be worthy of such honor."

"You are and you will. You're the one I've been waiting for."

His lips were soft when he kissed her, his tongue gentle in its inquiry as he waited for her to part her lips for him. The technique was perfect, but it lacked the fiery passion she knew lurked inside of Kian.

Obviously, since she was the one creating this scenario.

The one real kiss she'd shared with him was nothing like this polite, sweet thing.

"Kiss me like you did before," she whispered.

He lifted his head and looked at her with his glowing eyes. "Remember that you asked for it."

She nodded and he smiled, a wicked twist of lips that was the furthest thing from reassuring. In fact, it sent a shiver of fear down her spine. What the hell was she doing? Giving him a free pass to do as he pleased with her?

It's a dream, silly, it's not real. Let yourself go for once and enjoy.

With one large hand Kian cradled her head, entangling his fingers in her hair and using it as an anchor to hold her in place, while his other hand tugged on the nightgown. The thin straps snapped, and he pulled it off her in one swift motion, baring her to him.

"Beautiful," he hissed through his elongated fangs.

Stupid vampire romance was putting ideas in her head. But wait, Kian had fangs in all her dreams. Was her subconscious trying to tell her something?

But what? That he was dangerous? That she was craving danger?

She wanted to ask him about it, but as she opened her mouth Kian delivered on his promise and kissed her like she wanted to be kissed. With a light tug on her hair, he took ownership of her mouth, his tongue invading, his teeth nipping.

When his other hand palmed her breast, Syssi arched into it, remembering their first dream encounter and how he'd brought her to a climax with his lips and his teeth. Before that night, she hadn't known it was in her to orgasm like that; flying up and floating on a cloud before drifting back to earth.

She'd been on the receiving end of pleasure in both dreams and hadn't gotten to touch him, to explore him. She wanted to do it now.

"I want to see you naked," she whispered as he let her take a breath.

"Curious?"

"Dying. You're the most beautiful man I've ever seen. I want to see everything."

Kian flopped to his back and lifted his arms, tucking his hands under his head. "I'm all yours, sweet girl."

Syssi rose up to her knees, and appraised the mountain of man sprawled before her. His head was almost to the headboard and his feet reached the very end of the mattress.

"What should I go for first?"

Kian lifted his head a little and looked down at the large bulge in his pants, then waggled his brows.

She giggled, wondering if the real Kian would be as playful in bed. "Don't worry, I'll get there. But first, I want to explore this magnificent chest."

Leaning over him, she started at the top button of his shirt, wanting to go just as slow as he had done the previous night in her dream, but she was too impatient and in seconds had them all undone.

On an inhale, Syssi parted the two halves.

Smooth, with only the lightest smattering of hair on his chest, Kian was built perfectly. All lean muscle without an ounce of fat to be seen. He lifted up and shrugged off the shirt then returned to his previous pose with his hands tucked under his head. Not surprisingly, his arms and shoulders were amazing too. Not bulky like a body builder's, his lean musculature was athletic like that of a swimmer or a gymnast.

She ran her palms over his torso and whispered, "You're perfect, just as I've known you would be."

Kian hissed. "You'd better hurry up. I want to be the one doing the touching, and it's killing me to keep my hands away. I'm not going to hold back much longer."

His bunched muscles and strained face confirmed how hard it was for him to lie still and let her explore. In a moment, his patience was going to get rewarded.

With a quick flick of her fingers, she popped the button on his jeans, then carefully pulled the zipper down. He was so hard and his pants were stretched so tight over his bulge that she was afraid of hurting him.

She'd been right to be careful because Kian wasn't wearing any underwear, and his shaft came into view as soon as the zipper was halfway down, then sprang free when Syssi pulled it all the way.

She gasped. His manhood was as beautiful as the rest of him. Smooth and rigid, thick and long, and she couldn't wait to taste it.

With gentle fingers, she touched him, marveling at the velvety texture covering a rigid core. Kian inhaled sharply, then hissed as her hand closed around his shaft and she lowered her head to take it into her mouth.

The ringing started just as she was about to close her lips around it.

What the hell? Was it an alarm?

No. It was the damn bedside phone.

Ugh. Syssi wanted to hurtle the bloody thing against the wall, but of course, she didn't. Nonetheless, she was going to give whoever dared call her so early a piece of her mind.

"Who is it?" she barked.

"Good morning, beautiful. I'm ordering breakfast. What would you like?" Kian sounded awfully cheerful for such an ungodly hour.

With wicked satisfaction she thought that he wouldn't be as happy if he knew that his phone call had just cost him a blow job. The other him, but still.

"It's six in the morning, Kian."

"I'm sorry, is it too early for you?"

He didn't sound sorry at all.

"Coffee." She hung up and plopped back on the bed.

Naturally, she wasn't naked, she was still wearing the jeans and the T-shirt, and the laptop was open on the other side of the bed. The only reminder she had of the dream was another pair of wet panties.

So annoying. Syssi grabbed a pillow and shoved it over her face to muffle a frustrated groan.

47

KIAN

"How long are we going to be stuck here?" Anandur asked after they'd finished their breakfast.

More than two hours had passed since Kian had woken Syssi up, but she was still a no-show. She was either mad at him for waking her up so early and had decided to stay in her room, or she had gone back to sleep.

"I'll try to convince her to come home with me today."

Anandur scratched his beard. "Do you think it's smart to take her to the keep?"

"No, but I can't spare even one of you to guard her. We don't have enough men." It was true, keeping them here because he was obsessed with the girl wasn't fair to the guys. They had other things to do, and at a time like this the keep's occupants needed its few Guardians to be there at all times. But that wasn't the only reason.

"Thrall her. It's quicker," Brundar suggested.

Maybe he should.

"I'm going to knock on her door." Anandur wiped his mouth with a napkin and pushed his chair back.

Not a bad idea. If she was still mad over the wake-up call, Kian preferred for Anandur to get hit with the brunt of her ire.

The Guardian rapped his knuckles on her door. "Syssi, it's time to get up."

There was a muffled, "Shit," and then a patter of small feet rushing to the door. She opened it a crack, hiding her lower half behind the door, and cranked her neck to look at Anandur. "God, you're tall." She shook a head of mussed hair that was sticking out in all directions. "I'm sorry, I overslept. I'll be out in ten minutes tops."

"It's okay. Take your time, there is no hurry."

"Thank you." She closed her door.

Anandur came back to the dining table and sat across from Kian. "She is such a cute little thing."

The seemingly innocent remark had Kian seeing red. "Keep your opinions to yourself."

A red brow lifted almost to the guy's hairline. "Someone woke up grumpy this morning."

Kian ignored him and signaled an end to the exchange by lifting the *Wall Street Journal* and hiding behind it. The thing was that Anandur was right. Syssi was adorable and sexy as hell.

There had been a good reason for him calling her up when he had. She must've been dreaming something naughty because he'd been awakened by the scent of her arousal.

Sometime around one in the morning, the brothers had retired to the other bedroom. Kian had stayed up to catch up on his work, going over the files he'd brought with him until the words had started to blur.

Lying down on the couch to catch a little shut-eye, he'd been alone in the living room when the enticing scent had hit his system. It had been a struggle not to go to her and take care of her need, and he'd been thankful for the two Guardians sleeping in the other room. Their presence had helped rein in his libido.

That didn't mean, though, that he would've allowed them to get a whiff of what belonged to him alone.

Waking her up had been the first thing he had done, so no more of the aroma would filter into the living room. Next, he'd opened every window, and lastly, he'd ordered breakfast, hoping that the scents of baked goods and freshly brewed coffee would mask the last traces of her aroma.

As promised, Syssi emerged from her room ten minutes later.

"I'm so sorry to have kept you all waiting. I fell asleep."

"No worries. Here, I have fresh coffee for you." Kian gestured to the dining table where he had saved a thermal carafe filled to the brim for her. It had been delivered together with their breakfast, but the container it was in would have kept it warm. Something to eat was another matter. What he'd ordered could've fed six people, but had been barely enough for the two Guardians.

Syssi sat across from him, avoiding his eyes. Was it about the dream? Or was she embarrassed about keeping them waiting?

He poured her a cup. "What would you like to eat?" He handed it to her.

"I'm not hungry yet, thank you." She took the cup and he handed her the container of assorted sweeteners.

"Did you sleep well?" He couldn't help asking.

Her head shot up and she looked at him with suspicious eyes. "Very well. How about you?"

He stretched and pretended to grimace in discomfort. "Not at all. I've worked until late, and when I finally lay down, I discovered that the couch is not comfortable." He was lying through his teeth. The couch was perfectly fine. Granted, not as good as his bed at home, but not as bad as he'd made it sound.

"Why didn't you go home? Two men to guard me are more than enough. You could've been sleeping comfortably in your own bed."

Fuck, this didn't work. He needed another angle. Time to take off the kid gloves.

But wait? Did he really want Syssi to come home with him? Alone with her in his penthouse, there would be nothing to stop him from taking her. Other than his self-respect, that is, and Kian had a feeling that it would not be enough.

On the other hand, without her near him, he wouldn't be able to do shit, as he'd proven to himself yesterday.

This was so beyond fucked up.

It was all Amanda's fault. If not for her matchmaking, he wouldn't be in such a bind. Except, he knew it wasn't true. Even if Amanda had never mentioned Syssi to him, he would not have reacted to her any differently once he'd met her.

He would need to think of a solution, but until then Syssi had to come home with him. A financial empire was at stake.

"We could've all been sleeping more comfortably. Anandur and Brundar in their own apartment, and you in a perfectly appointed guest room that is even nicer than the one in this suite. Not to mention the amount of money we could've saved." He was such a manipulator. Kian couldn't care less about the money, but he knew Syssi did. It was a low blow, hitting her where he knew it would hurt, but she'd left him no choice.

With a sigh, she nodded. "You're right. If you'd agreed to drop me at my brother's as I've asked, you would have saved a fortune."

Stubborn woman. This wasn't the answer he was anticipating.

"As I've explained before, your brother's place is not safe. You would be putting both of you in danger by staying with him." That at least was true.

Syssi lifted her hands in defeat. "You win. I give up. Let's go to your place."

Hallelujah.

48

SYSSI

Once again Syssi was about to enter Kian's penthouse, unsure about the wisdom of the move and feeling awkward. Not that she had a choice. The only option left to her was to buy an airline ticket and join her parents in Africa. There was little chance the fanatics would follow her all the way there.

Except, it was akin to curing a headache by chopping off the head. Too extreme a solution for the situation. In a few days, they would know if those crazies had made a move to capture her or Michael, and if they didn't, she could go back home to her old life.

Fearing her own attraction to Kian was not good enough reason to flee all the way to the other side of the world. Besides, she hated heat and humidity, mosquitoes and God knew what other bugs. How her mother was tolerating it was beyond her.

"Are you hungry yet?" Kian asked the moment they stepped inside.

"Yes, a little."

"Good. I'll ask Okidu to serve us brunch."

It seemed that the guy liked to feed her. Which must have meant that he cared at least a little. Or maybe not. Maybe he was just being hospitable. She really didn't know what to think anymore.

Kian was unlike any other guy she'd ever met, and not just because he was leagues above anyone she knew. The guy was full of contradictions. At times she'd felt certain he was going to make a move, kiss her again or tell her something that would indicate he was interested. At others she was convinced she'd imagined it, nothing but wishful thinking making her see interest where there had been none. Because there was no way a guy like him would go for a girl like her. His normal fare was probably celebrities, movie stars and models, not everyday people like boring lab assistants or architect's interns.

But then she remembered that one kiss, the real one, and the way he'd looked at her. Syssi shook her head. She was driving herself nuts. The best thing to do was to let things unfold and see where they led.

The tricky part would be not to let herself fall for the guy, not any more than she already had. Not that her infatuation with Kian meant that she was falling in love with him. She needed to keep telling herself that.

Play it cool and guard her heart.

Easy.

Right.

Same as yesterday, Okidu served their brunch in Kian's formal dining room. Two people sitting at a table large enough for eighteen was awkward in itself, and not having Brundar or Anandur as buffers didn't help either. And to top it off, she tended to overeat when nervous, which meant that she attacked the delicious meal as if she hadn't seen food in a week.

When she was done, Syssi dabbed at her mouth with a napkin, attempting to look ladylike despite the way she'd gobbled up everything on her plate. The truth was that it had been delicious, and remarkably it had also all been vegetarian. Glancing at her plate, she realized that there was nothing left but a few crumbs from the delicious eggplant sandwich. If no one were watching, she would've picked those up too and stuffed them in her mouth.

But someone was.

Syssi could feel Kian's eyes on her even without looking at him.

When Okidu came in with the coffee, she was granted a few moments' reprieve, but once he left, the silence between them felt like a vacuum begging to be filled.

With nervous fingers, Syssi folded and refolded her napkin, then braved a quick glance at Kian.

Her breath hitched.

Reclining in his chair and sipping on his coffee, he was watching her raptly. Not the casual friendly look from before, but one that was appraising and unnerving.

Averting her gaze, she cleared her throat. "Thank you for a wonderful meal. I've noticed, though, that everything was made with vegetables and mushrooms. You didn't order any meat dishes for yourself when we ate out either. Are you a vegetarian? Same as Amanda?"

Kind of lame. She'd already determined he was a vegan yesterday, but it was the best she could come up with under his unnerving stare.

"It's a healthier way to eat, not to mention kinder. I think most of us are instinctively reluctant to kill a living creature. If people had to actually hunt and kill their own food, I'm sure many would choose not to—not unless they had no choice because there was nothing else. I stay away from all animal products as much as I can, although when the alternative is starving, well... self-preservation and all that. Amanda tries, but you know her, she has to have her Brie or goat cheese from time to time." He smiled a tight-lipped smile.

Syssi had to agree. Amanda hated rules. Her boss was a rebel.

"Yes, I know what you mean. What puzzles me though, is your comment about eating meat as an alternative to starving. Have you ever been in such a situation?" It took deliberate effort, but Syssi finally let go of the napkin, placing it beside her plate.

"There were times when there was nothing else, when I ran out of provisions, out in the wilderness or on a trek at some remote location. Hunting and killing for food was my only way to survive.

Yeah, I've been in situations like that." He shrugged as if it was of no consequence, and yet, his sharp expression told a different story.

"Are you into the whole extreme-survival-camping thing? Lately, whenever I go channel surfing, I stumble upon one of those reality shows. The theme has become very popular. Obviously, the shows are staged, but I assume that for some it's a real form of recreation."

Kian didn't strike her as the type. He embodied the sophisticated, worldly CEO, not an extreme survivalist. And yet, she could sense that just under the surface there was something wild lurking inside him. Maybe he had served in the armed forces at some point, a commando unit like Andrew's. Except, he was too young to have done both.

"No, for me it wasn't a recreational choice. Let's just say there were times in my life when I was forced to fend for myself in a hostile environment." There was a finality in his grave tone that suggested he wouldn't appreciate any further questions on the subject.

Syssi figured he couldn't talk about it, or wasn't allowed—

Like Andrew.

Yep, the little he had said sounded like Special Ops. "I admire your ability to do so. If left alone in the wild, I would probably become the food. I have no survival skills whatsoever. No sense of direction either. I would be lost and defenseless." Syssi shivered, remembering the nightmare and her desperate run through the woods with the demon-wolves snarling at her heels.

Unbidden, images of what had followed slammed into her mind, sending a powerful flash of arousal through her. Erupting in her core, it spread up through her chest all the way to the nerve endings of her fingertips, making them tingle as if zapped with an electric current.

Oh, God, please, let it stop!

God didn't answer her prayer. If anyone did, it must've been the devil. Because following that first crack, the floodgates burst open, and every erotic moment she'd spent with Kian in her dreams rushed through her mind like a fast-forwarded movie.

She tried to stop the moan from escaping her throat, but despite her efforts a quiet whimper managed to get away. Mortified, Syssi blushed and looked down, desperately hoping Kian would attribute that embarrassing sound to her fear of getting lost in the wild.

49

KIAN

Kian's body had reacted before his mind had time to process the torrent of sexual triggers slamming into him and knocking his breath out with the force of a battering ram.

Kind of like the one that had popped behind his zipper.

What the hell had just happened?

What had brought on that tortured moan? And why was Syssi suddenly emitting such a strong scent of arousal tinted by fear? It was nothing like the soft kind he'd scented this morning. This was powerful. Overwhelming. A trigger he couldn't resist.

It wasn't as if Kian was a stranger to that particular combination. Sensing his predatory nature on a visceral level, most females responded to him that way; their lust and their apprehension combining to create one heady aphrodisiac.

His favorite.

But coming from sweet shy Syssi that explosive mixture fueled his lust like nothing before.

And as it grew stronger, his control grew weaker.

Taking over, the predator in him overpowered the thin layer of civilized behavior he struggled to maintain. Kian pounced. In one quick move, he had Syssi on his lap, trapped there in the cage of his arms.

Taken by surprise, she squeaked.

She must've felt his cock swell and twitch under her butt because her eyes widened and her lips parted on a sharp inhale, the flush on her cheeks climbing along with her arousal.

"You see, Syssi. If you were mine, I would take care of you, defend you, provide for you. You would never be left alone to fend for yourself. The only wild beast to fear would be me."

Even to his own ears, he sounded like a Neanderthal, but every word was true. All that was male about him craved this. He wanted to be everything to her, the only one to take care of her in every possible way, the only one she would ever want or need.

Searching his face, Syssi smiled a little, probably thinking he was only teasing. But as she looked into his eyes, sensing the kind of animal she was trapped by, her smile faltered.

With his palm closing gently around the back of her neck, he held her gaze as he drew closer to her mouth, slowly, deliberately, prolonging her breathless anticipation until she was panting with it.

Abruptly, he tightened his grip on her nape and closed the remaining distance between them, striking her soft lips with an almost bruising ferocity.

Syssi melted into the kiss, pressing herself against him, surrendering to his invading and probing tongue, flicking it and sucking it in.

So damn good.

As he withdrew, breathless, she followed, licking his lips and pressing her own little tongue into his mouth.

Reluctantly, he refused her entry.

By now, his fangs had fully descended, following the rest of his body in preparation for what it assumed was coming.

He couldn't allow her to find out that he wasn't who or rather what she thought he was. Not yet, anyway.

Entangling his fingers in her hair, he pulled her head back and nipped her bottom lip in warning, then licked it to soothe the small pain away.

"No, sweet girl, I can't have you do that. I need to be in charge when we are together like that." He tried to mask the implied command with gentle words and a soothing tone, then kissed her again, softly, tenderly—teasing, testing her compliance.

50

SYSSI

Oh, God...

Syssi wanted, needed to intensify the kiss, but she needed to please Kian even more. Something in her craved his dominance, wanted to please him, wanted him to be in charge of her pleasure.

It turned her on like nothing had ever done before.

She was so aroused, her hardened nipples felt like they were pushing against her lacy bra and threatening to poke holes through the sheer fabric.

Mortified, she suspected Kian could feel not only her hard little nubs pressing against his chest but the wetness soaking through her stretchy pants as well. There was no way the scrap of her lacy panties could absorb all of what her arousal was pouring forth. Panting, she dipped her head, burrowing her forehead into his chest to hide her flaming hot cheeks.

A moment later, she sucked in a fortifying breath and tried to push off to get up, but he held her down, returning her head to his chest and stroking her hair as he leaned and kissed the top of it.

"Shh... It's okay, sweet girl. I've got you. I love how you respond to me. It's perfect, and it turns me on so much I'm afraid my zipper is not going to hold." Stroking her hair and running slow circles on her lower back, he waited for her to regain her composure.

On the one hand, she was even more embarrassed realizing Kian must've sensed how disturbed she was by her own reaction. But on the other, she appreciated his effort to ease her discomfort by admitting he was just as affected as she was.

Feeling the evidence of his arousal prod her butt, she chuckled and looked up hesitantly, not sure if Kian was joking or not.

His expression surprised her.

He regarded her as if she was special, precious, and not the disgrace to the feminist movement she'd felt like a moment ago.

Syssi didn't know what to say or how to react. Luckily, she didn't have to; his phone chimed, disrupting the sexually charged atmosphere.

Shifting his weight and wiggling to get the device out of his pants pocket, he kept his hold on her, delivering a quick peck to her forehead before answering the call. "Don't go anywhere," he whispered while covering the mic with his thumb.

As if she could.

With his hand drawing small circles on her back, and his hard muscular chest tempting her to rest her cheek on it, Kian's warmth and alluring smell lulled her into a hazy, dreamy state.

She heard him and the other guy talk, but the words didn't register.

The maelstrom of emotions and cravings were all new and uncharted territory for her. She had met the man just a few days ago for goodness' sake, and already she was dreaming about him, wanting him, needing him with an intensity bordering on desperation.

But what puzzled her even more was that despite his previous efforts to appear uninterested, he seemed to feel the same way about her. Was this crazy attraction the work of wild pheromones on steroids? Or was there more to it?

Words like destiny and fate floated through her mind, but she waved them away. Only fools and hopeless romantics believed in those.

Syssi didn't count herself as either.

Play it cool. Guard your heart.

Kian sighed as he returned the phone to his pocket. "As much as I hate to, I have to take care of a potentially combustible situation. Though believe me, I would've much preferred to stay here and stoke this one." Smiling suggestively, he quickly kissed her lips and lifted her off his lap.

"Make yourself at home. Okidu will show you around and help you get settled. Ask him for anything you need. I'll be back as soon as I can." He turned to leave.

"Wait. I don't think it's a good idea, Kian. I understand why I can't stay with Andrew, but I can join my parents in Africa. I'm sure I'll be safe there."

Moving into Kian's penthouse, even temporarily, would be a mistake. With the electrified currents sparking between them they might get carried away into doing something they would both later regret, albeit for different reasons. Hers would be a broken heart, his would be regret over breaking it.

Kian turned back and got in her face. With only scant inches between them, he took hold of her chin, tilting her head so she was forced to gaze into his hard eyes.

"You're not going anywhere. You're mine to protect, mine to take care of, and this place has the best security money and loyalty can buy. I will not trust anyone and anyplace else with your safety. So make yourself at home."

That predatory look that had made her heart flutter before was back, but as he smiled a tight-lipped smile, it transformed into something that was between sinister and lascivious. "We both know where this is heading, so why go through the pretense, Syssi? You might as well put your stuff in my bedroom. Anything else will be an exercise in futility."

Syssi tried to escape his hold and look away, but he wouldn't let go of her chin, forcing her to look into his eyes.

What a fool she'd been. The illusion she'd created in her mind, was just that, an illusion. The real Kian was a caveman, a big gorilla who thumped his chest and proclaimed all kinds of male bullshit.

Fueled by her deep disappointment in him, she felt her discomfort turn into anger. The polite, considerate guy she had gotten to know was gone, and in his place was this rude, presumptuous jerk who thought he could order her around. Worse, who was under the impression she would be grateful he invited her to share his bed just because he was a great kisser.

The guy sure had an inflated ego, probably fueled by numerous too-easy conquests. Not that she showed a lot of resistance, or any for that matter.

The thought made her absolutely furious, mostly with herself.

That's it, Syssi. For the first time in your life, you earned the official title of slut.

As much as she craved him, she was not about to become another notch on his belt.

"You may be right. I'm not going to deny this thing between us, but you offend me by presuming I'm the kind of woman who jumps into bed with someone she just met. I'm grateful for your concern for my safety, but if I'm not leaving for Africa, I would at least appreciate having a room of my own." Unflinching under the intensity of his gaze, she continued. "Face it, Kian, this whole situation is temporary, and in a day or two I'll be back at my own place—it's not like I'm moving in permanently. So please, don't make it harder for me than it already is."

It was so unlike her to react so strongly. She hated heated confrontations and tried to avoid them at all costs. Walking away was more her style. Surprisingly, though, Syssi didn't feel as shaky or disturbed by this as she normally would.

For some reason, she trusted Kian to respect her wishes. And even though she was still angry, venting some of it helped her realize that although crude, Kian hadn't meant offense by his words. Like many guys, his communication skills were not that great.

But she needed to make a stand, else he would walk all over her.

His expression softened, and he let go of her chin to rake his fingers through his disheveled hair. "Forgive me, you're right. Whatever makes you comfortable is fine with me." He looked at her apologetically. "I wish I could be more charming and debonair for you, or even just patient, but that's not who I am. A rough around the edges, insensitive jerk, that's more my style." He smiled a little, still looking contrite.

Syssi felt relieved beyond words that her original assessment of him had been right. Kian was a good guy. A little intense, a little crude, but his intentions were not dishonorable. Well, maybe a little. But that wasn't a big deal. He was, after all, only a man.

With composure that surprised her, she smiled. "Now you're just fishing for compliments," she said to let him know that they were still okay. "I like you, Kian, just the way you are. I'll take blunt and honest over charming and deceitful any day, but that doesn't mean I'll tolerate it when you behave like a jerk." She rose on tiptoes and kissed his lips lightly. "Go, do whatever you need to do, I'll be fine." She grabbed his elbow to turn him around, and when he did, slapped his butt to send him on his way.

"Getting frisky, are we?" He laughed as he walked out.

"Just payback, smooth talker," she called after him.

So that was it.

There was no going back. She'd admitted to Kian that she liked him, basically giving him a green light. Perhaps not for a quick seduction, she would make him work for it because he wouldn't appreciate her otherwise, but she was finally ready to step outside her comfort zone.

To live, really live and not just go through the motions, she needed to start taking risks. Kian was a big one, but he was certainly worth it. Because if she gambled and won, it would be like winning first prize in the lottery of life.

Problem was, she had no idea what her odds were like. The stakes were high, that was for sure. Because if she lost, it would destroy her.

51

KIAN

On his way out, Kian chuckled and shook his head.

Syssi defied characterization. How refreshing—a real person and not a facsimile of some preconceived set of attributes. She was different, and he liked that she didn't fit into any standard mold: shy and reserved in some situations, hot and wild in others. Taking her pleasure in yielding sexually, asserting her will otherwise.

She certainly stood up to him, as not many would, and even fewer could.

Reflecting on her spike of arousal at his little show of dominance, and how it had unsettled her, he suspected it had been the first time she'd experienced anything of that nature.

Syssi had no idea what to make of it, or how perfect he'd found her response to be. And although it had been only a tiny taste, Kian hoped to be the first and the only one she would ever explore this further with. Regardless of how far she would let it go, he would love anything she would allow. He would go slow, introducing her to the pleasures of submission one little step at a time, careful not to overwhelm her or frighten her.

A little fear was part of the game, but just a little. She needed to learn to trust him; to feel safe letting go with him.

Wait! Whoa... what was he thinking? There was no future for them.

And what a pity that was.

The more time he spent with Syssi, the more he realized how perfect she was for him. She was exactly what he wanted, just as Amanda had predicted he would, her courage to be honest and true to herself impressing him above all.

In contrast, Kian felt like a scumbag. A deceitful jerk. And the biggest joke was that she believed him to be an honest guy.

Trouble was, there was no way for him to come clean and tell her the truth, about anything really.

And that didn't sit well with him at all.

It had been a mistake—a momentary lapse of reason, a weakness—to start with Syssi something that could never be. He must've been possessed when he'd blurted that nonsense about her moving into his bedroom.

What the hell had gotten into him?

She didn't deserve to be talked to like that. Syssi was an amazing woman: smart, sweet, beautiful. In a few days, though, she'd go back to her old life, and he would have no choice but to scrub her memories once again.

This time for good.

For his own sanity, he needed to keep his distance.

Fuck, he was deluding himself if he thought he could let her go. He'd become obsessed with her, needing her to be near him to function.

He was so screwed. What the hell was he going to do?

I'm an idiot for starting this in the first place.

And it wasn't as if he hadn't known better.

What had he been thinking? That he would use her and then get rid of her like all the others?

Even if he were willing to sink that low, let his honor and self-respect go to hell, fate or perhaps his bloody hormones had taken the choice out of his hands. For some inexplicable reason, he needed her worse than a drug addict needed his next fix.

Perhaps he should book that trip to Scotland he'd been putting off forever. He hadn't seen Sari and the rest of the gang in ages. But more to the point, it would take his mind off a certain sweet blond that was threatening to ruin what had taken him nearly two thousand years to achieve: Letting go of an impossible dream and accepting a fate of an endless, lonely life.

With a sigh, Kian stepped into the elevator and glanced at himself in the mirror. He looked miserable, tortured. If only he could talk to someone about this messed up situation, get some good advice, find a way to be with Syssi without ruining her life or his.

The trip to Scotland sounded like a good idea in theory, but the truth was that he didn't have time for that. He was drowning in work, and taking even a few hours off required careful planning. Taking a trip to see family was out of the question, while getting any work done without Syssi around seemed impossible too.

Man, he needed help.

Pulling out his phone, he called the last person who he thought could do that.

"Hello, Kian," Amanda answered cheerfully.

"Where are you?"

"Having my nails done."

That would explain the Vietnamese he heard in the background. "When are you coming back?"

"Why? What do you need?"

Kian raked his fingers through his hair. "Could you invite Syssi to stay at your place?"

"Why? What have you done to her?" Amanda's tone had turned accusatory.

"Nothing. Yet. That's why I need you to take her away from me. She is driving me crazy. I can't be with her and I can't be without her. Maybe staying across the vestibule in your place will be a good compromise."

"Kian, Kian, Kian. Stop being such a sanctimonious prick and just have sex with the girl already. Be gentle, though. It has been a very long time for her."

"You have absolutely no morals, Amanda. And you claim to care for Syssi."

"I do, you idiot, and I care for you too. That's why I want you two to be together. You need each other."

"She is a human, Amanda. And the chances of her being a Dormant are nonexistent."

"You don't know that. You're just terrified of taking a chance. Stop being such a coward and take a risk. Live!"

"You're not helping."

"The hell, I'm not. I swear, if you don't do it, I'm going to involve Mother."

"You're bluffing."

"Try me!" She hung up.

Fucking hell.

Kian hurled the phone at the mirror, watching the device bounce off and land on the floor. Goddamned Shai had gotten him an indestructible cover after he'd pulverized the last one.

Now he had nothing to break. Unless he used his head. Banging it until it bled sounded like a plan. Maybe something would shift inside and he could go back to the way he'd been before.

With a sigh, Kian leaned his forehead against the cool glass. As much as he hated to admit it, Amanda wasn't completely wrong.

He wasn't living. He was functioning.

It dawned on him then that the only times he'd felt alive lately had been with Syssi.

Perhaps he needed to reevaluate his position. Take a chance. Maybe Syssi would turn out to be a Dormant after all, making him the happiest male on the planet.

He would never know unless he tried.

As the saying went, "Nothing ventured, nothing gained." He had to take a risk.

Problem was, unbeknownst to Syssi, she would be risking more than he, and unlike his sister, Kian believed that to do so was not only dishonorable but despicable.

52

AMANDA

With a smirk, Amanda slipped the phone into her purse and leaned back.

"What you happy for?" the nail salon owner asked. Holding Amanda's hand and painting one of her long nails with bright red nail polish, she looked at her expectantly. There was nothing these hardworking women loved more than a juicy piece of gossip.

"I found my brother his future wife. He fought me hard on this, didn't want to even meet her."

The woman frowned. "Why? She ugly?"

"She is beautiful, and smart, and sweet. He doesn't know how lucky he is."

The woman harrumphed. "Men are stupid. You good sister, find him good wife."

"I know."

"But if he not want see her, why you smile?"

"I had a little help from Lady Luck, and now my stubborn brother has no choice but to spend time with her."

She should send a gift basket to the Doomer headquarters, thanking them for helping her matchmaking plans along. Inadvertently, by bringing Syssi and Kian together, they might have saved their enemy clan's future. Except, not all of it had been good. The clan had lost Mark in the process.

Amanda sighed. They hadn't been tight, but she loved her nephew and was going to miss him dearly.

The Fates worked in mysterious ways, but they always demanded a sacrifice for bestowing their gifts. Had they taken his life in exchange for securing the clan's future?

It was a horrible thought to mull over, and therefore Amanda got rid of it as soon as it flitted through her mind.

The old woman smiled, her eyes sparkling with excitement. "You think he fall in love?"

"I'm sure of it."

The question wasn't whether they would fall in love with each other, but whether Syssi was a Dormant who Kian could turn into a near-immortal like them.

Amanda had a strong feeling that she was, but there was always a possibility that she might be wrong. It was a frightening prospect. Kian and Syssi's hearts were on the line. But there was no other way. The future of the clan depended on the success of this experiment.

The salon owner put the nail polish away and leaned back in her chair. "Good Karma for you. You do good, you get good karma. You do bad, you get bad karma. You find good woman for your brother, karma find good man for you. This how it work."

"You're sure about it?"

"I know it. Every day I see it. Like I told my grandson. If you nice, it come back to you twice."

Not really.

Sometimes the Fates were cruel for no good reason. Amanda hadn't done anything to deserve the tragedy that had befallen her all those years ago. At the time, her pain and her anger had been so great that she would've destroyed the world and everyone in it--the good with the bad. Fortunately, she wasn't an omnipotent being, and the only one she'd ended up destroying was herself.

On that terrible day almost two centuries ago, the old Amanda had ceased to exist, and the new Amanda who'd emerged from her ashes was a made up person with an impenetrable shield around her heart.

Fear, however, still managed to percolate through the tiniest of cracks in her protective layers.

What if the cruel fates weren't done with her yet?

What else would they take away from her?

Amanda was almost expecting it. This time, though, she was prepared. The walls she'd worked so hard on building around her heart would save it from breaking again.

TURN THE PAGE TO READ AN EXCERPT FROM

DARK STRANGER REVEALED

DARK STRANGER REVEALED

Syssi's fingertips were starting to prune.

As fun as the spa was, it was time to get out. Turning the whirlpool off, she stepped out of the tub and wrapped herself in one of the plush towels stacked by its side.

All during her soak, Kian's words from earlier had been playing over and over in her mind, providing a background soundtrack to the vivid images they were painting.

On one hand, all these new and intense sensations electrified her. It was like discovering a whole new world of pleasure she had never known existed. It was exhilarating. On the other hand, she was afraid that once she had gotten a taste for how it could be, she would do just about anything to get more of it.

Before, she had never understood what drove people to indulge in careless sex, despite the potential utter devastation it entailed. Unwelcome pregnancies, ruined marriages, family feuds, wars... Literature painted an abundance of catastrophic scenarios Syssi had used to believe were mostly fictional. After all, what was so difficult about keeping your pants on?

But now, as need gnawed at her like a hungry beast, she understood.

Standing on the cold marble and looking out the window at the dark sky, she grew nervous. Kian would be back soon. And then what? Was she strong enough to say no to him, or at least not yet? Or was she going to surrender to her longing and have reckless sex with a man she barely knew but wanted desperately?

Toweling the moisture off with the excessive vigor of her rising frustration, she questioned her indecision. What was really the point of delaying the inevitable? If not tonight, then the next, or the one after that. If Kian still wanted her, that is. He might have concluded that she was too much trouble, and go for the easy and available.

Everyone around her was talking about hookups and booty calls, instead of dates and relationships. People treated sex as casually as going to the movies or out for a drink. In this uninspiring, emotionally disconnected landscape, the pursuit of sexual gratification was the norm, and the rare relationship an exception. An oddity.

Still, she wondered if all these people were deluding themselves into accepting this sorry state of affairs as gratifying. Perhaps they were just desperately reaching out for any kind of connection, hoping something real would sprout from all that carnality.

She couldn't see herself living that way. Maybe she was old-fashioned, or just naive, but she needed at least the illusion of a relationship—if not the real thing—to get all hot and sweaty with a guy.

Oh, but Kian…

He was like an addiction, an obsession, calling to her, drawing her in like a moth to a flame. She knew she was going to burn, but at this point she didn't care.

She was going to do it, had to…

Catching her panicky reflection staring back at her from the mist-covered mirror, her hand flew to her chest.

Oh, God! She wasn't ready!

It had been so long since her last time, Syssi felt like a virgin all over again; nervous, insecure, frightened. So okay, it probably wasn't going to hurt like the first time had—thank heavens for small favors—but she felt anxious nonetheless.

What if she fell short of Kian's expectations, what if he found her unexciting... lacking...

What if, what if... stop it! She ordered the self-disparaging internal monolog to cease.

Rubbing lotion onto her hands, she decided a whole body rub would help with her jitters. Squirting a generous dollop of the stuff, she slathered it all over, watching her skin turn slick and soft.

She took a little longer than necessary to work it into the soft skin of her breasts, running her thumbs over her sensitive nipples and tweaking them lightly till they tightened into hard little knobs. It felt nice, but didn't come close to the kind of fire Kian's touch had ignited in her dream.

Would reality be as amazing as that fantasy? How would his hands feel? His lips? She closed her eyes, imagining, and as the slow simmer of arousal flared into searing heat, a quiet moan escaped her throat.

What am I doing? Syssi sneaked an embarrassed glance at the mirror as if catching herself red handed. Grimacing, she shook her head; how pathetic was it for someone her age to be so reserved. After all, she was by herself with no one to judge her one way or the other, but she still felt uncomfortable touching herself with the lights on and in the vicinity of a mirror.

With a sigh, she wiped her moist hands on the towel and began blow-drying her hair. Once she was done, she was ready to head out when a faint bang sounded from behind the closed door.

Cautiously, she opened it a crack.

It was dark, and coming from the brightly illuminated bathroom, it took a moment for her pupils to dilate enough to make out the large shape lying on her bed. As her eyes fully adjusted to the dim light, Kian's handsome but brooding features became clear.

He looks like the big bad wolf about to devour Little Red Riding Hood... Me. Syssi chuckled. Apparently, today was a fairy-tale day.

First Goldilocks and the Three Bears, then Little Red Riding Hood, what next? Cinderella, or Beauty and the Beast?

Syssi leaned toward the second one. As gorgeous as Kian was, she had a feeling that he was more of a beast than a prince.

"Oh, my! What a big, strong body you have, Grandma!" Purring seductively, she sauntered into the room. But as Kian's expression turned from brooding to menacing, she chickened out, and cursing her inability to put a muzzle on her stupid mischievous streak, she turned to flee into the walk-in closet.

"All the better to pounce on you, my dear!" Kian took to the role play with gusto, and leaping off the bed with the swiftness and grace of a jungle cat caught her from behind before she managed to reach the closet. Holding her back against his chest, he lifted her up.

She jackknifed, kicking her legs and trying to get away while laughing nervously and clawing at the strong fingers clutching hers on the towel.

It was futile.

In one swift move he swung and tossed her on the bed, then pounced, looming above her as he caged her between his thighs and outstretched arms. Still panting from the laughter and exertion of her failed escape attempt, she couldn't fill her lungs.

Or maybe her shortness of breath had nothing to do with exertion and everything to do with Kian. The long strands of his wavy hair falling around his angular features, he was insanely beautiful…

And terrifying.

There was no humor in that hard beauty, only hunger.

Caught in the intense glow of Kian's eyes, she felt trapped like a deer in the headlights of an oncoming car. Fear trickled down her spine in liquid drops of fire that pooled at her core, wetting the insides of her naked thighs.

He caressed her cheek then kissed the hollow of her neck, gently soothing her before bringing his palm to rest over her fisted hand. "Let go of the towel, Syssi," he whispered. Except, coming through his clenched teeth, his words sounded hissed, rough and demanding.

Not ready to let go yet, Syssi shook her head.

He kept at it, stroking her straining knuckles with his thumb, until gently, one at a time, she let him pry her fingers open.

Gazing into his hungry eyes, she was still apprehensive but didn't resist when he entwined their fingers and stretched her arms over her head, holding them there as he brought his face down to shower her with featherlight kisses.

He kissed her eyelids, her eyebrows, her cheeks, her nose, the hollows at the sides of her neck. He kept kissing her like that until she began to relax, her body growing slack. Only then, he released his hold on her hands and leaned back on his haunches to stare hungrily at her body.

Under Kian's searing gaze, laid out like a bounty before him, Syssi stretched out ready to be unveiled. There were no more thoughts, no more hesitation, only a burning desire.

Slowly, carefully, as if unwrapping a precious gift, Kian peeled away one side of the towel and then the other.

"Damn! Just look at you… perfection." He swallowed, gazing at her with an expression full of awe, as if he'd never seen a woman as beautiful as her. No one had ever looked at her like that. She basked, for the first time in her life feeling truly desired. And not just by any man, by Kian. The nearest male approximation of a god.

As his eyes lingered on her breasts, watching them heave with her shallow, panting breaths, Syssi felt her nipples stiffen. And when his tongue darted to his lip, her breath caught as she imagined him licking, sucking. Instead, he continued his tour of her body, his eyes traveling down until coming to a halt at her bare mound.

"Beautiful. All of you." He cupped her center.

With a strangled moan, her lids dropped over her eyes.

"Perfect," he whispered, bending to lightly kiss one turgid peak.

"Magnificent." He kissed the other, then waited until she opened her eyes and looked at him.

"I want you so badly, I'm going to go up in flames if you won't have me," he breathed. Running his hands along her outstretched arms, he reached her hands and entangled their fingers. His face a scant inch from hers, he searched her wide open eyes.

Gazing up at his beautiful face, she saw her own raging need reflected in his eyes. "I want you, Kian, so much that it hurts," she whispered.

It was a terrifying thing to admit, and the only reason she'd mustered enough courage to speak the truth, was the way he was looking at her. There was no way he was faking it. Kian's soul was shining through his eyes, and he was baring himself to her just as much as she was baring herself to him.

He closed his eyes in relief, but only for a brief moment. Then with a measuring look, he asked again. "Are you sure?"

She must've seemed shell-shocked to him, lying underneath his big body with her eyes opened wide, panting.

And in truth, she was.

Still, she needed this like she needed to take her next breath.

"I need you," she whispered.

The change in his expression was lightning fast. Sure of his welcome, Kian's last vestiges of restraint shattered, and he descended upon her like a hungry beast; smashing her lips with his mouth, thrusting his tongue in and out, and growling as he nipped at her lips.

Swept in the torrent of his ferocity, Syssi arched her back, aching to feel the length of his body pressed against hers—to feel his weight on top of her.

Except, he remained propped on his shins, his bowed arms supporting the weight of his chest, their bodies barely touching.

But with her mouth under attack and her arms pinned, there was little she could do about it besides moan and whimper.

Kian's mouth trailed south, kissing and nipping every spot

along her jawline and down her neck to her collarbone, then licking and kissing the small hurts away.

Syssi panted in breathless anticipation, her painfully stiff nipples desperate for his hands, his lips…

"Please…," she whispered, her need stronger than her pride.

He lifted his head, the hunger in his eyes belying his teasing mouth. "Tell me what you need, beautiful." He let go of one of her hands to caress her cheek, extending his thumb to rub over her swollen lips before pressing it into her mouth.

She sucked it in, swirling her tongue around it until he pulled it out to rub the moisture over her dry lips.

With the hand he had freed, she cupped Kian's lightly stubbled cheek, letting the last of her shields drop and allowing him to see in her unguarded expression all of the desire and adoration she felt for him.

He leaned into her tender touch. "My sweet, precious girl," he whispered, covering her hand with his own.

Holding her palm to his lips, he kissed its center before returning it to where it was before. "I like the way you look with your arms outstretched, surrendering to me, trusting me with your pleasure."

Hooded with desire, his eyes were pleading with her to give him that, promising only pleasure if she did.

Syssi felt powerless to deny him anything. Without a word she complied, stretching her arms and grabbing onto the headboard's metal frame.

How did he do that, she wondered, setting her body on fire—knowing what she needed better than she did herself.

To hell with precaution and consequences, she was done being careful. No more almosts, no more only ifs, no more maybe-next-times, this was it.

With Kian, she had finally glimpsed the path to the elusive bliss. And the only way she could traverse that road was with him in the driver seat. She needed to cede control to him. And to do that, she needed to trust him… which was scary.

It wasn't that she feared he'd hurt her physically, she knew he wouldn't. But to trust that he would not exploit the tremendous emotional vulnerability she was about to expose; that took real courage.

Or stupidity.

Still, she knew it was her one and only chance to take the plunge because there was no doubt in her mind that she would never even consider this with anyone but Kian.

Releasing a shuddering breath, she gazed into his eyes, and the way he looked at her, waiting breathlessly for her acquiescence, provided the final push.

She took the plunge.

"I don't know why I feel this way with you, trusting you to take control of my pleasure, but I do. I crave it," Syssi whispered, a rush of pure lust sweeping through her with the admission.

Kian groaned. "Do you have any idea how perfect you are? How much your trust means to me?" He dipped his head, pouring his gratitude and appreciation into a tender kiss.

Well aware that lovely, sweet Syssi was nothing like what he was accustomed to, and the set of rules she played by was different than his, he had to make sure she understood the rules of this new game he was introducing her to. But now that she had given him the green light, he was in serious trouble because there was nothing holding him back, and his damned instincts were screaming for him to rip off his pants, plunge all the way into her, and sink his fangs into her neck while he was at it.

Not going to happen. Kian took a deep breath and closed his eyes, forcing the beast to back the hell off.

First, he would make sure to take care of her pleasure.

Kissing and licking the column of her throat, he needed at least a moment between her thighs, even if only to feel her through the fabric of his pants. Pushing her knees apart, he aligned his erection with her sex, careful not to scrape her with his zipper as he rubbed against her.

Fuck, it feels good.

With a groan, he slid farther down her body until his face was level with her stiff peaks. For a moment, he just looked at their sculpted perfection, watching them heave with each of her breaths. Until he heard her whimper.

Only then, he took one tip between his lips. He pulled on it gently, twirling his tongue round and round, while lightly pinching its twin between his thumb and forefinger and tugging on it in sync with his suckling.

As he kept alternating between the sensitive nubs, suckling them harder and grazing them lightly with his teeth, Syssi's moans and whimpers were getting louder and more desperate.

She was loving it. Her hips circling under the weight of him, she held on to the headboard with a white-knuckled grip.

Kian eased up, giving her a small reprieve. "Ask me to make you come, baby," he breathed around her wet nipple, lifting his eyes to her sweat-misted face.

"Please…," she whimpered.

"That's not good enough. You can do better than that."

Syssi arched her back, and as she turned her desperate eyes up to her tight grip on the headboard, he felt an outpour of wetness slide down her thigh.

"Oh, God! Yes! Please… Please make me come… Kian."

As his blunt front teeth carefully closed around one nipple, and his fingers around the other, Syssi erupted. And as he kept increasing the pressure, turning the slight ache into what must've been an almost unbearable hurt, her climax continued rippling through her—her beautiful body quaking with the aftershocks as she wailed until her voice turned hoarse.

That was it for him.

Unable to hold it off anymore, he came hard, erupting spasmodically inside his pants. Except, it did nothing to soften his erection, he was still as hard as before.

Releasing some of the pressure took the edge off, though. Now, with the wild beast raging inside him contained for a little longer, he could watch Syssi climax again and again.

He would never tire of seeing her like that. Her dazed, blissed out expression suffusing him with tenderness.

My beautiful, passionate girl.

Cupping her breasts with his palms, he soothed her tender nubs, waiting for them to soften under the warmth of his touch.

As her ragged breathing slowed down, Syssi mouthed, "Wow!" her cheeks flaming.

Kian smiled, peering at her from between the hands he had cupped over her ample breasts.

Releasing her hold on the metal frame, she took his cheeks between her palms and pulled him up for a kiss.

"Did I give you permission to bring your arms down, sweet girl?" he said before sealing his lips over hers. He then traced the line of her jaw with kisses and nibbles, all the way up to her earlobe, catching the soft tissue between his teeth.

Syssi squirmed. "No," she said in a small voice, caressing his stubble with her thumbs. "My hands have a mind of their own. I just had to touch you." She pouted, pretending contrition.

"Be a good girl and put your hands back up, or I'll have to flip you over and spank that sweet little bottom of yours." He tweaked her nipple and smirked, watching her eyelids flutter as a shiver of desire swept through her.

"Is that a promise?" Syssi taunted, whispering breathlessly as she lifted and tightened the aforementioned body part and pressed her pelvis up to his belly. Still, she hastened to obey his command, and stretching her arms, returned her hands to the headboard.

The hint of trepidation in her eyes hadn't been lost on him. Syssi wasn't sure if he was just teasing or intended to make good on that threat.

"Could you be any more perfect for me?" Kian said, shaking his head. "My little minx has some naughty fantasies I would be more than happy to fulfill. I promise. If you ask really nicely… or behave really badly, you can bet your sweet bottom on it." He winked, and with a surge, dived down and pressed an open-mouthed kiss to her wet folds.

Syssi squeaked, lifting and pulling away from him, but Kian gripped her hips and pulled her back down. Sliding both hands under her bottom, he lifted her pelvis up to his mouth and licked her wet slit from top to bottom and then back up, growling like a beast.

At first, she stiffened. But Kian kept at it even though he knew she felt scandalized. This was such an intimate act, demanding a level of trust and familiarity that must've been difficult for her. After all, he had her spread out naked, her sex soaking wet from her earlier climax, licking and feasting on it while he was still fully dressed.

He was pushing her, testing her limits, thrilled that despite her initial reluctance she was letting him have his way.

He loved that ceding control to him turned her on. The more he demanded, the more he pushed, the more she responded with wild abandon, rewarding him with her moans and whimpers and more of her sweet nectar pouring onto his greedy tongue.

He could go on like that for hours, savoring and exulting in the pleasure he was wringing out of her.

It wasn't about him being a selfless giving lover, not entirely. Having his pants on and not allowing her to touch him was the only way he could stay in control. His hunger for sex, for her, was so intense, he was afraid of what he'd do to her otherwise.

The beast in him wanted to impale her sex with his cock and sink his fangs into her neck in one brutal move. And then go on fucking her for hours, biting her and coming inside her over and over again. Rutting on her like the animal it was.

Traumatizing her.

It was true that she would climax every time he sunk his fangs into her neck... or her breast... or the juncture of her thigh. The aphrodisiac in his venom would make sure of that. And yes, her pain and bruising would fade from its healing properties. And after he was done, he could easily thrall the nasty memory away.

Except, he was neither a sadist nor a mindless beast… well… not entirely, and not as long as he remained in control.

He cared too much for this girl to let go—even a little.

Before he slaked his need, he would make sure she was properly pleasured, sated, and soaking wet from multiple orgasms. And even then, he couldn't let loose the monster lurking inside him.

The man is wicked.

Drawing lazy circles around her nether lips and scooping her juices with his tongue, Kian groaned with the pleasure of literally eating her up.

He'd been doing it for so long, keeping her at a slow simmer, skirting the spot where she needed him most, that she had to bite on her bottom lip to stifle the sounds she was making. Her needy groans sounded like angry growls.

"Please, I can't take it anymore!" she finally hissed.

Kian lifted his head. "Tell me what you need, baby." He smirked, licking her juices from his glistening lips.

Hanging on the precipice, she was beyond shame or reserve. "You… I need you inside me! Please…" She groaned—panting from parted lips as he pulled his hands from under her butt and lowered her back to the mattress. Eyes trained on her face, he tightened his grip on her hip, anchoring her down, and slid one long finger inside her slick core.

Her channel tightened, clutching and spasming around the thrusting and retreating digit. It felt so good. Syssi moaned, closing her eyes and letting her head drop back.

"Look at me!" Kian growled.

With an effort, she lifted her head and looked at him with hooded eyes, her lower lip pulsing, swollen from where she had bitten on it before.

Holding her gaze, he pulled out his finger and pushed back with two. She inhaled sharply at the amplified pleasure. A slight burn started, reminding her how long it had been for her, and for a moment she got scared. But then as he lowered his chin and slowly, deliberately, flicked his tongue at her most erogenous spot, a flood of moisture coated his fingers, turning the intrusion from slightly painful to blissfully pleasurable.

His fingers pumping in and out of her, in that slow, maddening way, Syssi was hanging by a thread—straining on the edge of the orgasm bearing down on her. She needed him to move just a little faster, or pinch her nipple with the powerful fingers of his other hand, and she would've gone flying.

But Kian had other ideas. Joining a third finger, he stretched her even wider. Again, there was a slight burn, but she couldn't care less.

Let it hurt, just let me dive over that edge.

She kept her eyes on his face, watching him as a wicked gleam sparkled in his eyes, just a split moment before he closed his lips around the tiny bundle of nerves at the apex of her sex and sucked it in.

"Kiannnnn!" Syssi erupted, mewling and thrashing as the climax came at her violently, jerking her body off the bed. Kian didn't let go, pumping his fingers and suckling on her, he prolonged it, squeezing every last drop of pleasure out of her.

A moment later, or perhaps it had been longer than that, she came down from floating in that semiconscious, postorgasmic space and opened her eyes. A gasp escaped her throat. Kian was suspended above her—gloriously naked. Giving her no time to ponder the how and when he had shucked off his clothes, or to admire his beautifully muscled body, he speared into her with a grunt.

Syssi cried out.

It hurt. Boy did it hurt, and not in a good way. Not an erotic pain. Just pain, hot and searing.

As her channel stretched and burned, struggling to accommodate Kian's girth, Syssi wanted to push him off; memories of her first time intruding on and marring what was supposed to be something wonderful—casting an unpleasant shadow over the bliss that he had brought her before.

Tears streaking from the corners of her eyes, she panted, waiting for the pain to subside.

"I'm sorry," Kian whispered, kissing her teary eyes, as he tried to pull out.

"No, just give me a moment." She clutched him to her. This wasn't going to end like that, no way.

He didn't move, not even a twitch. With muscles strained and eyes blazing in his hard face, he looked at her, holding his breath as he waited for her body to adjust to his invasion. Only when the pain started to ebb and she began to moan and undulate—her lust and her pleasure overriding her pain—did he begin thrusting, carefully, gently, until she gasped again.

This time, in pleasure.

For what seemed like a long time, he moved inside her with infinite care, his thrusts slow and shallow, and eventually even the memory of pain was gone, there was only pleasure.

Syssi brought her palms to Kian's cheeks and pulled him down, kissing him softly. She was falling in love with this man, and there was little she could do about it. Right now she was overwhelmed with feelings of gratitude, for his patience, for his care. Kian was putting her pleasure first.

"I'm okay now. You can let go," she whispered against his lips.

His thrusts got a little deeper, but he kept going slow for a few moments, gauging her response. When she closed her eyes and moaned deep in her throat, he increased the tempo and force, gradually going deeper and faster until the powerful pounding rattled the bed, banging it against the wall and driving them both toward the headboard.

Kian braced himself by grabbing the metal frame above where she was holding on, his biceps bulging with the strain and sweat dripping down the center of his muscular chest.

As Syssi climbed toward another climax, Kian's grunts and her moans were accompanied by the sounds of the bed's feet sliding and screeching on the hardwood floor, and the headboard banging against the wall. A carnal soundtrack to the drama of their fierce coupling.

Forcing her eyes to remain open, Syssi stared at Kian's handsome face, awed. Straining, he was covered in sweat, his lips pressed into a thin line. And his eyes, those hypnotic blue eyes of his, were glowing with an eerie luminance.

I'm delirious, she thought, marveling at the sight.

Shifting those amazing eyes down to her neck, he dipped his head to suck and lick at her fast pulsing vein; strands of his soft hair caressing her cheek as he kept his relentless pounding.

On an impulse, Syssi turned her head sideways, startled to find herself silently pleading with him; *Bite me! Please...*

Oh, God!

The sharp pain of his fangs sinking into her flesh shocked her; the needlelike incisors clearly not human.

Fangs... He had fangs in my dream... was her last coherent thought as his seed jetted into her, and she fell apart, her climax erupting in waves of volcanic intensity.

The euphoria that followed left her boneless and exhausted. Unable to open her eyes, blissful and content, she sighed, surrendering to oblivion.

DARK STRANGER REVEALED

Praise for Dark Stranger Revealed

"—This second book of the trilogy is consumed by the budding sexual relationship between Kian and Syssi. In fact, the action-suspense plot regarding the danger Syssi is in moves forward slowly, sacrificed on the altar of sexy times. But I have to admit the sexy times were spicy and varied. —"

"There is nothing else to say except if you don't love this series you probably need to read car manuals! The entire series is suspenseful, hopeful, dark, violent, soft, romantic and positive. Hot characters who share the burdens of an entire species."

"I LOVE LOVE LOVE THIS SERIES! I was trying to find a series similar to the Black Dagger Brotherhood series by JR Ward and this hit the nail on the head! I finished the entire series within two weeks and I cannot wait for Book 9 to release! IT Lucas, please keep this story line going as long as possible. There are so many loose ends from Carol, to Andrew, to Bhathian, Anandur (needs a mate), etc... I cannot wait to see what happens to the rest of the clan!"

"Awesome story with intriguing characters. Romance and intrigue that draws one in. Better than Shades of Grey by a mile."

DARK STRANGER REVEALED

Don't miss out on:

The Children of the Gods Origins

Goddess's Choice

When gods and immortals still ruled the ancient world, one young goddess risked everything for love.

Part 1 of Goddess's Choice IS FREE WITH YOUR VIP CLUB Membership. To Join, go to: www.itlucas.com

Goddess's Hope

Hungry for power and infatuated with the beautiful Areana, Navuh plots his father's demise. After all, by getting rid of the insane god he would be doing the world a favor. Except, when gods and immortals conspire against each other, humanity pays the price. But things are not what they seem, and prophecies should not to be trusted...

The Perfect Match Series

Vampire's Consort IS FREE WITH YOUR VIP CLUB Membership. To Join, go to: www.itlucas.com

When Gabriel's company is ready to start beta testing, he invites his old crush to inspect its medical safety protocol.

Curious about the revolutionary technology of the *Perfect Match Virtual Fantasy-Fulfillment studios,* Brenna agrees.

Neither expects to end up partnering for its first fully immersive test run.

King's Chosen

When Lisa's nutty friends get her a gift certificate to *Perfect Match Virtual Fantasy Studios,* she has no intentions of using it. But since the only way to get a refund is if no partner can be found for her, she makes sure to request a fantasy so girly and over the top that no sane guy will pick it up.

Except, someone does.

Warning: This fantasy contains a hot, domineering crown prince, sweet insta-love, steamy love scenes painted with light shades of gray, a wedding, and a HEA in both the virtual and real worlds.

Captain's Conquest

Working as a Starbucks barista, Alicia fends off flirting all day long, but none of the guys are as charming and sexy as Gregg. His frequent visits are the highlight of her day, but since he's never

asked her out, she assumes he's taken. Besides, between a day job and a budding music career, she has no time to start a new relationship. That is until Gregg makes her an offer she can't refuse—a gift certificate to the virtual fantasy fulfillment service everyone is talking about. As a huge Star Trek fan, Alicia has a perfect match in mind—the captain of the Starship Enterprise.

The Thief Who Loved Me

When Marian splurges on a Perfect Match Virtual adventure as a world infamous jewel thief, she expects high-wire fun with a hot partner who she will never have to see again in real life.

A virtual encounter seems like the perfect answer to Marcus's string of dating disasters. No strings attached, no drama, and definitely no love. As a die-hard James Bond fan, he chooses as his avatar a dashing MI6 operative, and to complement his adventure, a dangerously seductive partner.

Neither expects to find their forever Perfect Match.

ALSO BY I. T. LUCAS

THE CHILDREN OF THE GODS ORIGINS

Goddess's Choice

Goddess's Hope

THE CHILDREN OF THE GODS

Dark Stranger

Dark Stranger The Dream

Dark Stranger Revealed

Dark Stranger Immortal

Dark Enemy

Dark Enemy Taken

Dark Enemy Captive

Dark Enemy Redeemed

Kri & Michael's Story

My Dark Amazon

Dark Warrior

Dark Warrior Mine

Dark Warrior's Promise

Dark Warrior's Destiny

Dark Warrior's Legacy

Dark Guardian

Dark Guardian Found

Dark Guardian Craved

Dark Guardian's Mate

Dark Angel

Dark Angel's Obsession

Dark Angel's Seduction

Dark Angel's Surrender

Dark Operative

Dark Operative: A Shadow of Death

Dark Operative: A Glimmer of Hope

Dark Operative: The Dawn of Love

Dark Survivor

Dark Survivor Awakened

Dark Survivor Echoes of Love

Dark Survivor Reunited

Dark Widow

Dark Widow's Secret

Dark Widow's Curse

Dark Widow's Blessing

Dark Dream

Dark Dream's Temptation

Dark Dream's Unraveling

Dark Dream's Trap

Dark Prince

Dark Prince's Enigma

Dark Prince's Dilemma

Dark Prince's Agenda

Dark Queen

Dark Queen's Quest

Dark Queen's Knight

Dark Queen's Army

Dark Spy

Dark Spy Conscripted

Dark Spy's Mission

Dark Spy's Resolution

Dark Overlord

Dark Overlord New Horizon

Dark Overlord's Wife

Dark Overlord's Clan

Dark Choices

Dark Choices The Quandary:

Dark Choices Paradigm Shift

Dark Choices The Accord

Dark Secrets

Dark Secrets Resurgence

Dark Secrets Unveiled

Dark Secrets Absolved

Dark Haven

Dark haven Illusion

Dark Haven Unmasked

Dark Haven Found

Dark Power

Dark Power Untamed

Dark Power Unleashed

Dark Power Convergence

DarkMemories

Dark Memories Submerged

Dark Memories Emerge

Dark Memories Restored

Dark Hunter

Dark Hunter's Query

Dark Hunter's Prey

Dark Hunter's Boon

Dark God

Dark God's Avatar

The Children of the Gods Series Sets

Books 1-3: Dark Stranger trilogy

Includes a bonus short story:

The Fates take a Vacation

Books 4-6: Dark Enemy Trilogy

Includes a bonus short story:

The Fates' Post-Wedding Celebration

Books 7-10: Dark Warrior Tetralogy

Books 11-13: Dark Guardian Trilogy

Books 14-16: Dark Angel Trilogy

Books 17-19: Dark Operative Trilogy

Books 20-22: Dark Survivor Trilogy

Books 23-25: Dark Widow Trilogy

Books 26-28: Dark Dream Trilogy

Books 29-31: Dark Prince Trilogy

Books 32-34: Dark Queen Trilogy

Books 35-37: Dark Spy Trilogy

Books 38-40: Dark Overlord Trilogy

Books 41-43: Dark Choices Trilogy

Books 44-46: Dark Secrets Trilogy

Books 47-49: Dark Haven Trilogy

Books 51-52: Dark Power Trilogy

Books 53-55: Dark Memories Trilogy

PERFECT MATCH

Perfect Match 1: Vampire's Consort

Perfect Match 2: King's Chosen

Perfect Match 3: Captain's Conquest

FOR EXCLUSIVE PEEKS AT UPCOMING RELEASES & A FREE COMPANION BOOK

JOIN MY *VIP CLUB* AND GAIN ACCESS TO THE VIP PORTAL AT ITLUCAS.COM

GO TO: http://eepurl.com/blMTpD

INCLUDED IN YOUR FREE MEMBERSHIP:

YOUR VIP PORTAL

- READ PREVIEW CHAPTERS OF UPCOMING RELEASES.
- LISTEN TO GODDESS'S CHOICE NARRATION BY CHARLES LAWRENCE
- EXCLUSI

VE CONTENT OFFERED ONLY TO MY VIPS.

FREE I.T. LUCAS COMPANION INCLUDES:

- GODDESS'S CHOICE PART 1
- PERFECT MATCH: VAMPIRE'S CONSORT (A STAND-ALONE NOVELLA)
- INTERVIEW Q & A
- CHARACTER CHARTS

IF YOU'RE ALREADY A SUBSCRIBER, YOU'LL RECEIVE A DOWNLOAD LINK FOR MY NEXT BOOK'S PREVIEW CHAPTERS IN THE NEW RELEASE ANNOUNCEMENT EMAIL. IF YOU ARE NOT GETTING MY EMAILS, YOUR PROVIDER IS SENDING THEM TO YOUR JUNK FOLDER, AND YOU ARE MISSING OUT ON **IMPORTANT UPDATES, SIDE CHARACTERS' PORTRAITS, ADDITIONAL CONTENT, AND OTHER GOODIES.** TO FIX THAT, ADD isabell@

itlucas.com TO YOUR EMAIL CONTACTS OR YOUR EMAIL VIP LIST.

ACKNOWLEDGMENTS

First, I want to thank you for reading my debut novel and joining me on this incredible adventure.

When I pressed the "Publish" button in July of 2015, I never expected the special connection I'd form with my readers. My circle of friends suddenly expanded exponentially.

I love answering your emails, responding to your Facebook comments and messages, and reading your reviews. You are literally the wind beneath my creative wings, providing the motivation for the endless hours that go into writing, editing, and publishing my stories.

Which brings me to my family. My husband and our four sons are so amazingly supportive and accepting. Thank you for putting up with my scatterbrained inattention and the scarcity of home-cooked meals. I love you all to pieces.

To Julia, thank you for working around my crazy schedule and delivering the corrected manuscripts in record time. You're awesome. To Jenna, Jean, and Nancy, I don't know how you gals do that, but thank you for proofreading practically overnight. And to my sisters-in-law, thank you for reading every book and hounding me for the next one.

Lastly, to Charles, thank you for bringing the stories to life with your incredible narration.

XOXO

Isabell T. Lucas

Dark Stranger The Dream

NOTE FROM THE AUTHOR:
This is a work of fiction!
Names, characters, places and incidents are products of the author's imagination or are used fictitiously and are not to be construed as real. Any similarity to actual persons, organizations and/or events is purely coincidental.